A SUN PRIEST'S MAGIC

Valor Book Three

✦S. M. SAVOY✦

بسالة

Published by
Ace Lyon Books
January
2017

Published by
Ace Lyon Books
Acelyonbooks.com
First Edition
Cover Design by S. M. Savoy
S. M. Savoy A Sun Priest's Magic
ISBN 978-1-947122-17-8

Books in this Series

Valor

A Warrior's Magic

A Sunpriest's Magic

Beyond Valor

TABLE OF CONTENTS

A SUN PRIEST'S MAGIC

Valor Book Three

-1-

AFTER THE RESCUE

Charlie cradled Sara in his arms and leaned against the curved side of the helicopter. The magic within him felt bloated as if it would burst from his body. Pressure only violence would ease, and he wanted to be violent, to slash and stab and fight with every ounce of strength he possessed.

He squeezed his eyes closed and tried to still his harsh, panting breaths, glad the roar of the engines drowned them out. Adrenaline still raged through him, leaving fiery pains behind as he fought his nature. Sara's presence eased him, and he squeezed her tighter, afraid the magic would make him rampage.

Her sheet-wrapped body lay still and cold, but the pulse in her neck beat steadily. Such relief and gratitude filled him that tears came to his eyes. Sara's matted, dirty, blond hair hid his face as he cried. Everyone on the helicopter pretended not to notice, giving him the illusion of privacy.

Team Valor had killed most of Sara's abductors. Team Beta remained at the house where she'd been held, gathering what evidence they could before the Canadian authorities arrived and took over.

A vehicle had fled the scene that Hawk was tracking on foot while teams Alpha and Valor followed in the helicopter. Rinto, the man Charlie really wanted, had already fled the zone. Oz casted Magical Locate every few minutes but hadn't caught a glimmer.

Guthrie spoke on the radio, his large hands dwarfing the small device. When the call ended, he squatted in front of Charlie. "You aren't going to like this—"

Charlie interrupted, "I'm not leaving her! It's non-negotiable." The mere thought made him feel ill, and the magic pressed harder beneath his skin, leaving him feeling uncomfortably bloated.

"I wasn't going to ask you too. Take Sara and Joy and go ahead of us. This could take Hawk a few hours, or even a few days."

"No. Team Valor stays together. I won't leave them either. Neither would Sara if she had a choice." Charlie shifted his grip on Sara, sitting her more upright and resting her head on his shoulder.

Sergeant Guthrie lowered his voice. "Look, your eyes are glowing; we can't have you blowing up the helicopter. The best way to help—"

"The magic is under control. I'm touching her. I'll be fine," Charlie insisted as he slid his hand onto Sara's bare leg. "If it gets bad, I promise we'll get off." He tried to smooth his face into calmness. "The team has to stay together."

Guthrie returned to his seat, a deep scowl on his brow.

Charlie closed his eyes and rested his cheek on Sara. Guthrie would just have to get over it. He wasn't leaving his team, any of his team.

Guthrie sat forward in sudden decision. "Okay, people, this is how it's going to be. Give me a status check. And, by God, it better be an honest one. If Joy is a one, and the top of your game is a ten, give me a number. Let's start with you, Drew."

"Six, Staff Sergeant, but my six is better than your ten!" Drew said with a cocky grin that faded as he glanced at Joy laying by his feet. He leaned down to smooth her hair back, his expression anxious. Charlie turned away, the sight angering him and making the sick, nervous feeling in his stomach worse.

Marcus laughed. "Roger that. Six here too, but I bet I could beat you in a race."

After the rest of the Scouts and Team Valor had reported in, Guthrie called Hawk.

"Okay, Hawk, we'll follow for four hours, but we need to refuel first. If we pick you up, will you be able to find the trail again?"

"Leave me here, go top off, and catch up."

Hawk didn't sound winded at all from the long run.

"Negative, we aren't leaving you alone."

Stasia touched his hand. "I'll go with him. Get the gas and meet up with us. No one will see us."

"Stasia, they wanted you too." Oz grabbed her arm and squeezed. "Those men wanted you girls most. Don't let whoever this is see you."

Stasia gave him a hard smile and rolled her eyes. "Please— nobody will see me, and I'll be careful."

The helicopter hovered; Stasia jumped out and sprinted down the road to catch up to her brother.

Charlie tensed, wanting with all his soul to follow, but Sara was defenseless, and he couldn't bring himself to leave her. Small swirls of blue magic grew to billowing clouds in moments.

Guthrie exclaimed as static sparked. The static grew into thin tendrils of lightning that zapped from person-to-person, waking the sleepers and making some exclaim.

Oz held out his hand as glowing motes surrounded it. "Are you doing this on purpose," he asked.

"Doing what?" Charlie frowned at Oz and shrugged irritably as the static flickered over him.

"What's he doing?" Guthrie asked at the same time.

"This is an enchantment. Well, not quite, but almost. Or, maybe… I don't know." Oz leaned closer and stared at his hand. "I see the connections but not what they do."

"Well, I'm not doing a thing," Charlie said.

Oz closed his eyes, clearly concentrating. Charlie eyed him thoughtfully, wondering what he saw. Guthrie rose the radio to his lips.

"You better land us somewhere private

ASAP," he said.

"Under no circumstance do you engage with our quarry! You're surveillance only!" Guthrie ordered on the raid channel. "This is worse than herding cats," he mumbled and then glared at Brenda when she snickered.

Oz tilted his head and waved his hands as if plucking strings, his frown deepening. "I can see the connections between us growing or maybe strengthening is a better word. I wish Hawk were here to see this. I think it's the part he sees as being in our group, but I'm not sure."

Gusts of warm air accompanied by the smell of ozone wafted through the helicopter. The flickers of lightning reverted to sparks of static, and the wild swirl of magic slowed and settled on the scouts, absorbing into their skin.

"I don't feel any different," Brenda said doubtfully as she rose to check them all again.

"Take us to an airport. Whatever was happening is over," Guthrie said and heaved an annoyed grunt. He held a hand to his ear and nodded. "Great," he said sarcastically and dropped the radio into his lap to rub his face.

"Whatever you just did, Captain Sanders reports a small cloud of magic covered him in the cockpit. He got hit by a few shocks, and the magic sailed away heading north. I assume to team Beta, but for all I know, it's looking for a new host.

"Sorry, Sarge, I have no idea..." Charlie trailed off as Stasia reported on the raid channel, her voice sounding scratchy and far away in his headset.

"A cloud of magic just overtook us. It zapped us a few times with no noticeable effect, then condensed to a blue ball about the size of a baseball and soared away heading north.

"I think it was strengthening the raid," Oz said, still with his eyes closed. He held his hands out and traced something in the air only he could see.

Guthrie shrugged one shoulder and straightened. "Let's worry about it later."

Charlie almost laughed at his put-upon tone.

The helicopter flew to the nearest airport to refuel and was back trailing Hawk in thirty-five minutes.

To Charlie's relief and dismay, Hawk and Stasia hadn't caught up to their quarry yet. A pale and winded Stasia returned to the helicopter by casting Waylay on Charlie as the helicopter hovered thirty feet above her head.

"On a scale of one to ten, I'm about a four now, I guess." With a tired sigh, she leaned back in the seat and closed her eyes.

Oz wrapped a conjured bandage around her.

She nodded her thanks but kept her eyes closed.

Charlie stole Sara's heal and used it on Stasia, angry with himself he'd let her get so run down. He should've made her eat and rest while they'd searched, but he'd ignored his team, wallowing in his anger. And she was a rogue. Anger wouldn't sustain her like it did him. Her magic was fueled by her energy, and he hadn't even brought a candy bar for her.

His angry gaze scanned his raid. On every cooldown, he'd healed someone, but they remained exhausted and filthy. He needed to be in charge of his anger, not let it rule him. He sat straighter and tried to breathe calmly.

By the time Beta team checked in, reporting the Canadian authorities were taking them in for questioning, and the cover story had so far passed unchallenged, Charlie had gained some measure of control. Beta also reported they too had been hit by small flickers of lightning and the magic had absorbed into them, not seeming to travel on.

Charlie no longer felt an almost overwhelming need to join Hawk. His anger was subsumed by plans to get his team somewhere they could rest before they hunted down the general.

His gaze landed on Guthrie and his lips pursed. He didn't believe Guthrie had been involved. He examined Drew thoughtfully. Rinto had been a teammate and a friend of his under Major Nelson's command.

Charlie was certain Drew's worry was sincere as he was certain Drew loved Joy. The magic that had gusted over him made his sincerity unmistakable. And, while he couldn't be certain what the worry was for, Drew's horror and anger were also sincere. He felt no guilt or fear of Charlie, and Charlie didn't think that would be possible if he'd had a hand in the betrayal.

Of the two generals who knew of Team Valor's abilities, Charlie's money was on Flores. His eyes narrowed as he considered Major Nelson's actions. He needed to question him, Glenn, and Harrison preferably while they stood in his magic.

Guthrie startled as a cloud of magic burst from Charlie. The magic gusted and danced over the Scouts, bringing their feelings to him with improved clarity. Charlie chuckled and called it back.

"I did it on purpose to see if I could," Charlie said as he concentrated, trying to release his magic purposefully again. Another blue cloud manifested with shocking suddenness. "Can you feel my anger?"

Guthrie nodded.

"Good. I feel your worry. I'll know if I'm lied too." Charlie flicked a glance at Drew.

Guthrie followed his gaze and nodded slowly.

Brenda, rising to recheck Joy, drew Charlie's eyes.

Guthrie scowled and fingered the first-aid kit he carried as Brenda examined everyone again.

She gave Guthrie, then Charlie, a reassuring nod. "Everyone is stable. When the sedatives wear off, Sara and Joy will be fine. No one has any injuries remaining. Some sleep and food and we'll be good to go."

Charlie clasped her hand in his blue one, hoping she felt how sorry he was she'd been injured, hoping the respect and love he felt for her were clear.

Her eyes clouded, and she patted his hand with her free one a moment before waving it through the magic that swirled around them.

"I love you guys, and I'm fine."

A burning hunger darted from him to her, growing as the magic darkened when Stasia placed her hand on theirs. Charlie released them, satisfied with their need for vengeance.

Thirty minutes later, Hawk reported in, sounding aggravated. "Sarge, we have a problem. My quarry left the road and is traveling by water. I can't follow."

Captain Sanders landed the helicopter as closely as he could to Hawk's position.

"Well, this is the ass end of nowhere!" Guthrie complained as he placed his hands on his hips and narrowed his eyes at the small inlet before him where a rough buoy floated in a murky brown river bordering a deserted stretch of dirt road.

"Can you tell anything about the boat at all?"

"Nothing," Hawk said, frustration evident in his voice. "Well, something actually. If they're using water to break the trail, they know how I track. And they left their car here."

"Yeah, Agent Lewis can probably make something of that." Guthrie called Agent Lewis and reported where they were and what they'd found.

"Okay, he's sending a team in. Mounties will

be here soon. Until they arrive, we guard the scene." After informing Captain Sanders, he climbed into the back to check on everyone.

Everyone sat quietly. Most had closed eyes and leaned back in the seats, their exhaustion apparent. They needed food and rest.

The Scouts were a mess. Kept sedated at first, then tied, they'd been without food and water for three days. Brenda and Rick had dried gore in their hair, smeared across their faces, and covering their clothing. Dried blood mixed with bits better left unidentified caked the side of Brenda's head and neck and matted in her hair. Crimson flakes fell from Stasia and Charlie every time they moved. A glance at his own uniform informed him he wasn't much cleaner.

The Scouts need food, clean clothes, and rest. He stepped outside the helicopter to make a call.

A sudden commotion made him jump back in. Sara was awake almost three hours early. In a complete panic to be free, she thrashed wildly.

-2-

ALONE

Charlie didn't think Sara knew where she was. When she started screaming to be let go, he was sure of it. She struggled wildly, constrained by the blanket around her. He ripped her loose, and she pushed away from him.

When her hands were free, she casted a heal on herself followed by a shield and a heal-over-time. Tears clouded her blue eyes and her dirty hair stuck to her cheeks. Charlie doubted she could see a thing she was crying so hard. Blind and deaf in her panic to escape, she didn't seem to hear him calling her name.

Stasia grabbed her, and Sara screamed and loosed her fear spell.

The cracked, hoarse sound of her scream enraged him. Color and sound sharpened and the magic within him again pressed against his skin. He wished there was an enemy to slay, he'd gladly kill a hundred men to still her screams and soothe her terror. Unable to gain her attention talking, he placed his hands on her cheeks, forcing her to look at him, and yelled, "Stop! Please, stop, you're safe. It's me, Sara, sweetheart, it's me!"

Her wide-eyed gaze met his, and she sobbed and reached a trembling hand to him.

"You're safe," he repeated in a quieter voice. To his relief, Sara's eyes met his, and she saw him. Still sobbing, she clutched his shirt, her wide terrified eyes locked on his. The terror in her gaze deepened when she glanced at her hands. She held both up and screamed a high, piteous wail that set his teeth on edge. Light formed in her hands and a heal hit him.

Blinding white light filled the helicopter as she casted frantically, using every major heal she had.

"Stop!" The panic on her face horrified him.

He grasped her shoulders, shaking lightly, trying to force her to listen. Every bone in her body stood out in sharp relief. Already thin, she'd lost an amazing amount of weight in her three days of captivity. Worried about hurting her, he lightened his grip. The light between her hands faded, and she collapsed and huddled on the floor against his knees. Static shimmered in arcs through the blue magic surrounding him as he crouched in front of her to smooth her hair back.

"I'm fine, this isn't my blood."

Black pupil obscured the blue of her eyes. The drugs she'd ingested affected her still, at least he hoped it was the drugs causing her panic.

Her trembling hands reached for him, and

she seemed to spot spotted Joy lying motionless on the deck. She scrambled back and shrieked as her gaze swung over the staring Scouts. Another light ball filled her hands, and she threw the heal at Joy.

"Sara—"

"Nooo..." she sobbed and formed light balls one after the other, casting as fast as possible.

Charlie grabbed her bony wrists and kissed her fingers as she continued to cast. "Please, Sara, we're all fine. Please, stop!" he yelled louder when she didn't.

Horror filled her eyes when her magic failed her. A continuous low moan came from her as she frantically flicked her fingers, trying to cast. Her distressed felt a knife to his soul, and he moaned with the pain of it.

Swirling madly, the blue magic surrounding him rushed to her. The static built up to yellow sparks that flared bright white and ozone filled the air. He jerked back as emotion buffeted him with painful clarity. Fear from Sara. Fury and worry from Stasia. As the blue cloud expanded, he sensed everyone in a confusing mix.

He ignored Sara's resistance as she tried to keep casting and pulled her into an embrace. The moaning stopped when she clutched him around the neck.

"Everyone is fine!" Charlie yelled, putting as much command as he could into his voice.

Stasia crouched behind Sara, biting her lip. Tears trailed down her dirty, blood-smeared cheek, and her eyes blazed blue.

"No one is injured," she said. "Joy is sedated,

but she'll wake soon."

Hands that had just minutes ago killed men gently smoothed Sara's hair and rubbed her back.

Charlie met Stasia's glowing blue eyes over Sara's shoulder. The magic brought her feelings to him as clearly as if she'd shouted them. He flushed as he considered they could feel the fire in his soul that was his love and need for Sara.

Dense, and roiling in thick streamers, the magic settled on Sara, coating every inch of exposed skin.

"Shh… sweetheart… You're safe, everyone's okay," Charlie kept murmuring. The tremors wracking her body as she clutched him scared him. Icy-cold skin shivered under his hands.

"The team is safe." Tears sprang to his eyes when she started sobbing. Still murmuring endearments, he closed his eyes and rested his head on hers, not knowing how to help her as she cried on his shoulder.

"Oh, my God, Charlie, they killed him! I'm so sorry." The tremors escalated as she cried. "Oh, God— your mother will never forgive me. I tried so hard, Charlie. I really did."

Charlie pulled away and framed her face with his hands. "Sara, Rick's fine. He's right here." He spoke slowly and tried to talk calmly, although it was futile, she could probably feel his anger as clearly as he felt her fear.

He met his brother's worried gaze as he kissed Sara's temple.

"I'm fine, Sara. You did save us. Brenda is fine too," Rick said.

Tremors shook the hand she reached to Rick.

A low keening moan came from her, and she fell to her knees. Her emotions seesawed wildly from fear to guilt and loneliness so strong it made Charlie yell his attack cry.

The cry stilled her whirling emotions, whether from the shock of it, or it helped her, he didn't know, and she fell forward. Charlie grabbed for her as she landed hard on her hands and spewed green bile followed by violent dry heaves.

Guthrie spoke, asking the Scouts to give them space, but Charlie didn't turn to look. All his attention was on Sara who gasped and gagged with dry heaves at his feet. Wisps of dirty blond hair stuck to his fingers as he smoothed the hair back from her face, trying to speak in soft, comforting tones, not the angry yell he wanted to use.

His conflicting emotions were so distinct, his actions so at odds with his needs that it scared him. It felt as if he could cease to be Charlie and become Chief, and he might have let it happen, except he didn't think if he were Chief he'd care if Sara needed kind words or comforting hugs. Chief wouldn't speak kindly, he'd kill and keep killing until his team was safe, and he wouldn't care who or how many he killed. Innocent or guilty wouldn't matter. The only thing Chief cared about was protecting his party. Enough Charlie remained in him that he knew that was wrong. It terrified him that he still considered giving in to it anyway.

Never before had it been so clear to him that he had two distinct personalities. He shivered in fear, glad the gathered Scouts could only feel it and not know its cause.

"Everyone is fine, sweetheart. Just breathe, take a deep breath." The muscles in her back strained as she continued to retch and gag.

Charlie wrapped the ripped blanket around her shuddering shoulders. "Please, Sara… calm down. Everything's okay. We're all okay, and you aren't alone." The retching stopped, and she clutched him again panting.

Now seriously alarmed, he swung her into his arms. "Hawk, she needs you."

The magic had kept her alive, but had used her body as fuel doing so. Kept in the dark with no food or water for days while severely injured it was a miracle she lived. Sunlight would help her. Hawk's calming aura would help her more.

"Carry her outside into the grass and let me hold her," Hawk said as he sat by a tree in the sunniest spot he could find.

Charlie hopped from the helicopter and placed her in Hawk's lap.

The panting stopped, and her breathing slowed as she calmed in Hawk's aura.

"You're okay?" She hugged Hawk, burying her face in his neck.

"I'm fine." Hawk rubbed her trembling hands in his. "Take a second to catch your breath. Don't try to heal me. I don't need healing." Hawk placed their clasped hands on Charlie's. "None of us do. You healed everyone. Just sit. I wish more sun shone for you, but tomorrow you can sit in the sunshine all day, I promise."

"It was so dark. I was so scared." She began

to cry, quietly this time, and released Hawk's hand to hug him again.

Hawk whispered reassurance as Charlie glowered. He glanced to the helicopter where Oz and Stasia stood, and his glower deepened.

"You aren't alone," Hawk said, bringing Charlie's attention back to Sara.

"We're here." Charlie beckoned to Stasia and Oz. "See? Everyone is here, and we're all okay." He didn't know if she heard or understood. The terrible aloneness she felt eased when the others gathered close and surrounded her in their magic. Sobs muffled her words, and he only heard sunlight, and alone clearly.

Stasia knelt beside her brother and hugged Sara. She whispered something too low for Charlie to hear but it seemed to help. The sobs lessened, and she stilled but didn't relax her hold on Hawk. The fear rolling off her in waves made him feel sick. By Stasia's expression, she felt ill too, but all he sensed from her was worry and anger.

Oz laid his hand on Sara's shoulder, then sat beside her, reaching up to pull Charlie down too.

"Sit, Chief. You need to relax too." He waved a hand through the blue cloud surrounding them. "Your aura is so strong even I can feel it. Sara needs peace and sunlight."

Charlie grimaced but let himself be pulled down. Oz spoke in a low voice, telling Sara about a book he'd just read and his plans to make a computer code. Charlie didn't understand a thing he said. He couldn't focus over the humming of the magic beneath his skin.

The magic surrounding him gradually dissipated, and he could no longer feel their emotions. The pressure beneath his skin eased. Oz, Hawk, and Stasia no longer had glowing blue eyes, and he assumed his had reverted too.

Colors once more resumed their normal depth and brightness, and tension he hadn't realized he'd carried slid from his shoulders. Oz trailed off into silence, and they sat quietly, resting in Hawk's aura. Charlie didn't know if Sara dozed or not. Her face was turned away from him. Stasia slept with her head on Oz's shoulder, clasping Sara's hand in both of hers.

Mounties arrived. Guthrie spoke with them wearing a disguise Oz had casted to cover his filthy uniform. The Mounties never asked about the boy in black armor holding the half-naked girl. They didn't see them. Hawk had casted his No-See-Um, making them invisible.

The cover story again passed without comment. In twenty minutes, they were ready to leave.

Charlie crouched before Hawk, rubbing Sara's back. "Can you get on the helicopter now?"

She stiffened and sat, pulling her hand from Stasia and waking her. Not meeting their gaze, she nodded. "Thank you, Hawk."

Hawk handed her to Charlie and kissed her cheek.

Charlie nodded thankfully as Hawk tucked the blanket around her. When they boarded, she hid her face in Charlie's neck.

Sara tried to sit on her own, took one look at Brenda's blood splattered uniform, and was violently ill again. "I'm so sorry," she moaned. "Oh, my God, Brenda, I'm so sorry!"

Too dehydrated to cry, she sobbed as she apologized. Blue magic sprang from Charlie, his earlier relaxation vanishing as Team Valor gathered about him. Their angry glowers met his as blue magic seeped from their skin and coated them. A burning need for vengeance passed among them.

The blue surrounding them became darker and denser. Bright arcs of static leaped between them, and beyond a shadow of a doubt, Charlie knew the team would seek out and kill everyone involved. The magic demanded it. He embraced his rage. He wanted those men dead.

Brenda stood back, away from the magic swirling over Team Valor, wringing her hands as Sara continued to gag and strain with dry wracking heaves that shook her entire body.

"Sara, look at me!" Charlie yelled and turned her away from everyone else. "They're fine. None of this was your fault. Stop it right now! Brenda is just tired and dirty, not hurt." He sat and leaned over her, hating how frail she felt in his arms and the guilt she felt.

"You didn't see what they did to her because of me. They shot her, Charlie. Her brains were on the wall." Sara's voice quavered, and she shuddered and gulped. "They shot your brother in the head because of me. I watched them die!"

"I'm okay, Sara," Brenda said.

"Me too," Rick added.

Charlie glanced at the staring Scouts grateful for their continued support. They could easily blame them for their abduction, but they didn't, it was clear in their worried gazes.

"They aren't dead. You saved them. They don't blame you. Nobody blames you. It was horrible for everyone, but not your fault." Charlie grabbed her hands as she started a cast. "No, you used all your magic! Give it time to replenish. Nobody needs any more heals."

Angry and thankful, he ran a hand along her cheek and rested it on the bare skin of her collarbone.

The gagging stopped. After taking a few deep shuddering breaths, she leaned into him, hiding her face in his neck again. Her warm breath on his neck eased the tenseness in his shoulders. A blue mist coalesced and swirled around him in thick blue streamers. Sparks of blue and white static swept over them as he slid his other hand onto her bare thigh under the blanket. She pressed harder against him. The mist settled on her exposed skin and disappeared. They stayed like that until the helicopter landed at the airport.

While they remained seated, everyone disembarked. Team Valor took turns leaning down and kissing Sara's brow, murmuring reassurance, before leaving her with Charlie. Guthrie told Drew where to find the jet that would take them home.

"Shower first. Let's give Sara a break. We're all gross. I'm sure there's a locker room or something you can use around here. Clothes and food should be onboard. The plane leaves in one hour. Stick together, groups of three minimum and someone carry Joy. Yes, I know you're better, but you're weak, so let us take care of you." Guthrie insisted as Joy protested. "Dismissed."

Once everyone had left, he turned to Charlie. "Do you want to clean up, or get right on the plane?"

Sara shrugged as she clutched Charlie.

"We'll go right to the plane. I don't think I should stop touching her." Charlie stood, holding her close to his chest. She clutched him so tightly, if he didn't have a healing buff, she'd be leaving bruises.

"We saw." Guthrie frowned at him.

"That was magic going to her. It had nothing to do with sex." Charlie glared. "Her magic is depleted. She used it all in that healing frenzy and needs more."

Guthrie rose an eyebrow. "You can tell what it wants now?"

"No, I can sense my magic in Sara, and her lack of magic and how that hurts her. Until she can regenerate her own, she needs to touch me. If she has none, it hurts. She needs orange juice and sunlight."

"Okay, bring her to the plane, but I want to know right away if the magic gets loose. We don't want a plane crash."

Charlie nodded and followed Guthrie to the plane. A pile of sweatsuits wrapped in plastic bags sat by the door.

He grabbed two bags and carried Sara to the lavatory. The room barely fit them both. Skin contact was easy to maintain in the small space. When his chest was bare, she leaned against him.

For ten minutes, the magic swirled around

them as they held each other. Ten minutes of ebbing fear and growing love. It took Charlie immense effort to let his rage go and concentrate on his love for her, and he wouldn't have been able to do it all if he couldn't feel how his rage upset her. His love and happiness to hold her close eased her, making it easier to let himself embrace his kinder emotions.

When the magic reabsorbed into their skin, she pulled away.

"Better?"

Without meeting his gaze, she nodded.

With both hands, he smoothed her hair back and framed her face. His voice cracked, and he had to clear his throat before speaking. "I would do anything for you, even before we had the magic to share. I love you, Sara." Tears filled his eyes over her misery. He closed them and kissed her.

"I'll be right next door in the other lavatory. Take your time. We're safe here." Charlie handed her a bag containing a plain gray sweatsuit and went into the other lavatory where he stripped off the rest of his clothes and used the small sink to wash.

The smell of vanilla filled the room from the hand soap he used to shampoo his hair. Bloody water splattered the walls and floor. More smears formed when he tried to wipe up the mess he'd made with his dirty clothes. Without cleaning supplies, the mess was hopeless.

He stuffed his dirty, wet clothes and boots into the plastic bag his sweatsuit came in and threw the bag into an overhead compartment.

The rest of the bags of clothes were gone and the staff sergeant nowhere in sight. A quick search turned up sandwiches, sodas, and water in a cooler by the doorway.

Adrenaline still hummed through him. He didn't know it was possible to be this angry. Every time he thought of the bruises and marks on her soft skin, a hot surge of rage passed over him, prickling like pins-and-needles.

The sound of her tear-filled voice made his hands clench and pulse skyrocket. The phrase a killing rage took on new meaning for him. His anger angered him more. What she needed from him now was comfort, not rage.

Soon, he promised his magic. Soon, they would find those responsible for this and kill them all. A hard smile crossed his face. Soon, he would be Chief again.

Calmer, his rage pushed down deep, simmering; he took two seats in the back of the plane and settled in to wait for Sara.

-3-

THE RIDE HOME

When Sara finally appeared, wearing the gray sweatsuit that was tight on him but dwarfed her, her feet were bare and wet strands of hair tangled behind her ears. She stood in the aisle and bit her lip.

"Come sit by me." Charlie had to clear his throat again before he could speak. Her sadness and uncertainty hurt him. "Want some food or water?"

The water bottle he handed her fell unopened to her lap as she tucked her feet under her and huddled in the seat next to him. A small sob escaped her, and she clung to him again crying, pressing her cheek against his neck. The tears stopped after a moment, and her grip lightened as he stroked her hair.

When she relaxed against him, he kissed her temple and pulled away to see her expression.

"Want to tell me about it?" The need to know roared through him with a fresh wave of rage that she flinched from, and it took real effort to keep his voice light and not pressuring. If she didn't tell him everything, he wouldn't know who to kill. No doubt or mercy existed for him. Everyone involved would die, his rage demanded it. The wait to hunt them was agonizing, but she needed him now.

Shivers raced across her pale skin. Unable to meet his eyes, she drew away and fussed with the water bottle a moment before gulping hard. Tears clouded her eyes, but she didn't cry, she just closed them. He didn't need the magic to feel her shame and embarrassment, it was etched in every line of her body. The fury he felt when he contemplated what they might have done to her when she was alone and defenseless tightened his muscles and flushed his skin.

She gave him a worried glance, and he tried to give her an encouraging smile, but by her grimace, his smile looked as sickly as he felt.

She took a deep breath and said, "No, but I think I have too. The fight with Brenda and Rick you heard about already. After that they kept me tied up and drugged." Her voice hitched. "I don't know what they did to me then."

Charlie remembered the handprints on her arms and thighs and nodded slowly. He was glad she had no memory but hoped imagined horrors wouldn't cause more harm. "Whatever happened is over now, and we're together and safe. We'll deal with it together."

She flushed and rubbed her arms, not taking

his hand again when she dropped them but grabbing the armrest. Fresh rage surged, and he had to close his eyes and breathe deeply for a moment while she spoke.

The knuckles on the hand grabbing the armrest turned white, and she took a deep shuddering breath before continuing. "At first, they kept me in a box, and then a pitch-black room tied to a metal table. The drugs they gave me kept me confused. Time was all mixed up, and it seemed like I was there for years. Whenever I woke, I tried to get away, but I couldn't, and they always injected me again. I was praying so hard for Oz to locate me. Everything hurt so much, and I couldn't feel my hands at all just pain." She stopped speaking to rub her arms again and stare at her hands as if assuring herself they were still there. The sight angered him so much he accidentally cracked the armrest he gripped.

"I thought—" a shudder wracked her— "I thought they cut my hands off. How did you find me?"

"Three days and twelve hours ago they took you. Oz found you. You summoned him. He arrived in the room with you as the men entered. The shot they gave you was supposed to last six hours."

Charlie pried her hand off the armrest and kissed it, pulling her close, and rubbing her back.

"He said I metabolized it quick. I was almost always awake awhile before they returned."

"So cruel, to keep you in the dark like that." Charlie leaned over, putting his cheek against hers.

"I don't want to think about it." She shivered and pressed her face into his shoulder again.

Charlie pushed the rage back down. *Soon*, he promised it. Her pain infuriated him. The fear she still felt made it hard to sit there being Charlie and hold her when he needed to be Chief and find them, to stop them permanently.

"No one is hurt?" The hand holding his clenched.

"All the Scouts are perfectly fine. Our parents are at a safe house, or they were at least. I don't know where they are now, but I'm sure they're fine." He grimaced and rubbed his face hard with both hands. He'd been so consumed by his rage he hadn't taken care of anyone at all. "Liz was shot. As of the last report, she was recovering, but I'm ashamed to say I didn't keep up with the reports on her condition. Guthrie will know. When he gets back, we'll ask." Charlie mentally smacked himself in the head. He needed to do better, lot's better. Wallowing would help no one. He should know where the people under his care were at all times.

"And Prince… who's looking out for him?"

He groaned and squeezed his eyes closed, *poor Prince and the kitten*. The kitten had likely died locked in that box. Prince might be alive. That kitten had saved her life, and he'd let it die in a box. If he hadn't gone there and found Liz, if he'd waited to see Sara until the next day, Rinto might have managed to hide her. With enough of a head start, Rinto might have been able to take Oz too, leaving Charlie with no way to find her.

He'd hesitated too long.

"Prince is dead?"

"I don't know. I'm sorry, sweetheart, I was distracted. Prince never crossed my mind," Charlie admitted.

Both of her hands clutched his now.

Prince meant the world to her; he should've checked. He pulled his hand from her cold one and opened her drink. "Drink some please."

The small sip she took made her gag. "I can't yet. I'm sorry. You eat. I need a little time." Huddled in the blanket, holding the water, she sat back in her chair with her feet under her.

Marcus and Joy boarded, followed by Tony and Brenda. They grabbed sandwiches and sodas and settled into their seats, leaving Sara and Charlie alone in the back.

Tears brimmed in Sara's eyes when she saw them, but it was her guilt that made him moan.

Dark and black he could feel it without magic it was so strong. He might have thought it his own feeling if it hadn't hit so suddenly and intensely. He didn't know if the reason he still felt her without magic swirling around her was because she had his magic and he was holding her hand, or his was trying to warn him, but her despair felt awful.

"When we went to Iraq and got Rick, I thought we were saving him, saving them all, but look what I did to them."

"They look okay to me," Charlie said, trying to imbue his voice with sincerity. He had no idea if she felt him as he did her. He hoped she didn't. Every spike of guilt from her was met by an equally strong surge of anger from him, and he didn't want her to think he was angry at her.

"If we asked them, I bet they would say they would rather be here than buried in the sand of Iraq."

She closed her eyes and turned away as if she couldn't bear the sight of them. "They might have been rescued in time. We changed their fate. What happened to them was awful, the worst thing I've ever seen or even imagined."

"Yeah, but that wasn't our fault. We didn't do it. No one is angry at you just the men who took you."

"My head agrees, but my heart doesn't. This huge weight of guilt is smothering me, so much worse than anything I've ever felt." Sara hid her face against his neck again and cried.

Soft talking from the front of the plane as the rest of the Scouts boarded had her sitting up wiping her eyes before Charlie could formulate a reply.

Stasia, Oz, Hawk, and Rick arrived with Guthrie and grabbed sandwiches. After nodding to Charlie, who signaled them to stay, they took seats in front, letting Charlie and Sara sit alone in the back.

Guthrie rose and addressed everyone. "This plane is headed to Camp Pendleton. We should arrive in six hours, around one a.m. Write your reports before you sleep, every detail no matter how insignificant it seems. When we land, you'll all be debriefed." After assuring everybody started the reports, he sat by Charlie and Sara and handed her an orange juice. "Sara, if you could answer some questions?"

When she nodded, he turned on a recorder.

"Do you remember who took you?"

"No, I woke up in a room with six men." Pale and shaky, she kept her eyes closed and fidgeted with the unopened orange juice as she told Guthrie what had happened to Brenda and Rick when she'd first woke.

Every word she spoke sent a fresh wave of rage through Charlie. Rinto had a lot to answer for, not only Sara's pain but his brother's. The general who authorized Sara's abduction would pay with his life.

"When you were home, what's the last thing you remember?"

"Prince playing in the living room. When I finished packing, I went to wrap presents. The wrapping paper was by the tree. Liz had made a fruit salad that morning. I took some, and a soda, and started wrapping. Prince wanted to play with the Christmas ribbons, so I lay down on the floor to play with him. That's the last thing I remember."

"Did the food or drink taste funny or seem off at all?"

"No, not that I recall anyway."

"Can you describe anyone?"

Lines formed on her brow as she concentrated, giving descriptions of all the men she remembered. For over an hour, she described every man she saw and every detail her photographic memory held.

"Two men I never saw spoke Arabic and talked about getting Anastasia. They either didn't know or didn't care that I understood."

Charlie leaned forward and took her hand. Just mentioning them made her fear spike to all new highs. He frowned as he listened. Her inner fear didn't match her outward demeanor. She spoke calmly and didn't glance at him. Color bloomed around him as if the world had been clouded and he knew his eyes had flared blue. She was trying to keep him calm. Whatever those men had really said had terrified her.

"They'll never get either of you," Charlie said. She glanced at his face and winced and patted his hand.

Color resumed their normal brightness as he half-laughed over her comforting him. She gave him a real smile and turned back to Guthrie. Charlie was just glad her fear had lightened.

"Whenever anyone came in, I pretended to be asleep. They talked over me like I wasn't there, and I couldn't see them in the dark."

"When you say getting her, can you be more specific?"

"They said something like, 'The general promised us both the girls. We'll get Anastasia ourselves, and the deal is off.' One said I was only half, and they argued about money for a few minutes. The other man said, 'We can get the others ourselves, we don't need them.' They talked about cutting the general out and sending their own men to get you guys. I was in and out of consciousness while they were arguing. The drugs they injected me with made it hard to focus when I woke and cloud my memory. One of them said, 'We stick to the plan,' and I heard them say make it worth it or something like that. Then they debated over telling their men what we could do. But, I don't know how that argument ended, that's all I remember."

Charlie's grip had tightened when she'd said the general. "Oz heard them call their boss the general. Is it Major General Campbell?" He'd wanted to keep that knowledge secret and go investigate themselves. Privacy laws and red tape wouldn't stop them when they investigated. Nothing could be hidden from Stasia. But, since Sara had mentioned him, he might as well find out what they knew.

"First I've heard of it. Excuse me; I need to speak with Oz." Guthrie hurried to the front where he sat beside Oz and shook him awake.

"I never even thanked him," Sara whispered as they watched the staff sergeant speak to Oz.

"We will, but he knows."

Charlie stared at Oz as he gave his report caught by conflicting needs. Chief wanted to learn of the enemy's movements, and Charlie wanted to stay with Sara.

"Go listen if you want. I'll be okay." But she gripped his hand.

"It doesn't matter what they say. Stasia will find out everything we need to know," he said absently and lifted Sara, placing her on his lap, putting his cheek against hers. "Right now, I need to be with you." Snuggling her next to him, he reclined his seat as far as it would go.

A contented sigh escaped him as she ran her hands under his sweatshirt and pressed harder against him. The pilot had turned the main lights in the cabin off. Only a few small lights remained lit as the Scouts wrote reports, leaving the cabin shrouded in shadows. Most of the Scouts were already asleep or busy writing. With a small shrug, he pulled his sweatshirt off and laid back down, pulling Sara on top of him. A soft blue glow covered him. Sara pressed as close to him as she could get, and the glow intensified.

"Take your shirt off," Charlie whispered. "The blanket will cover us."

With a glance to ensure no one watched, she took off her shirt and lay on his bare chest. When their naked chests touched, she gasped.

Another small sound of contentment came from Charlie as he ran his hands over her bare back and snuggled closer. The blue seeped into her skin, and she relaxed as his magic filled her.

"Am I hurting you?" she whispered.

"Not at all." Emotion made his voice crack. "It feels good. I can feel it make you better." He kissed her temple. "You feel good. If we had no magic at all this would be enough."

Both closed their eyes, enjoying being together. The monotonous hum of the plane engine soothed him to sleep.

Warm tears on his neck woke him. When he became aware of her distress, his magic left him in a rush and surrounded her. "I'm here," he murmured as he stroked her bare back. The magic made her fear and loneliness clear to him. She sobbed and tightened her grip on him. "Nothing will hurt you while I'm here and I'll be with you forever. I love you. Everyone is fine." Slow and easy, he rubbed her back and then kissed her temple before pulling her further up his chest to rest his cheek on hers. "How can I help you?"

A headshake was his only answer. The change in pressure from the descending plane caused his ears to pop. The thought of being separated from her on landing upset him too.

"I swear to you, Sara, no one will ever separate us again. I'm staying with you. You won't be alone." The crying stopped, but her grip didn't relax. Anxious, and not knowing what else to do, he murmured more endearments and kept rubbing her back until she relaxed. Blue magic lit with static swirled around them and settled into their skin as her grip eased. With gentle touches, he kissed her hair and neck.

She pulled him to her lips. When he started to pull away, she used both hands to hold him. For the first time, he became aware of her bare breasts against him. Until now, it hadn't been sexual. Pressed so tightly against him, his arousal would be obvious. It didn't need the magic to make his feelings clear.

Heat flooded his cheeks. She needed comfort, not pawing. Doing what he could to minimize his reaction, he grasped her waist and kissed her until she was breathing harder and let him go, putting her face back in the crook of his neck. He was relieved she felt better, less afraid and comforted from her deep loneliness. The feelings he sensed from her became harder to decipher as the magic dissipated until he had only her reactions to go by. He bit back his frustrated growl. Her reactions gave him no real clue to her feelings. He wanted to know what she felt, not guess.

Others in the cabin started moving around as the plane continued to descend. He made sure the blanket covered her before he pushed the seat up more, and reached over to grab a sweatshirt and helped her put it on. Dim lighting in the cabin revealed her bloodshot eyes. He smoothed her hair.

"I love you," he repeated, staring into her teary eyes. "Anything you need, I'll get you—anything! The team will make sure you're safe."

Not wanting to let her go, he hugged her again, ignoring the seatbelt light, and ran his hands under the sweatshirt over her back. Gradually, she relaxed against him. He continued to rub her back in long slow strokes until the plane landed.

Guthrie kept an eye on them. Hoping alertness would forestall any unfortunate magical excesses, he stayed on watch the entire trip. Half of the flight he spent on his phone both hearing and making reports while watching them. The blue glow brightened, and he saw how it dissipated. It wasn't quite sexual, but it wasn't platonic either. He left them alone. He didn't understand the magic; no one really understood the magic. Sara and Charlie obviously needed each other in a completely new way. As long as they didn't blow up the plane, he would let them be. Let his parents worry about Charlie and his girlfriend, he would worry about his team.

-4-

THE PROPOSAL

Charlie stared out the picture window overlooking a tranquil pool. Dull, predawn light lit the uninhabited apartments and shimmered on the wet hair soaking Sara's gray sweatsuit. No supplies were available in the bathroom except a bar of soap they'd stolen from the plane.

The empty room was shrouded in gloom, lit only by the light from the bathroom she'd just come from. No furniture or personal items of any kind softened the echoing emptiness of her small apartment.

From now on, this would be his home too. The magic needed her, but he needed her more. No one would ever touch her again. From this day on, he would take care of her. His presence eased the aching loneliness she felt.

Loneliness was too small a word for the feeling he sensed from her when his magic touched her. She was alone in a way he didn't have words for, a way that grew until he could feel it without magic and eased when his magic coated her. He'd concentrate and surround her again in his magic until the feeling eased, and each time he did, it took longer for the loneliness to build back He hopped the feeling would soon leave her entirely. Just feeling it second-hand was so unpleasant he cringed remembering it.

They'd just gotten in. The plane had landed three hours ago, but Sara had given another statement, and they'd both wrote out quick reports. Guthrie had given him the keys to this place. The apartment held no furniture but was somewhere to be alone, and the shower worked.

When the sun rose, they would go outside. His brother had offered to get them bathing suits when the stores opened so Sara could absorb as much sunlight as possible.

Even after a half hour long hot shower, her hands remained icy cold. The nausea seemed to be passing though. She'd been able to keep down the orange juice she'd drank, which relieved him.

Physically fine, stress caused her illness. Dark circles ringed her eyes. He was exhausted too. This wasn't how he wanted to ask her. In his daydreams, he'd imagined a romantic dinner and moonlight, but he couldn't wait. If she said yes, he would move in with her. His parents would be unhappy but would have to accept it. Sara needed him. In fourteen months, when he turned eighteen, they could marry with or without parental blessing. Meanwhile, he would live with his fiancé. If anyone tried to stop him, he would take her away.

He held her close in front of the window, cleared his throat, and spoke softly. "I love you; I'll always love you."

A cold cheek rested against his as she stood on tiptoe to kiss him.

"I've told you that before. We're both very young, but neither of us is a child anymore." With a hopeful look, he knelt before her, taking her hands in his. "Everything I am, everything I have or will ever have, will be yours. I want to marry you, to be your husband, to take care of you forever. We'll never be separated." The intensity of his feelings caused his magic to swirl around him as he spoke. "Sara Mitchel, will you marry me?"

Sara's eyes widened, and her hands trembled in his as she pulled him to his feet. "I love you too. I want to be with you and be your wife." Her blue eyes began to glow. "I will love, honor, and cherish you forever."

A soft blue glow covered her exposed skin and static arced between them.

He grinned at her. Love shone in her blue eyes now and danced along his skin, the magic transmitting her feelings. With all his heart, he wanted to be her husband and see her beautiful eyes shine with love and happiness every day. "Sara, we belong together. When we legally can, I swear, I'll marry you, but from this moment on you *are* my wife."

The magic swirling around them collided violently when they kissed. White and blue lightning struck, immobilizing them. Charlie didn't have time to do more than gasp before pain grabbed him and rooted him to the spot.

Drew and Joy were crossing the courtyard when the window blew out. Instinctively, they took cover. Charlie and Sara stood frozen in place in the second story window outlined with blue and white lightning. The lightning surrounding them flowed out the window where it traveled up the side of the building and onto the roof where it was lost from sight.

"Shit, Joy, call Guthrie!" Drew yelled. "The last time that lightning struck, they needed CPR. Get us some help." Without waiting to see what she did, he ran across the courtyard and into the building.

The door to Sara's apartment was locked. A dull thud and a small dent were all he managed when he kicked the door as hard as he could. Frustrated, Drew ran back outside.

Joy spoke on the phone, staring in the window. Lightning still coruscated over the roof. Sara and Charlie stood unmoving, outlined in brilliant white.

"Joy, boost me up!" he yelled, gesturing to the broken window.

"You boost me. You can throw me right to the window!" Joy ran over to him still on the phone. "Damn, wait. Guthrie is on his way and says to wait for him."

Joy backed up until she could see in the

window again. "How long?"

Drew glanced at his watch. "Four minutes, thirty seconds."

"I'm tempted to jump in the lightning; maybe it will give me magic," Joy whispered.

"That's a big risk, Joy, it might kill you, and there's no healer here."

"Where's Hawk?"

"HQ, which is over six minutes away. If you die, you die for good. Please, don't do it." Drew took her hand.

Joy nodded and bit her lip.

Five minutes and fifteen seconds later, the lightning disappeared. The light pulsed as it traveled down the building, back into the room, and absorbed into Charlie and Sara. Joy spoke on the phone again, describing what she saw.

Sara's knees folded unable to support her. Charlie caught her, pulled her closer, and sat abruptly with her on his lap. The pain faded as if it'd never been, leaving him weak and shaking.

The lightning had changed him again. This time it hadn't given him magic, it had given him Sara. Somehow, it had connected them. Love, amazement, fear, worry, one after another her emotions flashed through him all much clearer than when they stood in the magic. Where the emotions matched his, they echoed. The ones that didn't match stood out, a wrong feeling, an itch he couldn't scratch. When he touched her bare skin, her emotions came clearer yet. He could almost hear thoughts in them. Physically she felt different, softer more fragile and at the same time stronger and warmer than she had been.

A low sound of contentment issued from her when he ran his hand over her arm. The contentment came through clearly followed by love. His love and happiness met hers and echoed, magnifying what he felt. When their lips touched, he froze. The merging of awareness intensified the light kiss until he was lost in the sensations, not knowing whose emotions he sensed.

With his eyes closed, he could see her. A yellow ball of energy made up of hundreds of individual threads of varying thicknesses and brightness snarled together, yet somehow beautiful and perfect. With a small shock, he realized the yellow ball was himself as well. Bright lines connected to her pulsed with energy. When he opened his eyes, he expected to see them, they were so bright and clear, but he saw nothing. Visually, she appeared the same. He closed his eyes again and kissed her while watching the energy. One strand flared and then another and another. The light passed through the ball that was them, leaving glowing edges and pulsating shimmering strands. To learn what each was would take a lifetime.

The power of the kiss lessened, and he realized she wasn't echoing to him now. Instead, she seemed removed, distant. A frown of concentration furrowed her brow, and he realized she was trying to figure the connection out.

With a grin, he kissed her again purposefully breaking her concentration. Wet hair tangled in his hand, and the heat of her skull warmed his entire body. Desire for him flared hot and bright and echoed his own for her. Caught up in the intensity of their feelings, he lost track of time.

This connection amazed him, and he hoped it wasn't temporary.

-5-

WEDDING RECEPTION

Drew called out, interrupting his enthrallment with Sara. More than anything, he wanted time to explore this new connection.

"We're fine," he shouted. "We need some privacy. This is no one's business but ours." He pulled her face against his chest, smoothing her hair back, even as he yelled at Drew.

Disappointed, sad, and a bit anxious now, again her emotions echoed him. Tingles of embarrassment came from her. The mismatching emotion was an itch; he wanted to be in sync. His anger probably felt off to her too. This would take getting used to.

"Sorry, Chief, but your window almost killed us," Drew said. "The lightning hit you again, and you froze for five minutes. Are you both okay?"

"We're fine," he repeated in a more normal tone. "Look, Drew, this is a private moment for us, could you—"

"Too late, we already called," Joy said. "The lightning worried us. What happened?"

"We got married," Sara said in an amazed voice.

Charlie tightened his grasp on her, kissed the top of her head, and smiled at Drew. The connection to Sara was clear and unmistakable; they were truly married. He hadn't expected this, but he liked it. Irrevocable his now, every fiber of his body felt connected to her. The anticipation swirling through her when he kissed her hair sent a bolt of desire through him. Knowing she wanted him to kiss her, to touch her, and how much she wanted it, was amazing.

"You what?" Drew asked in bewilderment.

Charlie smiled. "We got married." Heat suffused him when his lips touched hers. Aggravated with Drew, he cut the kiss short. "The lightning married us. It might not be legal, but it is binding." Still holding Sara, he stood and jumped to the ground.

The glass from the window had blown out in one solid piece and lay twisted up on the ground. The grass by the pool would be sunny soon. Afraid to tear apart the ball of energy that was them, he sat with her in his lap, keeping her close. Craving, he assumed was for the sun by the way she held her face to the sky, flickered over her in waves mixed with fear.

"The sun will be up soon, sweetheart. Rick is getting us bathing suits. We'll sit here in the sunshine all day." Another swirl of emotions came from her settling into uneasiness and need that eased when he touched her bare skin.

Cold hands warmed against his back as she ran her hands under his sweatshirt, getting as close as possible.

Drew and Joy exchanged dubious glances.

"You know what she's thinking now?" Joy asked hesitantly.

"I recognize she needs to touch me, and I need to touch her, but no, I can't read her thoughts." This new connection would be hard to explain. It wasn't just her feelings he sensed, but her. As much as any other part of his body, she was a part of him now.

How can you explain to someone how you know your foot is attached to you? He thought and sighed in frustration. In the same way the hurt from a stubbed toe traveled from his foot to his thoughts, her emotions built. Even when she felt nothing strongly, he felt her like he did every other part of his body.

Sharp spikes of emotion emanated from her as he spoke. Love for him and embarrassment when he told Joy she wanted to touch him. When his hands touched her, she felt safe and content.

The awareness was fleeting, small moments of connectedness, stronger with skin contact. Most of her emotions were so subtle if he didn't try to notice them, he wouldn't. Some spikes were bigger, unmistakable. When his hands slid under her sweatshirt and rested on her bare back, she sighed and felt loved.

Closing his eyes, he laid his head on hers, basking in her love, letting her enjoy his. The echo built until it hummed so strongly he almost expected it to become visible. It wouldn't surprise him if she suddenly glowed golden, her love for him visible to everyone. He laughed when she glanced at him puzzled by his smugness.

Drew and Joy exchanged glances. Both looked relieved when Guthrie arrived.

"Is everyone okay here?" He placed his hands on his hips and inspected them with narrowed eyes.

Charlie sighed heavily, just wanting to be alone with Sara without having to explain or defend their actions, to sit in the hot sun and feel her grow stronger.

Get this over with, he thought and sat up straighter. "We're fine. I'm sorry I broke the window. I'll replace it." He hoped Guthrie would let it go at that, even though he knew he wouldn't.

Guthrie made a dismissive gesture. "The window doesn't worry me. Joy reported you frozen in place nonresponsive for five minutes. That's what I'm worried about."

"We didn't plan that. The magic sealed a vow. Sara's mine now, and I'm hers. We married each other. We'll never be separated again," Charlie said.

Guthrie put his face in his hands and visibly counted to ten.

Joy snickered. Drew poked her, making Sara giggle. Charlie stifled a laugh.

"That's romantic and all, but you're too young, you both know that," Guthrie said as he dropped his hands.

Charlie shrugged and grinned at Sara. "Yes,

we're too young to be legally married. We know that. It doesn't matter. It's too late. We're as married as two people can be."

"Okay, kids, I realize you're in love and have a magical bond, but that doesn't mean you can just say you're married."

Charlie laughed. "What you say or think doesn't matter. Sara is my wife. A piece of paper won't change anything. My magic is now hers. Everything I am is now hers. Our connection is real. Nothing anyone says will change that." He kissed the top of Sara's head, her confidence and pride in him came through loud and clear. She trusted him, and he wouldn't disappoint her. No one would separate them.

"What about what your parents say?"

"What they say will be between us." Charlie sighed and kissed the top of Sara's head again before meeting the sergeant's eyes. "As much as we could we've cooperated trying to understand the magic. We trained to help people and want to help them. But, this is private and has nothing to do with anyone except us. I don't know why, but our magic likes to be together, and it's helping us do that. You want us to give it to someone else, and maybe someday we'll be able to, but today we need to be together, just us."

"And tonight?" Guthrie asked.

"Forever," Charlie replied evenly, as Sara's grip tightened and worry replaced her earlier love. "She's my wife, and we won't be separated."

"You're too young—"

"Are you more of a man than I am? I can take care of her. In fourteen months, I'll be eighteen and able to legally marry. Does it matter that much to you? Will I suddenly be a man then? What will make me a man in your eyes?"

Guthrie sat beside him. "No, you're right. You're a man, a young one, but still a man. You haven't been a boy for a while now. But, she's still so young, Charlie."

"You think she'll change her mind, or be sorry she married me?"

Guthrie threw back his head and laughed. "No, I surely don't." He stood and dusted off his sweatpants. "I wish you both happiness. Congratulations. I'm not telling your parents for you though, and they'll be here tomorrow. This has to be reported." A troubled glance flitted between them. "I wish I could say this would remain a private matter, but we all know there'll be questions and lots of them."

Hands on his hips again, he gazed at them a moment. The pool was peaceful and serene, the twisted, broken glass in the grass a stark warning. "Stay here in the sun today. Tomorrow, there'll be meetings to attend. I assume you both want to be involved with what's going on. Liz will be here, Sara, and sends her love."

He leaned over, gripped Charlie's shoulder for an instant, and kissed Sara on the top of the head. "I love you guys. Take care of each other and get some rest. In a few hours, I'll make sure there's food here." After one more troubled glance, he pulled Joy aside, and they spoke a moment. Joy returned, and he left.

Drew and Joy stayed with them, sitting quietly, watching the rising sun dance on the water. "We should celebrate," Joy finally said. "Wait here; I'll bring back food."

"And bathing suits," Drew added.

"Call Rick. He's picking up ours and could probably get more." Charlie didn't look up. All his attention remained on Sara.

Drew rose and loped after Joy.

"Alone at last," Charlie murmured.

Sara sighed and ran her hands over him.

Contentment eased her fear when she touched him. His lust didn't seem to bother her. Unable to stop his desire, he didn't even try to. But he kept his caresses on the bare skin of her back and his kisses light.

She needed time. Her feelings for him were a complex tapestry. The warm deep glow of her love bathed him. A deep need flickered, easing when he touched her. Brighter and hotter, was a sense of worry, a dark fear. Rubbing her back and kissing her neck eased her fear. He wondered if this closeness would last.

Stasia, Oz, and Hawk showed up, followed seconds later by the Scouts. Sara's feelings of guilt grew as they arrived, a black, heavy weight.

When he closed his eyes, he could see it. A dimming of the golden radiance that was her.

"Stop it! You have nothing to be guilty about. If they took Stasia instead, would you expect her to feel guilty? Well, she doesn't expect you to either."

With one arm, he waved Brenda over keeping the other around Sara. Sara's guilt grew. No outward sign betrayed her, but her distress suffused him.

"Sara is horrified that you got hurt and blaming herself," he told Brenda.

Sara plated the grass with nervous fingers, avoiding their eyes.

"I'm fine. I won't lie, it was horrible, and I'll probably have nightmares, but I don't blame you at all. If anyone should feel bad, it's me." Brenda touched Sara's shoulder lightly. "My job and duty is to protect you. If I hadn't been there, they wouldn't have hurt you."

Sara's guilt worsened; her pain his. Unsure how to ease her distress, he hesitated before speaking. "Sara, if you'd never met Brenda, and she was rescued and sent on another mission, a convoy or whatever, and been badly injured, she wouldn't have blamed the people who sent her there. She's a soldier, and it's her duty. There's nothing to be guilty for. It's hard because you love her, but she would've done the same thing for anyone she was duty bound to protect."

Charlie sensed only the slightest easing of her crushing guilt and wasn't certain her worry, worry that grew heavier as he spoke, was just obscuring it. This level of mental pain wasn't something he could help with. She needed professional help, someone to counsel her through this. The guilt was irrational but hurting her just the same. Tomorrow, he would ensure she got the help she needed.

Sara nodded and slid off Charlie's lap, keeping his hand clutched in hers. Charlie could tell she still felt horrible, but she was trying to hide it. In an effort to ease her distress, he spoke of normal things.

"Did you receive your housing assignments?" he asked.

"Yes, they aren't ready for us yet though, so we'll be camping out in them until we get furniture. Joy asked everyone to come here. She says we have something to celebrate, and you'll tell everybody."

Charlie smiled. "When my brother gets here, I will."

Sara released his hand and went to Oz. Charlie closed his eyes and tensed, expecting discomfort and possibly even real pain when her energy separated from his but felt nothing. The ball of energy that was them separated into two distinct balls with entwined strands, fading as she moved away from him until he couldn't see it anymore. The connection to her remained. Emotions still came to him, albeit with less strength and clarity. When he opened his eyes, she stood with Oz.

He couldn't hear what they said, but her gratitude, worry, and affection were clear. No excitement or anticipation swirled through her when she touched Oz. The love she felt for Oz didn't make him jealous. No passion or lust existed for Oz just a deep love the same as she experienced when she looked at Hawk or Stasia. The same love he felt for them. She didn't need Oz like she needed him.

Filled with gratitude, she took Oz's hand, and they went to Stasia and Hawk. Oz pulled away from her, rubbed his hand on his pants, and said something that distressed her.

Charlie rose to go to her, but they came to

him.

Brenda left to talk with Drew, making way for them to sit together.

"When I touch Oz, it hurts him." Sara bit her lip in worry.

Charlie held his hand out to Oz, who dropped it in fifteen seconds.

"Stasia, you try," Oz said.

Stasia took Sara's hand and held it for a few seconds before dropping it. With a small grimace in anticipation of pain, she grasped Charlie's hand.

"That doesn't hurt?" she asked, as she held his hand determinedly. After forty seconds, she had to let go.

Hawk leaned over and gripped both their hands. "Whoa!" he yelled and released both. Cautiously, he reached out, grasped Sara's hand, and dropped it after thirty seconds. Then he took his sister's and Oz's hands. "What's going on? I can still touch them with no problem."

Charlie pulled Sara into his side, kissed her temple, and grinned, the grin widening when she smiled back. "We got married. I guess its hands off for everyone now."

"You what?" Stasia yelled, clapped a hand over her mouth, and looked around guiltily. "You what?" she repeated much softer.

"We married each other," Charlie said firmly.

"When, where? How come I wasn't invited?" Stasia said, sounding hurt.

"A few minutes ago, and it was just us." Sara went to hug Stasia but stopped and gave her a wry smile.

Charlie explained what had happened.

"And you can read her thoughts now?" Oz asked, sounding intrigued by this new magic.

"No, her feelings. I'm more aware of the magic now. I have more of it, or maybe I have access to Sara's." Charlie glanced at Sara thoughtfully.

"Try one of her spells." Hawk leaned forward eagerly.

Charlie nodded and tried to cast a heal and instead jumped forward. "Hmm, same keybinds. Let me try again."

For ten minutes he tried, but couldn't cast any of Sara's spells, just his own. "I'll need access to the lab to see if my spells are stronger now. I feel stronger, or more complete, more— I don't know… more something," he said in frustration.

"Are you, Sara?" Stasia asked.

"No, I'm tired, but maybe after I get some sun. You have no idea how much I missed the sun. They planned to keep me in the dark forever." A shiver traveled over her.

She shook her head and changed the subject.

Such fear consumed her that Charlie expected to be able to see a black cloud surround her, but it was only visible with his eyes closed as a diming of her radiance. He pulled her closer, offering what comfort he could with his presence.

Sara leaned on him. "Guthrie said Liz will be here tomorrow, and Prince is fine too. It's so silly to be so relieved the cat is okay."

"No, it's not," Hawk disagreed. "I'm going to get a dog, a big one. It'll be the best-trained guard dog on Earth. When I was little, we had a dog, but a car hit it. My mom was so upset she wouldn't let us get another one. I'll train my dog to stay away from roads."

"This will be weird." Stasia's quick glance at the surrounding apartments was troubled. "Not living with my mom. I'm not sure… I'll miss my mother."

"You don't have to stay here," Oz assured her. "Live with her if you want."

Stasia nodded, but still looked troubled. Sara went to hug her again and stopped.

Stasia laughed and grabbed her in a quick hug, then held her longer. "When I'm not touching your skin, it's fine, and even that's fine for ten seconds or so."

"This is the first Christmas we've spent apart." Hawk glanced away.

"Jeez, I forgot today was Christmas!" Sara exclaimed.

"Well, it makes it easy to remember our anniversary." Charlie grinned at her. "Merry Christmas everyone."

"Next year we'll have an extra special holiday to make up for this one." Oz patted Sara on the hand.

"This was the best Christmas of my life," Sara said fervently. "And I can't thank you all enough."

"That was nothing." Oz touched her hand again, then squeezed Charlie's shoulder. "You would do the same for us. This did get me thinking though. I'm going to take time off from school. I have an idea for a computer program to help me do my locates, but I'll need time to work it out. Too many people go missing. Someone has to do something about it."

"Will they let you?" Charlie asked.

Oz shrugged. "How can they stop me? I'm not a soldier, and I have no contract or anything. My father will let me, I'm sure of that." He stared into the distance, a troubled expression on his face. "I want to stay here and keep up my practices with you, but spend my time on this project. It's more important to me than reading Chaucer or Shakespeare."

"We should all start thinking about the future more." Stasia put an arm around her brother. "What about you, Chief? Will you join the service?"

"I don't know. We haven't talked about it. Maybe we should stay private contractors. I don't want to take a chance they separate us. Do you want to join?"

"I'm not sure either," Stasia admitted. "On one hand, I want to be a full-fledged Scout, on the other; I would hate to be assigned away from you."

"You are a full-fledged Scout, silly." Hawk lightly pulled his sister's ponytail.

Stasia just shrugged.

Charlie understood what she meant. She wanted to belong to the team, to have the same responsibilities and privileges, to fit in with them. On missions, he was a real Scout. At home, he was just Charlie. He too wanted to be a permanent part of the team. To earn the right to wear the uniform in public, not just clandestinely on missions.

Later, he would talk to Sara about it, but not today, not for a while probably. Not until this threat to them was handled. With effort, he put it from his mind. Sara tensed up when he thought of the danger, his anger leaking through to her.

"It's okay, Sara, I was thinking of something else. Let's keep today for us, no work, no plans for tomorrow. Let's lay here in the sun and enjoy being together. We should go to an island, somewhere hot." The thermometer read sixty-two degrees. The coolness didn't bother them thanks to Hawk's buff, but she would appreciate the heat.

Sara nodded and slipped her hand under his shirt. He took it off, and she leaned on him with a sigh of contentment, contentment that grew, his contentment with her presence close to him feeding it.

"Are you hungry?" Charlie asked.

"No, you?"

"Not yet. I can wait until Joy brings back food." Charlie examined his exhausted friends. "We'll be here all day. Go sleep if you want too."

Stasia shrugged. "We might as well sleep here. We have no beds or blankets anywhere else. Are we intruding?"

"No, not at all," Charlie said, knowing it was true for both he and Sara.

"Good. I don't especially want to be alone either," Stasia said. "I do want a lawn chair though, or a towel or something." She took out her phone and went shopping.

Charlie leaned back in the grass, bringing

Sara with him, wishing the day were warmer for her. He stroked her back occasionally, enjoying knowing she was safe beside him. His hand resting on her bare waist made her feel better. Gradually, she relaxed against him, and they both dozed off.

"Mrs. H is going to freak," Oz whispered.

"Maybe not, she likes Sara," Stasia said.

"Doesn't matter what anyone thinks." Hawk shrugged. "We all felt that. Their magic has changed."

"I wonder if ours will too. I envy them their closeness." Stasia sighed. "We should get them a wedding present."

Oz grinned. "I know just the thing. See if you can find someplace open to pick up a bed today."

Stasia rolled her eyes and laughed. "Oh, god, Mrs. H is gonna kill us," she said, as she used her phone to look it up.

Joy returned, carrying four large bags, followed by Rick who lugged a stack of chairs. "There's more in the car, guys. Give me a hand."

Everyone got up to help and brought back lawn chairs, towels, and two coolers full of drinks and snacks. Charlie and Sara slept through it.

Stasia and Joy exchanged grins when Rick asked if they were celebrating Christmas.

Before long, everyone was settled by the pool.

Stasia placed her lawn chair as close to Rick's as possible. One of the towels Rick brought back made a good blanket. She wanted to take his hand but didn't quite dare. Instead, she curled up and fell asleep.

At one o'clock, Guthrie found them sleeping by the pool and helped himself to a chair. Joy and Drew woke, saw him, and went back to sleep. At two, Joy's phone alarm sounded. She turned off the alarm and went to pick up the food. Thirty minutes later, she returned with a carload of food.

Drew and Brenda helped her set it out on towels. Before long, everyone woke and ate ravenously. Sara sipped water and nibbled on fruit. Charlie enjoyed her happiness as she watched them eating and laughing.

When the sandwiches and chips had been devoured, and the boxes of cookies opened, Joy handed out paper cups and poured everyone champagne.

"A toast— to the bride and groom!" A grin on her face, she lifted her glass.

Half of the people there looked confused, and she burst out laughing.

Sara blushed hotly.

Charlie stood.

"Thank you, Joy." He met his brothers disbelieving gaze and grinned. "Sara and I got married this morning. You guys are the first we've told."

"Seriously," Rick said in such a surprised tone Stasia laughed. "How could you? There hasn't been time, and you're too young to even get a marriage license."

Charlie gave him the by now familiar explanation. "She's more a part of me than any license or preacher could make her. It isn't just our magic; we want this too."

"Did you tell Mom and Dad?"

"Not yet. I'll call them later." Charlie tried to project reassurance to Sara whose worry and guilt had spiked at the mention of his parents.

Rick hugged Sara and kissed her cheek. When he hugged his brother, he jerked back.

"Yeah, sorry," Charlie said sheepishly. "I forgot it's so new. Only Sara can touch my bare skin now."

"I'm happy for you both." Rick smiled at them. "But, you surprised me. I wasn't expecting this for a few more years." Still looking shocked, he faced the assemble Scouts and lifted his glass. "To my new sister."

The Scouts laughed and drank and made toasts to the new couple. "This calls for music and dancing," Brenda said and borrowed Stasia's phone. She turned the music up as loud as it would go.

Stasia and Drew left to get a real radio.

Rick handed out the bathing suits, and before long everyone lounged in the pool.

As the sky grew dark, and the air grew colder, Oz used his flame shock underwater until the water warmed.

To Charlie's relief, happiness surpassed Sara's guilt. The relief she experienced might be temporary, but any respite was welcome.

Dark shadows encroached the pool until true night fell and swaddled them in darkness. Sara grew more worried by the minute, so worried his touch didn't ease her, which made him worry. The worry echoed between them, growing to uncomfortable proportions. The darkness took on shape and detail, and Charlie knew his eyes had begun to glow. He wished he'd brought his sword.

"Call Stasia please, Joy," she finally asked.

It relieved Charlie Stasia's absence caused Sara's worry, not the night itself or the thought of being alone with him. They needed to work this out; feelings could be easily misinterpreted. His relief eased the echoing worry, and he was able to separate her feelings from his.

Drew answered on the first ring. "We're fine. Her shopaholic instinct kicked in. We'll be back soon."

"Can everyone make sure not to go anywhere alone for a few days?" Sara asked. "You can take care of yourselves, but can also be outnumbered. They wanted you too."

"Everyone will be on base, Sara. No one will leave alone," Guthrie assured her. "That's an official order by the way, not a request. Today, we should be safe enough. They couldn't know we came here to get operatives in place, but by now, I'm sure they do. Everyone keep alert, stay in groups and report suspicious activity. This area is guarded and fenced, you need a passcode to enter, but take nothing for granted. They were willing to pay a lot of money for you. You'll be reissued sidearms, and we expect you to carry them at all times. We can talk more about this tomorrow, let's not spoil tonight," he finished with an apologetic grimace at Charlie.

Charlie glared at him, every word Guthrie said scared Sara more.

Charlie nodded in thanks when Guthrie

stopped talking and kissed Sara's lips quickly before jumping from the pool.

"You need food." With one hand, he lifted Sara from the pool. "How about soup? Joy brought back chicken soup earlier, we can heat up."

Sara nodded.

Brenda and Charlie soon had the food reheating.

Drew and Stasia returned with the radio. Team Beta arrived and greeted everyone with hugs and handshakes.

The party continued but grew quieter as the evening progressed. The Scouts broke up into small groups talking quietly or lounging in the pool, some had fallen asleep again in the grass.

Finally, Charlie rose from the lounge chair.

"Thank you for sharing our special day with us. Everyone has a busy day tomorrow, get some sleep."

The Scouts called well wishes after them. When he closed his eyes, embarrassment made a rose-colored tinge on Sara. The strands that he recognized as himself were faintly tinged as well; he was embarrassed for her sake. His smugness and anticipation weren't visible with his eyes shut, but he was sure she sensed it.

-6-

HURRIED DECISIONS

Stasia watched Sara and Charlie leave, sighed wistfully, and glanced at Rick who spoke quietly to Harrison and Tony. She gathered her courage and approached. They made room for her in their circle.

"I just came to say goodnight." Heart beating faster, she took a deep breath. "I don't want to be alone tonight, will you come with me?"

"Stasia, I'm flattered but..." Rick trailed off.

A jerky nod was all she managed. Her throat was so dry she knew trying to speak would make her cry. A hot flush scalded her cheeks. She shouldn't have asked him, especially not in front of anyone.

"I'll stay with you," Harrison offered.

When she nodded and held her hand out to him, he grinned. Without another word, they walked away hand-in-hand. The door of her apartment closed, leaving them alone together.

Harrison hugged her. "Rick is a fool for turning you down. No pressure, we won't do anything you don't want to." When she relaxed, he laughed. "Let's just sleep."

"Thank you, you're a good friend," Stasia said. "I'm not afraid to be alone. I just wanted..." Forehead wrinkled in thought and confusion she trailed off.

"Me too," Harrison said. "Sometimes you just need to be held, it isn't about sex. Not that I would say no," he finished hopefully.

She laughed and led him to her room.

"Oh, god, a bed, this gets better and better." A delighted smile lit his face. "I was picturing us curled up on a towel on the floor."

"Hot water, new fluffy towels, soap, and shampoo too. Take as long as you like. And, Harrison, I really appreciate this."

Rick stared after them in shock. He couldn't believe that just happened. Just like that, she'd left with Harrison.

"Dude, your mouth is hanging open," Tony said with a small laugh.

"He's older than I am!" Rick said indignantly.

"But, not as stupid," Tony said with another small laugh. "I wish I'd thought to offer."

"That's not funny," Rick growled.

"Wasn't trying to be," Tony said seriously. "If you don't want her, move out of the way. Any of us would happily take your place."

"For god's sake, she's fifteen!" Rick yelled.

"I'm willing to overlook it if she is." Tony chuckled.

"That isn't funny. She's fifteen, a minor! Never mind it's illegal, it's also wrong." Rick glared and clenched his fists.

"Don't get your knickers in a twist. It's not me she wants. I'll grant you fifteen is too young, but her experiences belie her years. She's killed hundreds of people for you. Was she too young to do that?" Tony asked as he walked away.

"Yes!" Rick yelled after him. "She was too young. She's too young for all of this!"

Rick scowled as he stomped away.

Guthrie caught up with him. "Can you make some deliveries for me? The MCX will have uniforms for everyone ready for pickup at oh-six-hundred. Can you get them and drop them off no later than oh-seven-hundred?"

"Yes," he snarled.

Guthrie put a hand on Rick's arm. "I didn't agree with lifting the ban either, but it *is* lifted. If you don't like how this is playing out, do something about it."

"What am I supposed to do?" Rick asked bitterly.

"Well, that's up to you. You're a resourceful guy." Guthrie patted his back hard and walked away. "Night!" he called in parting.

Rick snorted in disgust and went to his room. A damp towel spread on the hard floor made his bed, and now he had to lie in it.

-7-

MAGIC AWAKENING

Charlie noticed the dent in the door where Drew had tried to kick it in and made a mental note to have it repaired. A large bouquet of red roses sat on the small kitchen counter, perfuming the air with their delicate fragrance. Snacks and bottled water rested alongside it.

Sara read the message and her eyes clouded with tears. "Stasia and Drew picked this up for us. Everyone signed the card, but I'm sure this was her idea."

In the bedroom, Charlie found another surprise and grinned at the double bed. Two, new, white robes lay across a thick, blue comforter. "Man, she's the best friend ever."

"She really is." Sara grabbed a robe and headed to the bathroom. "I'm going to take a shower." A moment later, she yelled, "She bought soap, shampoo, and towels too!"

Charlie's smile grew. Sara's happiness bubbled beneath his skin like the champagne he'd drunk.

A few minutes afterward, she returned, toweling her hair.

Charlie gave her a quick kiss as he headed to wash up. Stasia had thought of everything. Razors for them both sat on the sink, and a frilly pink nightgown hung from a hook. When he saw it still there, his smile widened.

In the bedroom, crisp white sheets, illuminated by the light from the bathroom, covered Sara's slim form, making his pulse quicken. A mixture of nervousness and anticipation bounced between them.

"Do you want the lights on?" The bathrobe slipped to the floor unheeded as he climbed in beside her.

"No, the light from the bathroom is good." Warmer now, not ice-cold like earlier, she snuggled against him. "I love you."

"I'll always love you," he replied and kissed her, stroking the wet hair from her face.

Shared emotions echoed back to him, growing stronger with each passing minute. Desire from him, a need and loneliness that eased when she touched him from her, mingled until it became impossible to differentiate who felt what.

"There's no rush. We have all the time in the world. When we're both ready...."

She silenced him with a kiss.

Thirty minutes later, Sara panted beneath him. "You're sure?" Charlie stifled a laugh as she arched against him. Soft sighs and impatient hands urged him on as he knelt between her legs.

Her hands trailed across his back, pressing him closer. Relief filled them both at the small sharp pain. No one, except him, would touch her like this. Emotions mixed with physical sensations in a confusing cacophony.

As he tried to sort the perceptions, he held still, letting her adjust to him until anticipation obscured her discomfort. Excitement quickly put all thoughts out of his mind, and he finished in moments.

Somewhat embarrassed at his loss of control, he gathered her in his arms and rolled over until she lay on top of him. A mix of pleasure with a tinge of embarrassed disappointment swirled through her.

"Next time will be better for you." A blush heated his cheeks, and he hid his face in her hair.

In sudden alarm, he realized she was crying. Happiness mingled with contentment, but she cried.

"I'm okay. I don't know why I'm crying." Warm tears trailed onto his chest. Shaky and tear-streaked, she clung to him, her damp hair sticking to his sweaty skin.

Charlie kissed her brow, and pulled her closer, running his hands over her softness, relieved she wasn't upset.

"I'm surprised I'm not crying too." A small chuckle escaped him. "That was amazing. I love you so much, just saying that doesn't seem adequate. Those aren't big enough words for what I feel for you. We could do this a million times, and it wouldn't be enough. I want you more than ever. I want you desperately!"

Still kissing her, he rolled over until she was beneath him, pressing her into the mattress. With effort, he pushed his own desire away and concentrated on her response to his touch, feeling her need, but not knowing how to ease it.

The magic showed him what she liked, and he learned to gauge the small sounds she made, gaining confidence as her excitement built.

Afterward, as she relaxed, small tingles of embarrassment came to him.

"Everything we did was beautiful." His voice was deep and husky with emotion and he had to clear his throat before continuing. "The sounds you make and how you respond excite me. You know it, you share my enjoyment, don't be embarrassed," he murmured as he kissed her neck. "I want to do this a million more times."

Mild embarrassment still emanated from her, but she was mostly happy. With his eyes closed, he could see her exhaustion, a dimming of her brightness as she yawned and snuggled against him. His hands wanted to roam her soft skin, but she needed sleep. They had the rest of their lives to make love. He debated getting a cloth to wipe them off but didn't want to disturb her. Already, she dozed in his arms, perfectly content. *The hell with it. We can clean up in the morning.*

The bed shifting woke him. Damp from washing, she snuggled into his side after using the bathroom; he didn't remember falling asleep. Hot tears trickled onto his bare chest, and her fear infused him. He kissed her brow and smoothed her hair. "Bad dream?"

Soft, silky curls, brushed his cheek when she nodded, but she didn't speak.

"Want to tell me about it?" When she shook her head, he kissed her temple and pulled her up higher to kiss her lips. "Nothing you say will scare me away. Please, Sara, let me help you."

"It's just a dream. I'm okay. I'm sorry I woke you." Her fingertips flitted over him, resting on his chest.

The crying stopped, and the terror receded, and he couldn't help his smug flickers of pride that he could soothe her. He rubbed her back while kissing her until all that remained was happiness and soft sounds of contentment. Nightmares and the fear she experienced required patience. He would speak with a doctor tomorrow and assure she got the help she needed. A glance at his watch made him sigh. Two-hour naps weren't enough.

Patience, he reminded himself and resisted the urge to caress her.

"Go back to sleep, sweetheart. Nothing will hurt you. The raid and I will keep you safe." Relaxed and comforted, she fell asleep again in his arms while he rubbed her back in slow circles.

At five fifteen, he woke again. After washing up, he grabbed two water bottles from the kitchen. When he lay down again, she stirred. Soft, sleep-warmed skin instantly aroused him, and he wished they could spend the day in bed napping and making love instead of attending meetings.

"Don't go anywhere, I'll be right back," she said as she rose.

The toilet flushed, and water ran in the sink before she returned and knelt on the bed. Pale-gray morning light now permeated the room, revealing her body.

His breath caught in his throat; he'd never imagined anyone as beautiful as her. Blond, sleep-mussed hair formed a wild tangle down her back. The unopened water bottle slipped from his grasp as he tangled his fist in the unruly curls and pulled her close for a kiss, running his other hand over her body. The heat of her skin excited him, the echo of her response felt stronger now. He loved the lust she felt when he touched her.

Sara's eyes closed, and her head tipped back as he caressed her. Calloused from his sword, his hands were large and very strong. She was delicate and fragile, and he would have to be careful not to hurt her.

As he watched his hand on her body, a frown crossed his face, and he was abruptly angry remembering the bruises. Men had touched her roughly, so roughly she'd almost died. His hands were suddenly hyper-aware of the jutting bones caused purposefully.

Sudden confusion and fear emanating from Sara brought him back to the moment. His gaze snapped to her face.

Tears gathered in her eyes, which glowed with magic. The fright on her face as she covered herself and hunched away from him made his anger grow.

"I'm here for you. You're safe here." The sheet tangled around them as she flung herself into his arms and cowered, shaking in confusion and fear.

Someone had purposefully done this, terrified her so she shook in his arms where she should feel safe and loved. Rage filled him anew, frightening her, and he didn't know how to stop.

"No, sweetheart, I'm not angry at you."

A shudder shook her, and she flinched back.

"This anger isn't for you. I'm mad someone hurt you." Magic swirled around him in agitation, rushing to Sara and covering her in blue mist lit with bright sparks of static. It was like turning the dial on a radio to maximum. The feelings he'd sensed became almost overpowering they were so strong, and he realized the magic was amplifying as well as transmitting them. The rage roaring through him was scaring her badly.

"Rage is my magic's need to protect you. I'm a Protection Warrior. My hands will never touch you in anger, I swear it!" How could he still his anger when her body trembling against his, enraged him more? The fury that filled him couldn't be stifled.

Unable to stop it, he embraced it instead. Everyone who'd hurt her would pay. Team Valor would hunt them down. None would escape. The rage subsided, replaced by fierce anticipation as he promised himself and his magic they would ensure Sara's safety.

"I'm not at all angry with you, I swear it. This will be confusing for us. We need to trust each other. Are you afraid of me?" he whispered in sudden worry as she continued to shake in his arms.

Her grip on him tightened as she shook her

head. The warmth of her breath on his chest comforted him. When her cheek rested on his heart, anxiety supplanted the anticipation of violence. The fear he sensed from her receded as he combed his fingers through her hair, teasing the snarls apart until his fingers slid smoothly through the thick mass.

The shaking stopped, her terror exchanged for small spikes of uneasiness and worry. "It's only love for you, Sara." The sheet slipped as he leaned over and kissed her, and her feelings clarified further with the skin contact. "I can't help being angry when I think about what happened to you."

Her body stiffened in his arms and fear swirled through her again. The magic within him churned unpleasantly. A feeling he'd gotten familiar with the last few days. His worry enhanced the sensations until his skin felt bloated. He wasn't surprised when his magic burst from him.

"Let your magic mingle with mine. Mine is worried about you." A dense, dark-blue cloud surrounded them as their magic merged. White sparks flashed, and the smell of ozone wafted through the room. With both hands, he framed her face and pulled away to meet her eyes.

"I'm sorry this scares you, but we need to talk about it for a minute." He tangled a hand in her hair and pressed her against his chest. The warmth where his palm cradled her head comforted him. The scent of her skin calmed him even more when he kissed her neck. Magic surrounded them, magnifying her emotions, making them clearer until her feelings became his and he could almost hear thoughts in them.

The desire they shared flared to life, and he smiled against her hair. "I adore our connection, experiencing what you do, but feelings can easily be misunderstood. We'll have to trust each other. Believe me when I tell you an emotion isn't for you, and I'll do the same. We won't lie to each other. If you don't want to tell me what the emotion is for, that's okay too. We don't have to talk about things that scare you, but you need help. I'll speak with the doctor too, to learn to handle my rage better."

"I do need help," she said bitterly.

Misery radiated from her in almost visible waves.

"Nothing will separate us. I wish I knew how to comfort you more, but I don't. You need more help than I can give you."

He kissed her and rubbed her back, hoping to ease her, but his words upset her more.

"I don't want you to suffer like this," he finally said to say something, afraid his dismay and worry were being misunderstood as not wanting to deal with her problems.

He took a deep breath and tried again. "When you're ready, you can talk about what happened. I can't promise it won't make me angry, we both know it will, but the anger won't be for you. I'll stop talking about that," he said hastily, worried over how frightened she was growing. "Will you see a doctor for me?"

Deeply unhappy, she nodded.

Embarrassment, shame, fear, loneliness, and

worry swirled through her in a wild kaleidoscope of varying degrees hard for him to separate. Unable to help her, afraid of making things worse, he fell quiet, not knowing what to do. The sheet caught on his legs as he shifted. He yanked it away, held himself above her, and kissed her. In minutes, they were caught up, desire echoing between them until every kiss and touch of her fingertips made him groan.

The magic surrounding them settled into their skin, and with its disappearance her emotions faded to a vague background sensation, making it easier to differentiate their emotions.

"This emotion is for you." His voice was a deep, husky murmur as he trailed light kisses across her bare shoulder. "This will be awkward. I'm bound to feel lust when I think of you. Believe me when I say the spikes of lust from me, are for you, even if you're nowhere near. Trust me, and I'll trust you."

Sara's eyes blazed with magic, glowing blue in the gray morning light. "I adore you!"

His brown eyes smiled into hers. "I know. If the magic did nothing except this, it would be enough."

Tears filled her eyes again, but this time they were happy tears. "You really do love me."

Charlie smiled and brushed her hair back. "I'll always love you, forever and ever, my beautiful wife." He kissed her again, trailing his hand carefully along her soft skin.

A giggle tickled his neck, her breath a warm caress. "You're so smug."

His laugh ruffled her hair. "Yeah, I love

feeling your reaction to my touch." His voice deepened at her surge of lust. "You're so beautiful."

She tilted her head and made a contented noise as he kissed under her right ear.

"I won't be able to concentrate on anything. I'll be thinking about this all day," Charlie said as they made love again. Shaky and tear-streaked, she clung to him afterward.

Despite their lovemaking, she remained unfulfilled; craving something he had no name for, a hunger for him past desire.

Still experiencing an urgent need himself, he rolled over, letting his weight rest on top of her. He'd thought making love would sate him, but he wanted her more now, wanted to touch her everywhere; he didn't know what he needed, but he needed something. The sex wasn't enough; it made the need worse.

Urgent, not knowing why he possessed such an ache to touch her, he sat and ran his hands over her.

Pressed as tightly as she could against him, her hands skimmed his body.

"What is this, Charlie?" she asked in a quavering voice.

The pulse in her neck soothed him when his palm brushed it. "I think it's the magic. Rest your hand on my heartbeat, sweetheart."

She slid down his chest until her face was over his heart and put a hand on his neck, the other on his wrist. Her magic surrounded him again, and she relaxed against him.

As she calmed, the wild hunger for her eased.

One hand placed on the pulse in her inner thigh, the other on her heart, he breathed in relief. "It's the magic" he repeated, "It wants to know you're okay. My magic loves you too."

A moment's concentration called the magic out. Every time he did it, it got easier. It took him a few seconds of intense concentration to guide it over Sara. When it touched her, she sighed, and he felt her ease as his magic disappeared into her skin.

Intentionally, he called it out again. It was easier to guide it this time, and it flowed eagerly to Sara. Magic churned, flowing in wispy clouds, entwining around them, the magic's happiness dancing along his skin.

"The magic is alive," he said thoughtfully.

Her magic surrounded him in blue, smoky swirls lit with sparks of static. With a small shock, he realized he felt emotion from the magic, not just Sara. The differing degrees of fear he felt from her wasn't her, but it. She wasn't lonely; it was. Or maybe both were. In sudden worry, he wondered if she even knew the emotion wasn't hers.

His worry made her tense, and he tried to put the thought from his mind. They could worry about it later.

"Yes," she agreed. "My magic loves you too."

Both silently contemplated that. The magic wasn't static— it was alive. Not an ability, but an entity. The magic wasn't something he possessed, but something that possessed him. Unsure of how he felt about hosting an alien being, he was sure he liked his magic's love for Sara.

After a moments reflection, he decided he still wanted the magic. Other than when it had inhabited him, the magic had never harmed him and gave more than it took. The connection to Sara alone was worth almost anything. To please her like this and share her release, was amazing.

Even now, when they weren't making love, her emotions suffused him. Delighted by how much she wanted and needed to touch him, he grinned. Static flickered over them as he gathered her close and stroked her hair.

A deep sigh that he knew was contentment, brushed his collarbone when she laid her face over his heart.

Charlie closed his eyes and concentrated on the magic, trying to communicate, but all he managed was sensing and calling it out. Unable to achieve any meaningful connection, he gave up.

Sara was concentrating, but he doubted she would be able to connect either. Not only was she still worn-out, but he distracted her. Every small twitch or sound he made caused her concentration to waver.

"I'm too tired now. Later, when I'm rested, I'll try again." Relaxed against him, she yawned and nuzzled her face into his neck.

Charlie laughed and kissed her. "I'll go see about our clothes. I wish we could sleep in, but we have meetings. Go shower." When she snuggled closer with an indistinct murmur, he couldn't resist kissing her again.

Finally, with an unwilling growl, he left her in their bed. A look back from the doorway, and he almost returned. Mussed hair, rosy lips, and glimpses of soft skin enticed him. With another small groan, he turned away. A light laugh followed him out, and he basked in her love.

-8-

EARLY MORNING MEETINGS

When Charlie stepped into the hallway, Rick was dropping off bagged uniforms in front of Stasia's door. Before he could greet his brother, Stasia's door opened, and Harrison appeared, shirtless with his pants unbuttoned.

Harrison nodded to Rick, picked up Stasia's clothes, and returned to her apartment.

Rick stood motionless, his shoulders rigid.

Charlie was surprised, he hadn't known about Harrison and Stasia either— he wondered if Sara did. Quietly, he closed his door.

Thirty minutes later, Sara knocked on Stasia's door and gave her a quick hug. "Thank you so much! You're the best friend anyone ever had." A slight blush crossed her cheeks.

Stasia grinned. "Went well then?"

Sara wore a matching grin. "Perfect. We learned a lot about the magic. Charlie is calling Oz to fill him in, and he can tell you about it. If we didn't have to work today, it would be even better. Charlie said you spent the night with Harrison. When did that happen?"

"It's like living in a fishbowl." Stasia beckoned Sara into her apartment. The rooms were identical to Sara's right down to the lack of furniture except for a bed. "Nothing 'happened.' We're just friends. I didn't want to be alone, and you didn't need me hanging around either." An insincere smile flitted across her face, and she turned away. "I wanted company."

"Charlie and I will always be there for you. This will take getting used to, but it doesn't affect how we feel for you, for any of you."

"Oh, I know, and if I'd been desperate I would've come over, but Harrison agreed to stay."

"Why didn't you ask Rick?"

"I did. He turned me down flat." Stasia peered out her window, resting her forehead on the glass.

Sara hugged her again, being careful not to touch skin. "I'm so sorry."

Stasia nodded but didn't speak. Sara put an arm around her shoulders, and they stood together for a few minutes.

Finally, Stasia broke away. "It's stupid that his rejection upset me. I realize he has no interest in being with me. I even understand and agree with his reasoning, but it still hurt." Tears shone in her eyes when she faced Sara. "Harrison was a perfect gentleman. He made it clear he was interested but didn't push at all. I wish I were eighteen."

"I hear ya; if we were older no one would question our choices," Sara agreed.

"Did Charlie tell his parents yet?"

"He's calling them now. Not that he said anything, but he's afraid they'll disapprove of me. The idea of coming between them makes me ill, but I won't give him up."

Stasia returned to the small kitchen, grabbed a granola bar, and offered one to Sara.

Sara held up her hands and waved them in front of her. "No thank you." Tight-lipped she turned away and swallowed hard.

"Still can't bear the sight of food, huh?"

"Every time I think of food I see them being shot. No, I just can't." She went to the kitchen sink and splashed cold water on her face.

"You haven't eaten anything since you've been back?"

When Sara didn't answer but continued splashing her face, Stasia frowned and went to the bathroom. In a moment, she returned with a towel and handed it to Sara.

Sara dried her face, her voice muffled by the cloth. "I ate last night. I'm fine. A bit more sun and I'll be good as new. No need to worry about me. Worry about the boys. Those men talked of killing them to take us."

"That's so retarded. How did they think they could keep me? No chains can hold me, and I can disappear."

"Would you though if they also had someone

you love?"

"I don't know." Stasia pushed her hair behind her ears and rubbed her eyes. "We need to find and stop them."

"Yes, and fast. The boys need to be protected." Sara glanced at her watch. "I have to go; we're setting up an early meeting with Guthrie. Charlie wants me to get help with my, um, eating disorder." Flushed, she handed Stasia the towel, avoiding eye contact.

"Good, you need help. Don't be embarrassed. Everyone needs help once in a while. Speaking of help, who did your hair?"

Laughing now, Stasia pulled Sara by the sleeve into her bathroom and pointed at the toilet. "Sit. I bought supplies. Give me ten minutes and I can hide the circles under your eyes and fix your hair.

Fifteen minutes later, Stasia stepped back and gave a nod of approval. "Much better. Give me five minutes to finish my makeup," Stasia said as she walked Sara to the door. "We'll work out a plan today to keep everybody safe. Summon us so we have a timer. I kept thinking you would last night in your sleep again."

Sara blushed. "We didn't actually get much sleep. But, I'll summon you now, well, as soon as Charlie calls and warns Hawk and Oz. I'll have to be careful. Not only might they be seen disappearing, but Oz drives now. If I summon him from a car he's driving, I could kill someone."

"Be careful," Stasia agreed "but if you need us, do it, no matter what."

Sara nodded, looking uneasy, and left.

Sara had gone to talk with Stasia. She hadn't known about Harrison either. Charlie took the opportunity to call his father. "Hey, Dad, is Mom there too?"

"Yes, we're at the airport—"

Charlie interrupted, "Could you put me on speaker phone?"

"Yes." His father sounded worried now. "Is everything okay? They told us you were fine."

"Yeah, we're all fine, but I wanted to tell you something myself before you heard anywhere else. I'm sure you'll need time to get used to the idea. When you get here, we can talk."

"You're scaring me, son."

Charlie laughed. "It's nothing bad." He took a deep breath. "Sara and I got married yesterday."

A shocked silence filled the other end of the line.

"Sara was hurt bad. The details are classified. She's fine now physically, but fragile mentally. If you reject her, she would be heartbroken. I know this is a shock, and I hope you can forgive me for doing it this way, but she needs me."

"I don't know what to say. How did you do it? You're underage. Sara can sign legal contracts, but you can't."

"I'll tell you everything when you arrive. She'll be back soon. You and Mom are very important to her. I realize I have no right to ask this, but—"

His mother interrupted him. "You know we love Sara, but, honey, you're too young; you're both too young."

"Yes, we are, but we've grown up fast this last year. Mom, I'll never leave her, no matter who disapproves."

"It isn't disapproval exactly." His mother spoke slowly, choosing her words with care. "It's concern."

"The first chance we get, we'll talk more about this, but I have to go now. Things are happening fast around here." The soft snort of laughter from his father made him grin. "I love you both, and I really am sorry to surprise you like this." After saying goodbye, he called Guthrie and set up a meeting, then called Oz.

Charlie was just leaving the bathroom, after his shower, when Sara returned.

"Everything's okay. My parents know, and while they aren't thrilled, it's the age thing, not you." He placed a hand on the nape of her neck, careful of her fancy ponytail, and pulled her closer for a kiss. "Guthrie will meet us in twenty minutes. Want breakfast?"

She shrugged and picked up a cookie she pretended to eat. He helped himself to fruit and a granola bar.

"Stasia wants me to summon them for a timer. She's afraid I'll do it at an inconvenient time."

"Her and Harrison are a couple now?" Charlie pictured his brother's tense shoulders when Harrison left Stasia's room and frowned.

"No, he kept her company last night is all. They're just friends. She asked Rick first, but he turned her down." Sara leaned on him and put her cheek on his. "Mmm, you smell so good." She kissed his neck and ran her hands under his T-shirt.

Her desire for him mixed with his for her, magnifying it. The touch of her hands on his body was exquisite torture. Heat filled him, and he knew his enjoyment excited her. Emotions bounced between them, making it hard to tell who felt what. His magic wanted to manifest, the familiar feel of pressure beneath his skin grew as he kissed her, but he contained it.

Every touch amplified the echo. Charlie loved this connection. When she tugged him toward the bed, he laughed in delight, a laugh that turned into a groan when he saw the time. The meeting was less than twenty minutes away, they had no time to make love again.

"Oh god, this will suck. I don't want to go anywhere today, but we can't put this off."

Her grip on him tightened, and her desire faded, replaced by anxiety.

This did suck, Charlie thought angrily. His wife needed him.

"I'm not angry at you, just the situation," he said as her anxiety spiked.

She needed peace and sunlight, not meetings that stirred up bad memories, but they had no choice. With a moment of concentration, he called his magic out. The magic flickered in waves, appearing and disappearing in a cloud around his exposed skin before settling to his hand as he'd intended. He placed his glowing hand on her face.

Communicating with the magic became easier every time he did it.

When his magic entered her, she sighed in relief and did the same to him. He kissed her and stepped away, letting distance dull the connection.

"I'll call the guys."

Charlie called Hawk and Oz and told them Sara would be summoning. Already awake and dressed, they agreed. With small deliberate movements, staring at her fingers, she casted summon. When they appeared, she felt relief so strong it buffeted him like a blow. Still staring at her fingers, she reran the pattern faster and faster until Charlie took her hands and kissed them.

She'd needed to see her Call-for-Help work. He hugged Sara and mouthed thank you to Stasia over her head; Stasia had been right to have Sara summon. Stasia nodded and smiled sadly at him and then rested a troubled gaze on Sara who had clenched her fingers as she hugged Charlie, obviously trying to stop herself from running the pattern again.

"Sorry there's no time to get together now, we have an early appointment with Guthrie. After the meetings, we'll talk, okay?"

The rest of Team Valor nodded agreement. Charlie took Sara's hand and led her from the apartment.

Joy, Drew, and Harrison walked ahead of Rick on the way to the meeting. He ran to catch up, wanting to speak with Harrison, but not sure what to say.

"So, you guys had a good night too, I see." A laughing Harrison was saying to Joy when he arrived. Rick didn't know how it happened. He had no intention of hitting him, he just did.

Harrison saw the punch coming, Rick's furious face, and ducked back, holding up both hands to show he didn't want to fight.

Rick didn't care, he swung again. Harrison changed his hand position to block the blow.

"Dude, what's your problem?" Harrison hollered as Rick swung again.

"You goddamn pedophile, you're my problem! How could you take advantage of her like that?" Rick swung again and followed with a kick. The swing missed, but the kick connected, sending Harrison backward.

"It isn't like that!" Harrison yelled. "And it isn't any of your business. You had your chance!" Harrison sounded pissed off now and came back swinging.

"Knock it off," Joy said.

Other people stopped to watch. Harrison and Rick rolled on the ground, fighting for real. Rick was past reason, wanting to kill him.

"Stop this right now! That's an order!" Joy yelled and grabbed the back of Rick's pants to pull him off Harrison.

Furious, he swung at her while trying to shake her off.

With magical speed, she ducked and leg-swept him. "Stay down, Rick. Stand up, and I'll hurt you," she yelled in a furious whisper.

Drew grabbed Harrison and strode away, keeping a tight hold on his arm.

"Jesus, Rick!" Joy said, her whispering tone changing to exasperation. "We don't have time for this shit! Get your head in the game! You've just swung on a superior officer in front of witnesses. Luckily for you, you're out of uniform." Joy indicated the Army fatigues he wore. "Get up and go right to the meeting. No breakfast for you, and clean up. You're a mess. And, Rick, this better not happen again. You were completely out of line!"

Rick glared at her as he rose and dusted himself off. "I heard what he said."

Joy shrugged. "Drew and I are a couple, so what?"

"He shouldn't be a couple with Stasia! You know that, Joy." Rick ran his hand through his short brown hair, standing it on end.

"He isn't, but if he were, it wouldn't be any of your business. He isn't wrong, Rick. Everyone knows she would've preferred you. You did have your chance."

"Listen to yourself, Joy! She's fifteen! Harrison is twenty-two! That doesn't bother you?"

"Some," Joy admitted. "I do think she's very young to make the choices she does, but I'm trying to see her as an individual, not just as a fifteen-year-old kid. You're both still teenagers, but that wears off before you know it."

"There's a big difference between fifteen and

nineteen, and I'm almost twenty!"

"And she's nearly sixteen. The gap will always be there. In five years, no will care at all about the different ages," Joy added matter-of-factly.

"If I met her five years from now, it wouldn't be a problem," Rick agreed bitterly, "but it isn't then, it's now."

Joy nodded. "You do have a problem; I'll agree with you there. But, you're a smart guy. I'm sure you see the solution." Joy turned and followed Drew and Harrison, leaving Rick standing alone in the road. Most of the people watching had already cleared out; only a few remained to see him punch a nearby telephone pole so hard it shook.

-9-

GENERAL ASSEMBLY

Charlie was surprised to see General Campbell in attendance at the morning meeting. He'd assumed the general would still be under investigation. The rage he kept locked barely under control surged. Tense, and coiled to spring, his intellect at war with his instincts, he hesitated while Sara shivered, and the general stepped away from him holding out both empty hands.

"The general the men referred to wasn't me. We believe it was General Flores," General Campbell said in a calm voice.

With iron-will, Charlie forced the rage down.

Soon, he promised the magic in what had become a calming mantra. The man before him wasn't a target. Brave, or perhaps foolish to face him when he was so on edge, but safe from his wrath as long as he posed no threat to Sara. The rage settled.

General Campbell and Guthrie backed away from him as he approached, showing his rage had bolstered his protective aura. Satisfaction as they cowered from him and Sara's fear eased filled him, and she relaxed even more, trusting in his protection.

"Come in, and take a seat. Give me a minute, the printer is out of paper." Guthrie rose.

"Stay; I'll get it," Sara offered. "Charlie can talk to you alone."

Her relief was strong, so Charlie agreed. *Probably better to speak to them alone anyway.* Without her standing there, he could be blunter about his worry.

Guthrie told her where she could find the office supplies, and she left quickly, almost running.

Guthrie labeled the last folders and pushed them aside. "What's this all about? Not having second thoughts already?"

"Never," Charlie said with a smile. "Sara is just having a hard time with what happened to her. She's acting like she's fine, but it's an act. I feel her pain and fear. Nothing I say eases it. She needs—" He doubled-over, clutching his stomach. Her terror hit him like a punch in the gut. This wasn't a fleeting moment of fear or startlement but full-blown panic. He let out a sharp oof as he stumbled to his feet.

"Sara!" he bellowed and jumped over the table to grab the door handle. Her terror rose followed by pain so severe he screamed. Her need for him was desperate, making him feel sick with its intensity.

"What?" Sergeant Guthrie yelled as Charlie slammed through the door and leapt towards the stairs.

Men up and down the hallway poked their heads into the corridor.

"Back in your rooms, and close the doors!" General Campbell snapped.

Charlie leapt for the stairs, not caring who saw him. Her pain and fear beat at him.

"What the hell is happening?" Sergeant Guthrie called from behind him. "Charlie, she's fine. There are a thousand Marines here—"

The fire door Charlie kicked open reverberated off the wall with a loud clang, drowning out the sergeant's voice. Charlie ignored the stairs and jumped to the bottom floor, landing hard, and nearly ripped the door off the hinges in his haste to reach her. He heard Guthrie swear as he landed on the landing above him, but didn't spare a glance backward. He cursed himself for not wearing his headset. If someone had taken her again, he needed Hawk right now.

"Get Hawk," he shouted.

A growl of frustrated anger burst from his lips, but he kept running, hoping speed would make the difference. He didn't know where she was. The only direction he had was a supply closet. If they got too far ahead, he would lose them. The thought of losing her again enraged him, and he screamed his attack as he leapt forward into the lower hallway.

Men poked their heads into the hallway again. His pulse pounded so loud in his ears he almost didn't hear her weak cries for help. She was still in the supply room, and God help anyone in there with her. He casted Fury and rushed through the door.

"Help," she cried weakly between sobbing pants.

Small balls of light from her heal flickered over her, hard to see over the radiance of her Hand-of-Sun.

She lay on the floor trapped beneath a heavy shelf. Something had cut her face although no wound marred it now. She screamed a gasping cry and casted another heal. The shelf was crushing her.

"Get the light," Charlie snapped to Guthrie who'd followed him into the room as he yanked the shelf from her. "Heal yourself, sweetheart."

Supplies tumbled from the shelf, and she grunted and cried out. Small spikes of pain stabbed Charlie.

Her fear had lessened with his arrival. It lessened even more when the light went on.

"Get her out!" Charlie picked up the shelf and tried to set it upright, but the supply covered floor made that impossible. He couldn't release it to go to her. With a frustrated grunt, he picked the shelf back up.

Guthrie grabbed Sara and hauled her to the doorway. Bright lights flicked from her fingers, and her pain disappeared. She still wanted him with a feeling past need. He threw the shelf, not caring what he broke and grabbed her, swinging her into his arms as he ran back out the door. So strong were her emotions he expected them to manifest as a dark cloud or storm. He wished they would manifest so he could fight them for her. She huddled into his embrace, shaking.

"Nothing to worry about," Sergeant Guthrie said to the men who'd gathered in the hallway. "Get a clean-up crew here. A shelf fell, but she's fine. Get back to work."

Charlie kept his movements in a normal, human range but couldn't help the magic that swirled about him. He had no idea who'd seen it before he'd entered the stairway. In his arms, Sara took deep gasping breaths and laid her palms on his neck.

"I'm here," he murmured. "I felt you. I'll always come when you need me. You're safe. You're safe," he repeated, willing her and himself to believe it. He took the stairs two at a time. He needed to be somewhere private while he got control of his magic.

The magic swirling around him picked up speed and a feeling he didn't have a word for came from her, almost overpowering in its intensity. He groaned and stumbled to his knees. "You're safe," he repeated desperately.

General Campbell stood at the door of the meeting room with a worried expression on his face. He took a step forward as if to offer Charlie assistance in rising, then stepped back and gestured them inside.

"Is she okay?"

"No," Charlie said as Sara said, "Yes."

Charlie snatched a chair with one hand as he entered and plopped it before the window. "Sit in the sun. Maybe that will help."

"I'm okay," she said in a shaky voice. "Sorry I scared you."

"What happened?" the general asked.

"Someone turned off the light, and I panicked. I knocked a shelf onto myself as I ran for the door," Sara said in a mix of anger and embarrassment.

Guthrie returned and handed Charlie a box of tissues.

Charlie dabbed at the blood on her face. She spoke calmly, and if he didn't have this connection with her, he'd have thought she was fine. Maybe embarrassed and a hair shaken, but she wasn't fine, not even close to fine. The feeling he didn't have a word for grew in intensity.

She wanted something he wasn't giving her. She more than wanted it, she needed it. She needed it so strongly it was becoming pain.

"I'm here," he said again.

Her magic burst from her with shocking suddenness. One corner of his mind noted General Campbell and the sergeant ran for the door, but most of his attention was on the magic that crashed into him. It hit him so hard it knocked him to his ass and fluttered the papers on the table. She screamed a small gasping cry and fell forward, the sound drowned by the rolling peal of thunder that shook the windows in their frames.

A smell of ozone filled the air and the hair on his arms lifted. Another peal of thunder rattled the windows, and the magic surrounding him deepened in color. Tiny sparks of static expanded to lightning bolts that flickered about him and crashed into the metal objects in the room.

To Charlie's surprise, she wasn't afraid but concentrating hard. He was terrified. His skin felt tight as if the magic would possess him and the pressure would explode him from within.

"I need your anger," Sara gasped and reached for him. "Help me."

An alarm began blaring in the building. Charlie ignored it, his attention on the feelings emanating from Sara and the magic. Her calmness calmed him, and he closed his eyes to better see the energy that was them.

Fire danced over his exposed skin. The lightning hurt where it connected. It wasn't Sara's need he felt, but her magic's. It needed him, or more specifically it wanted protection. It was frightened. He held his arms out and tipped his head back, letting his simmering rage reach the surface.

"I need… I don't know what it needs," Sara said on a gasping groan.

Charlie took her hand, and the magic pulsed wildly. He yelled his attack and thunder sounded.

"Get my team," he shouted, hoping Guthrie lurked outside the door.

He snatched an empty chair and beat it against the metal table top. The magic calmed as he spent his rage, but it still wanted. Fear and confusion emanated from his wife. The fear growing as he destroyed the room.

"It's okay, Sara, I know what it wants. Get them here now," he shouted. "We need them!" He grabbed a broken chair leg and snapped it then lunged and spun, doing his attack rotation, feinting with the broken chair. "The magic is afraid and wants our protection." He casted every spell he could against the furniture in the room, leaving a trail of destruction behind him.

He let himself remember his fear and anger and pulled her tightly to his chest. "You're mine," he shrieked.

The door behind him opened. "She's mine," he screamed as he spun.

Hawk held up his empty hands and peered around the room. Oz pushed past him and stepped boldly into the magic. He grunted and stumbled when it engulfed him. The cloud of magic surrounding Charlie grew denser.

"She's ours too," Oz said and casted an instant fire wave across the table. He followed it with a fireball that blew a hole through the wall into the next room.

Saint Elmo's fire appeared and flickered over Hawk who still stood in the doorway. He held his arm across the door blocking Stasia's advance.

"Let her in," Oz said and held his hand out. "I can feel the magic's need. You're right, Chief, it is alive. It needs us. Jesus, it's so afraid and alone."

Hawk took Oz's hand and stepped into the swirling magic. Oz held his other hand to Stasia. They all cried out when she entered the magic. Thunder sounded again, and the lightning flickering in the magic grew larger.

"Cast something," Oz said and casted another fireball.

Stasia laughed and unsheathed her daggers.

Like Charlie, she stabbed and spun, going through her damage rotation, wrecking the furniture in the room and gouging the walls.

The magic surrounding Charlie slowed its wild swirling. Another wave of Saint Elmo's fire coated them as a softer peal of thunder shook the windows. In his arms, Sara trembled.

"We're okay. We can protect you." She kissed his neck on his wildly thudding pulse, leaving her lips on him. "We're okay," he repeated and stilled, running his hands under her shirt onto the bare skin of her back. She was so thin he could feel her heartbeat. The steadiness of it soothed him. His team still casting around him steadied him even more. The magic retreated, leaving him feeling exhausted.

"You're mine, Sara, and I'll kill anyone that hurts you."

Sara didn't like how he felt, but the magic did. He felt her unease and the magics satisfaction at his possessiveness.

"Holy crap," Hawk said.

Charlie glanced over his shoulder and winced. They'd destroyed the room they stood in and the room beside it. Oz was casting Freezing Rain to put out the fires he'd caused while Hawk stamped on burning papers. Stasia crouched on the dented tabletop. Her eyes glowed blue, and her body was tense.

"We'll kill them all Stasia," Charlie said.

Sara's grip on him tightened.

Stasia nodded and sheathed her knives. Charlie kissed the pulse in his wife's neck before speaking. "I know you don't like it, but the magic needs them dead. I need them dead. This is who we are."

Sara made no reply just burrowed against his chest, leaving him awash in her worry and fear.

"Give them a minute," Oz said.

Small sounds told Charlie they'd left the room, but he didn't pick his head up from Sara's shoulder.

"Everything under control?" General Campbell asked as Oz exited the room.

Oz closed the door quietly behind himself.

"It will be. Give them a minute. We sort of wrecked the room."

Stasia snorted with laughter.

Guthrie rolled his eyes. "We closed the building, and the Scouts are guarding."

"What happened?" the general asked.

"Not only is Sara frightened, but her magic is as well. It wanted reassurance."

Guthrie pursed his lips.

Oz shrugged and spread his hands in a what can you do gesture. "I'm telling you, I felt what it wanted. Well, sort of. We have to guess what the feelings are for, but its relief was clear when we casted. I think it needed to know we were with her."

Hawk nodded thoughtfully. "What caused that? She was fine this morning."

"She got stuck in a dark room," Guthrie said dryly.

Stasia winced. "Damn. Maybe I shouldn't have asked her to summon us, but I thought it would ease her mind to call us and have us appear."

"And I'm sure it did," Oz said reassuringly. He threw an arm around Stasia. "This isn't a problem with a simple fix. As much as Charlie would like to slay whatever scares her, this problem is too big for him. She's going to need professional help. Hell, he is too. Man, if you could feel his anger…"

"You felt it?" Guthrie asked.

"We all did," Stasia said.

Hawk rubbed his arms and looked worried. "The magic likes his anger, but Sara doesn't. I felt your eagerness to fight, sis. I want our enemies dead too, but you and Charlie are a little too enthusiastic about it."

"Fuck that."

Hawk jerked back, and Oz hugged her closer.

"No." She shrugged away from Oz and spun to face her brother with her hands on her hips.

"Everyone involved will get what they've got coming to them. Should we let them take us and torture us?"

General Campbell laid a hand on her shoulder. "No one wants that. And yes, you have a right to defend yourselves, but I think your brother is worried you won't stop with the guilty parties."

"You mean you're worried."

"Stasia…" Oz said warningly. He grabbed her shoulder and yanked her back to his side. "Sorry, General, but we're a little on edge. The magic's need is pretty intense. Hell, sharing our feelings like that is pretty intense. There's no need to worry though. We're in control."

Hawk snorted in derision. "I'm in control. I'm not so sure about you two. Sara is scared to death and Charlie is on a ragged edge. General Campbell is right to be worried."

Stasia glared at her brother as she said, "Because I'm angry? Don't be stupid. Of course, I'm angry. My magic isn't rage based like Charlie, but I'm a damage class. I want to fight. I long to fight. She's our fucking sun-priest!"

"Hawk," Oz cut in before Hawk could reply. "Stasia is speaking for her magic. Didn't you feel your magic want Sara's magic?"

"Yes." Hawk sighed hard and ran his hands through his hair. "Look, I'm not saying we shouldn't find who did this and stop them. I'm just saying we need to be careful our game personas don't overpower us."

"I am who I am," Stasia said.

"And I love who you are, but I won't love a cold-blooded killer."

Stasia nodded tightly.

Oz snorted. "I plan on killing Rinto."

"Me too, but I don't want to destroy this base to get to him," Hawk said.

Stasia let her hands fall to her side and sounded exasperated when she said, "Dork, it was one room. Well, two, but the magic needed to see us cast."

Hawk laughed and hugged Stasia. "I'm not arguing that." His laugh faded replaced by an uneasy expression. "Charlie's really angry, and

Sara's really afraid. If we don't want to lose them in their magic, we better do our best to calm them."

"I'll send for some potted plants. You sit beside them at the meeting," Guthrie said.

Hawk nodded.

Stasia glanced over her shoulder at the closed door. "Nothing is going to help him except the death of his enemies."

Charlie knelt with his head in Sara's lap and his arms around her waist. She leaned over him, running her fingers through his hair. He straightened when the door opened but didn't rise.

"Sara needs a minute," Charlie said before the general could ask what happened.

Her terror jittered along his nerves. More than ever before, he needed her safe. His magic pushed at him, demanding he help her. Somehow, joining his magic to hers had empowered it, making the magic stronger, more active.

Flickers of embarrassment came from her as her terror receded, but he needed the contact. She stroked his hair and relaxed as he did.

"What happened?" the general asked.

Tremors shook Sara's voice. "The box of paper was in my hand when someone turned the light off. The door slammed shut, and I panicked. I turned to run to the door and ran into the shelf.

It fell over and trapped me."

Shivers coursed through her body, growing as her fear grew. Terror and panic formed a roiling black emotion Charlie could see with his eyes closed.

"You're safe now. I heard you. You'll never be trapped. I'll always come for you." Charlie took her hands and placed them on his heart.

A deep shuddering breath slowed her tremors. He leaned forward and put his face against hers. With his eyes closed, he watched the darkness fade to gray. The dark didn't disappear completely, but it did diminish, leaving gray tarnished streaks and random spots of black on her shining brightness. They sat that way for a minute before Charlie returned to the table.

When she started to follow, he gestured her to stay. "No, stay there, in the sun." With no effort, he picked up the battered table and moved it back so she could rest in the sunshine.

General Campbell and Guthrie remained standing.

"We wanted to meet with you before the meeting today to talk about a private matter," Charlie said and took Sara's hand. "Sara is fine physically, but she needs help. I want her to see a professional counselor, the sooner, the better. Can you arrange that for her?"

"Of course. It's probably a good idea if you all speak with one." The general frowned at them. "What just happened? Not the shelf trapping you, but this." The general gestured around the destroyed room.

The gray surged too black. No outward sign

betrayed her, but inwardly she was scared to death.

Charlie leaned over and whispered, "You're not trapped there in the dark." He wasn't sure what was frightening her now whether it was remembered fear or fear of the general's reaction, but she was afraid again. "No one is mad about the stupid room. We won't talk about it," he said louder and turned to Guthrie. "Please stop talking about it. You're upsetting her. I'll send in a full report, but she can't talk about this yet."

The general's frown deepened. "I'll arrange for the counselor."

"The sooner, the better." Charlie rested his fingertips on her pulse. "She isn't able to eat anything, and my magic can only do so much. Broth and toast won't be enough."

"I've read the latest reports about the changes in the magic. Could that be why she's having difficulties?" General Campbell asked.

"There've been bigger changes than we thought," Charlie said. "Last night we conducted some experiments."

Sara blushed so hotly, he almost laughed. She glared at him, feeling his mirth.

"Magical experiments," he clarified and winked at her. "The magic isn't a static thing. It's learning or perhaps evolving."

"I think it's growing up," Sara added.

"Growing up like a person?" General Campbell jerked back in surprise.

"Not a person, no, or maybe… I don't know." Sara held up her hand in a questioning gesture as she spoke, then rubbed her neck. "But, it does have wants of its own. As far as we can tell, it's simple requirements, like a baby has. Our magic likes to be together. It's stronger together. I think it became aware of itself recently."

"Our marriage strengthened it. When we want something" –Charlie narrowed his eyes in thought— "I mean, really want something; it tries to give it to us. When we first got the magic, we wanted to win that tournament. Which is lucky or we would've died. We were those characters; I think it's how it perceives us. We can't communicate with it unless we really desire something. Communicate is maybe too strong a word."

Frustration evident in his voice at not being able to put his insight into words, he gestured with his hands as he tried to explain. "We wanted to win, to be better warriors, or sun priests, or mages, so it made us able to. I don't think the magic realized it was a game. I desired Sara, so it desired Sara. When we made our vows to each other, we both wanted it with all our hearts. I promised Sara no one would touch her again and no one can. What we want, it wants."

"At least right now it does," Sara agreed. "It can't force us to do what it wants, but it's uncomfortable to not comply with it. Right now, it only wants to mingle with Charlie's magic, but it can't do that unless we're touching. Both of us can call it out now, and I think we could guide it to someone else, but I don't think we should. If it is just a baby and is growing, what if it wants something else someday? Something we don't want to do."

"You're saying it grants your wishes?" Guthrie asked doubtfully.

"No, more our feelings… our desires. Not I wish I had a new house or a million dollars," Charlie said.

"Maybe it would, Charlie," Sara interrupted. "We don't want those things, but I agree it tries to fulfill what we desire most. We'll need time and a safe place to experiment."

Charlie laid their clasped hands in his lap. "Sara was magically depleted, it's mostly my magic she has now. The connection to my magic remains. I feel what she does. That's how I knew she was hurt. That's how I know she can't bear hearing us talk about it. I don't know if it's a permanent effect or not."

"But, you think it understands you now?" Guthrie persisted.

"It definitely does. When it wants me to touch Sara, I can ask it to wait, and it does. I can ask it to come out and go to her, and it does that too. I feel its impatience with me when asked to wait, and love for her, but this" – he gestured about the destroyed room— "I think it needed to know the team was with her and that we wanted to protect her. It isn't just Sara who is afraid. Her magic is scared too and very lonely."

"When our magic mingles, I sense its contentment and happiness," Sara said. "No anger, or any bad sensations, just its desire for me to touch Charlie so my magic can be with his. But, this is all new. I think our marriage made it stronger, more aware, more itself."

The general glanced at the time. "In another

thirty minutes, we meet in the main conference room. Go get Sara cleaned up. I'll want written reports from both of you, and I'll arrange for the therapist. Dismissed."

Charlie and Sara left the room.

General Campbell turned to Guthrie. "Well, this changes things. If it isn't an effect, but a being of some sort, it's a whole new ball game."

Guthrie rubbed his stubbled cheeks. "I don't know. Their perceptions could be skewed by their recent experiences. I'm not saying they're lying, but perhaps they misunderstand or are putting their own desires on the magic. I agree with Sara. They need time and testing."

"Go gather the team. This will be a long day." General Campbell took out his phone.

-10-

JUST THE FACTS

Scouts gathered in the conference room, sitting in rows behind a long rectangular table that faced a large projection screen. Computer monitors on carts and rolling whiteboards stood in the corner. Pierce Taylor, Agent Lewis, Major Nelson, Captain Sanders, and Guthrie sat at the table. Team Valor took seats with the rest of the Scouts.

Charlie sat by Sara; this was bound to distress her. Hawk sat on the other side of her beside a potted palm and a half dead fern.

Charlie smothered his laugh. The general was doing his best to keep Sara and he calm, and he appreciated the gesture, but a forest of towering trees couldn't dent his rage.

General Campbell entered the room, and the Army personnel rose and saluted him.

"At ease." After he returned their salute, he

waved them to their seats and handed a folder to Sara and Oz.

Sara's nervousness mounted. *To hell with military protocol*, Charlie thought and held her hand in his.

The general placed his briefcase on the floor, removed his laptop, and took a seat at the center of the table facing them, his back to the large screen.

"First, let me say, good work everyone. Our security protocols are being overhauled to prevent this sort of thing happening in the future. We got careless, thinking our secret secure and had lowered the guards to one and that only while you were expected to be home. I'm truly sorry about that. It made it much too easy for them to tamper with your food. The private security firm we hired lost three good men, but there were no casualties on our teams. Major Harris will arrive in a few hours, and Sara should be able to complete her recovery." The general keyed on the projector, and a picture of Sergeant Rinto appeared.

"This man was in the original Marine team sent to retrieve you in Iraq. Three months later, he left the service on an early release program he shouldn't have qualified for."

The general showed another picture. "Brigadier General Flores signed and put through his release papers. Within the last year, General Flores released two hundred of his men early but kept them on the books reassigned to a fictitious unit. That unit collected pay, but more importantly, it withdrew supplies."

A list of the pilfered supplies filled the screen. "Flores requisitioned a large number of guns and ammunition, rocket launchers, tanks, even helicopters. As you can see, it was a fully supplied unit. Stockpiled in three large warehouses, he had everything from food and medical stores to three types of helicopters. Most of the stolen goods have been recovered. But the amount still unaccounted for is worrisome. We think he was systematically stealing small amounts his entire career and when he realized what he could get for Team Valor decided to go all in. He withdrew his savings and cashed in his stocks and bonds. Our accountants tell us he must've had over two million dollars stashed away somewhere as well."

General Campbell flipped to another page. "Large supplies of Diprivan and Ketalar, which is a type of Ketamine, where also sent to this fictitious unit. I'm sorry to say it only triggered an alarm two months ago, and the investigation hadn't started. Both drugs laced the blood sample Brenda took from Sara." He changed the picture to a close-up of Sara's hands after her rescue. Swollen grotesquely and black from bruising, they barely resembled human hands.

Sara inhaled sharply and closed her eyes, clutching Charlie's hand harder. His anger was so strong he could barely feel her fear.

"We see multiple injection sights. Doctor Elliot thinks they were trying to make it impossible for her to use her fingers with the Ketalar and using the Diprivan to keep her unconscious. Used together like that is very dangerous. I'm sure Sara's ability to regenerate saved her life."

The next clip displayed both her arms. "Fourteen distinct needle marks showed on her arms. Locations and bruising make it impossible to tell how many punctures are on her hands, but you can see six clear ones."

General Campbell cleared his throat and stood, leaning forward braced on his hands, his expression intent. His gaze landed on Sara's bowed head and traveled to the hands clutching Charlie. "The reason I bring this up is that Doctor Elliot is sure that Sara couldn't move her fingers. The anesthesia, coupled with the restraints and broken bones would have made that impossible. He thinks she casted Call-for-Help using only her mind. Because she was so desperate to cast it, she somehow did. The events of the past day make me think he could be right. I want you to remember that if you're ever unable to move your hands."

Sara's fear spiked. Shallow panting breaths and wide eyes revealed her terror, but Charlie didn't need external clues. Her fear slammed him like a blow.

"We're fine," he whispered in her ear. "They can't be held against their will."

General Campbell nodded having caught the exchange. "That's true for some of you more than others. Anastasia can almost certainly escape. Oliver could wink out of any bonds holding him, and you, Charles, could use intervene to get out of bonds, but not through walls. Sebastian and Sara both could be held.

They also have a call for help, but we'll need to work out escape scenarios for them. We want you to try casting with just a thought." He returned to his seat, placing both empty hands on the table before him.

"In the file I gave you are pictures of the two hundred men in that phony company. Look through them as I show them on the screen. If you remember anything at all, about any of them, we need to know it."

For two hours, they went through the list. Sara confirmed seeing twenty-two of them. Six of whom she thought she might've killed in the fight.

Oz recognized eighteen that he was sure were dead.

Team Alpha identified another forty, some of which they confirmed dead.

Team Beta confirmed sixty-four dead, some of whom overlapped the rest of the sightings.

Charlie admitted he remembered no one in particular. The men he'd killed blurred in his mind. They weren't people; they were The Enemy.

"Thirty-six men are in custody now from that list. We think they're innocent soldiers sent home on early release to help legitimize the ones released who stayed. Every move they've made is being tracked, but they had good service records with no prior criminal involvement unlike the remaining one hundred and sixty-four. That leaves sixty-two men unaccounted for who we assume were involved."

General Campbell put another picture on the

screen. "This is the man who owned the house where Sara first woke. He has known connections to ISIS. Another batch of pictures to go through are in the black folder. Same deal, if you have any information on any of them, we want to know." Pictures flashed across the large screen.

"Wait," Stasia said an hour later. "Isn't that the guy who delivers pizza?" The Scouts had recognized a few men from the house in Canada, but they were dead now. This man they didn't recognize. "I swear it's the guy. Put a red ball cap and apron on him, and he was at your house once a week at least, Charlie."

"Easy enough to check," Guthrie said. "If it's the same man, this could be a good lead. That man had no clear ties. This would open a new avenue of investigation."

Pierce turned to Charlie. "Write the name of the place, and any time you're certain you ordered pizza delivery, and I'll have men on it today."

Team Valor conferred and remembered over ten dates they were sure they'd ordered takeout. Pierce took the list and made a call.

The general continued the slide show. "Stop," Hawk said. "That guy we tied up in the basement of the house where we found Rick when we went to Iraq."

By the end of the presentation, they had spotted four more men from Iraq.

"Those three men were in the custody of the Iraqi police," General Campbell said. "We tried to get custody of them ourselves. They should still be in custody. More investigators will need to be sent there. Agents are going over every department at Incirlik base. More people there could be involved. They didn't all necessarily join that fake company. So, one hundred and six known people involved with this plot remain at large. Sara reports the majority of the men holding her had no idea of the magic or of what she was capable. So, again, an unknown number of mercenaries could be involved.

"Oz, we think they'll try for you next. It's likely they'll attempt to kill you if they decide they can't hold you. They know you can locate them given enough time. The car that Hawk found led us to a woman who recalled a man using a payphone. She remembered it because it amazed her people still used them with cell phones so readily available, and he used it at the same time every day for a week. Agent Lewis tracked those calls to a liquor store in Montreal. One of their employees is missing, and another was killed four days ago in a car accident. The missing man owned a boat, and we think he's the man who picked up Rinto. Agents are tracking both men's whereabouts and associates. So, we have those leads to follow too.

"Beta team brought us a live prisoner, and we had the man from Anastasia's and Sebastian's home. He's the one that led us to the house they took Sara too first. The original plan was to go from there to the airport, but because Charlie had the alarm out so fast and all planes were grounded, they went to the backup plan.

"That man says the plan called for Anastasia and Sebastian to be taken separately. We know they planned to drug them. Drugs found on their bodies confirm his story and link to the supplies General Flores stole. We found their vehicles as well, an ambulance and two vans. The vans belonged to an antique dealer. Three boxes in the van held restraints and IV's. They planned to remove both you and your mother by ambulance and switch vehicles. The owner of the antique store claims no knowledge, and the vans weren't on his books. We're still investigating him. He was, however, in the process of putting a big order together to be sent to Dubai. The order seems legitimate enough. In two days, he would've shipped. His order was filled and waiting at the docks. The company he was shipping to checks out as legitimate, and in fact, has dealt with this dealer before. We're still investigating to be sure our bad guys used them, and they weren't involved.

"The baddie from Stasia's house had no idea what she could do. So far, he claims he doesn't know who hired him. The sunny climate of Guantanamo might jog his memory. He's there now in isolation and still doesn't know what he saw. Stasia's attack he didn't see, but he saw Oz and thought he was using a homemade flamethrower. He was here legally on a tourist visa claiming to be visiting family. This led us to the house where they first took Sara as I said earlier. We don't think that house was a planned stop. Because of the flight ban, they had to change their plans. We think they went there to pick up team Alpha and decided to take pictures while they could."

Sara swallowed hard, and her grip tightened on Charlie's hand until his fingers turned white. He tried to project love and not rage. She was concentrating intensely, and he didn't know if it was to block her fear from him or because she was interested.

The general put a picture of the room where she had woken on the screen. Sara made a small sound of distress, dropped Charlie's hand, slapped both hands over her face, and ran from the room.

"She's sick. I'll get her," Charlie said and ran after her. The sound of retching led him to her in the bathroom across the hall.

He rubbed her back and held her hair from her face as she continued to dry heave. His magic swirled around her. To his relief, the magic seemed happy with him an unafraid. This was all her fear, not inspired by the magic. When she crumpled to the floor in a shaky heap, he got a wet paper napkin and wiped her face.

"Better?"

Pale, with shaking hands, she nodded, pushed herself from the floor, and washed her hands and face in the sink.

The magic returned to him and settled into his skin. He shrugged irritability, annoyed with his inability to control his magic. Sara's worry spiked, and she stopped splashing her face to peer over her shoulder at him.

"I'm annoyed I can't control these magical displays, not with you. We need to control it better, or it's going to be a real problem."

"Sorry," she said and turned back to splash

her face again, saying," I'm hoping once I have more magic of my own yours won't want me so much."

"Not your fault, sweetheart. Don't worry about it either. We'll figure something out."

He rubbed her back and handed her a stack of paper towels to dry her face.

Stasia entered. "He's done with those pictures. Are you okay?"

Sara nodded again. "Yes, let's get this over with." Still pale, she avoided their gazes and led the way back to the conference room.

Stasia and Charlie exchanged worried glances.

They sat on either side of her. Charlie took her hand. Stasia put an arm around her shoulder being careful not to touch her skin. Static crawled over them, brief flickers of blue and white. Hawk rose and placed the plants behind Stasia, then sat directly behind Sara, leaning forward to rest a hand on her shoulder.

Charlie gave him a grateful nod. The frown on Oz's face deepened, but he said nothing, turning back to the report open in his hand.

The general cleared his throat and tapped his notes on the table before continuing. "Both video and still photos were taken at the scene. We don't know if they had time to pass them along or make copies. From what Oz remembers overhearing, we don't think they did. He heard talk at the house of pictures being their payday. The way they said it implied they hadn't sent them yet. No pictures were found at any of the crime scenes. So, somewhere, pictures of Sara doing the impossible are floating about. Hawk says only one man exited the car he tracked. We think it was Sergeant Rinto and he has the evidence. His trail leads back to Iraq."

A new picture appeared on the screen. "General Flores was last seen entering a helicopter at Incirlik base on Christmas Eve. That helicopter was found forty miles from Mosul. The pilot had been shot point blank after the helicopter landed. This is interesting to us because General Flores was alone on the copter carrying a large case. We can infer he had no confederates left on the base he wanted to save. Whether the pilot was one, we're still investigating. If the general left accomplices behind, they must not know what's really going on. I can't imagine he would've left someone behind who could reveal his whereabouts or subvert his plan. Of course, we're investigating everyone there, but it will take time."

General Campbell changed the picture again. "This is a village near Mosul. Satellites show us it's heavily guarded and armed. We're going to go take it over."

Charlie's magic burst from him as he jumped to his feet without thought. The general paused.

"Sorry," Charlie mumbled and regained his seat. It took him a few moments to recall his magic.

Sara peered at him worriedly, and he gave her a reassuring smile while patting her hand.

Oz pressed on Charlie's knee, and Charlie shrugged at him. Oz rolled his eyes and sighed hard, then smacked his shoulder,

The general resumed speaking when the magic dissipated. By the pressure beneath his skin, Charlie knew his eyes glowed. Eagerness like he'd never felt before churned like a physical thing inside him. He almost couldn't hold himself back from rushing for the door. He knew where The Enemy was.

We don't have permission from the Iraqi government. It'll be done clandestinely. If General Flores is there, we want him alive. If Sergeant Rinto is there, we want him to escape."

General Campbell held up his hand to silence Stasia's angry protest. "We want to follow him to see where he goes and who he talks with. General Flores was the leader, and evidence leads us to suspect Rinto was his second in command. Major Nelson tells us Rinto was always a guy with a backup plan; he always wanted to be doing the planning and was a discipline problem. Sergeant Rinto might have had made plans on his own to cut his boss out.

"Hawk will be tracking, and a satellite is assigned to this operation. Two Force Recon teams, four Ranger teams, and two Navy SEAL teams will be working with us. We want him to run in a panic and lead us to his confederates. We deploy at fifteen-hundred—" the general sighed and leaned back while Charlie again regained control of his magic. When the last whirl had disappeared, he continued, "Our hope is they don't realize we're on their trail. Oz, we want you to run a locate on everyone on both lists. I'm sorry, Sara, I want to give you the opportunity to recover, but every moment we wait gives them that much longer to disperse and spread the news."

General Campbell glanced at his watch. "Okay, break for lunch. Everybody report to hanger eighteen at fifteen-hundred. The mission briefing will be conducted on the plane. Your gear will be there. I'm assuming you're good to go?" he asked as he stood and examined them.

"Arghhh Oorah," the Scouts yelled. The general nodded and glanced at Team Valor.

Charlie jumped to his feet. "You have to be kidding me! Sara is in no way ready to go!"

"Scouts, you're dismissed. Team Valor, a moment, please. Remain in this building. I'll have lunch brought to you. I want Sara to speak with Doctor Gotlieb, a psychiatrist here on base. He's being briefed now. We want more blood samples, Sara. I'm not going to bother asking if you're up for this. I'm not happy sending you in, but the mission requires it."

His worried gaze flicked from Sara's white face to Charlie's furious one. "Being in a close team is an asset and a liability. Your survival is our highest priority. If that means letting a Scout die, they accept that. They know they're expendable, you aren't. I hate putting it to you that bluntly, but it's a fact. They're replaceable, you aren't. Don't, under any circumstances, risk yourselves for them!"

"Yeah, sure she can talk to the doctor, but she isn't going!" The room sprang into startling clarity, and he knew his eyes were glowing.

"Of course, I'm going," Sara said in exasperation. "You can't go without your healer.

Don't be stupid!"

"Sara…" Charlie paused to reign in his anger. "You can't even eat! You'll run out of magic and be helpless. No! You're not going!" Sara's anger pushed at him, and neither he nor the magic liked it one bit.

"Charlie, we're strong together. If I don't go and this fails, and everyone escapes, I'll be in even more danger. If I stay here and you die, then what?" Tears filled her eyes. "Don't leave me alone here."

Charlie was torn. She was his wife. His to protect, and she wasn't ready. She was weak both mentally and physically. He also knew she was right. He couldn't leave her alone. The very thought of being alone scared her to her soul, darkening the light he saw with his eyes closed in a way that scared him. If they wanted to succeed in this mission, they needed her, and his soul cried out for him to kill those men to make her safe.

"Damn it, Sara!" He yelled in frustration. Her fear and the magics loneliness beat at him. The blue receded from his eyes as he clutched her and buried his face in her hair. "Don't get hurt! Promise me, you won't get hurt!"

She said nothing just hugged him tighter.

General Campbell glanced at his watch. "Sara, Doctor Gotlieb will be waiting in the room where we met this morning. You're dismissed."

Team Valor headed out the door.

Pierce Taylor leaned back in the seat and tapped a pen on the stack of papers in front of him. "Sara isn't ready, but we do need her. They won't abandon the Scouts or any other group of soldiers you send. It doesn't take a master profiler to see that."

The general sighed heavily and paced the room. "I know. I also know we're pushing our luck with Charlie. The strength of his aura is increasing. He's a hair breath from attacking us."

Pierce sat up straighter. "No, not us. Well… unless we threaten her."

"Pfft," the general made a derisive sound. "We *are* threatening Sara. Sending her into harm's way is a threat, and he knows it. The fact that we mean her no harm just saved our lives. When they engage… no one will be able to stop him. I'm worried he won't stop with the men there but continue to Mosul. Hell, maybe all of Iraq."

Pierce said nothing.

General Campbell heaved an even heavier sigh and took out his cell phone.

~11~

COUNSELING

Rick was waiting for his parents when their plane landed. As soon as they appeared, he grabbed them in a tight hug. Liz Harris nodded greetings but didn't intrude. Rick took his parent's bags and led them to the conference room.

"Did they tell you we ship out in less than two hours?" Rick asked as they walked.

"Yes, but not where you're going. Does it have anything to do with the abductions?" Worried brown eyes met his son's identical gaze.

"Yeah, but I can't talk about it." Rick glanced away. "I really let her down. Sara was seriously hurt because of me. Charlie has her seeing a counselor right now."

"And their wedding, where you there for that?" Mary asked and rubbed his shoulder as they walked.

"No one was." Rick explained what had happened.

"So, they aren't really married then." Mary and John exchanged relieved glances.

"If you believe marriage joins two people together, they're very, very, married. They couldn't be more joined unless they merged into one person." A red blush climbed Rick's cheeks. "I meant magically, not..." Still blushing, he avoided his mother's gaze. "I'm sure they've, um, merged that way as well."

An uncomfortable silence lingered until they reached the conference room. Rick placed the bags inside the door. "Mom, don't try to separate them; it won't work. You'll only hurt Sara, and she doesn't need more pain."

"On the way here, we decided to accept this," his father said. "When you said they weren't legally married, I admit, I was relieved, thinking we could talk them into waiting, but that bird has flown." A small frown marred his father's forehead when he turned to face his son. "This'll take getting used to, but we love Sara. We just always assumed you would marry first."

Rick winced and looked away. Stasia, Oz, and Hawk returned carrying bags of food and Mary went to greet them.

"Charlie's this way." Without waiting for his mother to return, he took his father's arm and dragged him away. When they entered the stairwell, Rick stopped. Unable to face his father, he turned away, hanging his head.

"Son?" John laid a hand on his son's bowed back.

"Everything's so screwed up, Dad," Rick said in a tortured voice. "What happened to Sara.... I've hurt both the girls so much. I failed in my duty to protect Sara, failed badly. We aren't allowed to speak of what happened, but even if we could, I wouldn't tell you, it was that bad."

"Son, Sara loves you. I'm sure she'll forgive you," John said softly, laying a comforting hand on his son's hunched shoulder.

"Oh, she has already. She never blamed me, but I blame me," Rick said bitterly.

"Well, you need to forgive yourself then. Maybe you should see the counselor too."

Rick shrugged but didn't answer.

"What did you do to Stasia?" His father asked and narrowed his eyes.

"Not what you're thinking I did!" Rick told his father what happened.

"I see," his father paused. "Her feelings are hurt, but she'll get over that. The bigger question is, what will you do now?"

"Nothing. What can I do?" Rick shrugged and kicked at the bottom stair.

"If she was nineteen, what would you do?"

"She isn't; so why does it matter?"

"Because you have a choice to make and it'll suck for you either way. You know that already. There are only two things you can do— leave her alone, or you don't. If you leave her alone, I'm sure she'll find someone else. If you don't, well... You're an honorable man, and would need to wait a few years until she was old enough to date." Brown eyes serious, he pulled his son to face him and squeezed his shoulder hard. "And,

Rick, there's no guarantee she wouldn't change her mind. You might wait for nothing."

Rick nodded unhappily.

"Is she worth waiting for?" his father asked.

"I don't know," Rick said. "I care for her, and of course she's beautiful, anyone can see that, but how do I know when I can't let myself feel anything for her?"

"Rick, I'm not going to lie, they're both hard choices, but I'm sure you'll do the right thing here." After giving his troubled son a hug, he headed up the stairs to find his youngest one.

Charlie knocked on the office door, wincing at the dents and scuffs visible from this side.

"Come in," a man in his mid-fifties called out in a friendly way.

Charlie entered quickly, closing the door behind them.

"Ah, Charlie and Sara Hayes, correct? I've been expecting you. It's a pleasure to meet you both. I'm Doctor Gotlieb, a physiatrist here on the base." He extended his hand to shake. "Major Nelson briefed me, and I spoke to Major Harris by phone." A smile lit his face, and he gestured absently around the destroyed room. "I'll admit, at first I thought I was being punked."

Sara called her Hand-of-Sun, holding her glowing hand out for the doctor to examine, and he laughed in delight.

"Ahh, proof!" Doctor Gotlieb gestured Sara

to a chair still shaking his head in wonder at the magical display. "Because of your pending mission, our time today is limited. When you return, I'll want to speak with you both, but for today, I'll talk with Sara alone. Before I do though, I wanted to tell you both that nausea is a common side effect of ketamine and should wear off soon. I realize that the nausea is enhanced by memories, but in a few days, it should lessen. Charlie, if you could wait outside please?"

Charlie kissed Sara's cheek. As he left the room, Doctor Gotlieb asked Sara if she would like to sit in the sun and he smiled. The doctor was a fast learner.

The hallway was quiet with little activity. Charlie sat with his back to the wall and opened the file. If they encountered any of these men, he would recognize them. Sara was calmer then he thought she would be. He tried not to intrude on her privacy, but it was hard to ignore her sharp spikes of emotions. Calmness faded replaced by fear and guilt. The folder slid unheeded to the floor. Her pain was intense, and tears of sympathy clouded his eyes.

The door opened, and Sara squatted before him. "I'm sorry I'm hurting you." Her eyes swam with tears at his distress.

"I'm okay. I'm not hurt, that's your pain you feel. Don't worry about me, please, just talk to him, it's fine. I can't help feeling what you do, but don't let that stop you." Charlie rose and gave her a quick kiss. Gently, he ushered her inside where the doctor waited.

"This is more complicated than usual."

Doctor Gotlieb gazed at them with pursed lips over his tented fingers. "Unless care is taken, you could become trapped in a negative feedback loop, sending bad emotions back and forth until you forget what caused them or even whose they were. Both of you try to keep clear on who's feeling what. Sara, Charlie doesn't feel bad, you feel bad. Let's finish our talk and try not to worry about what he's feeling. He's safe right outside the door."

Sara nodded and hugged Charlie. "I'm sorry," she repeated.

"No need to be," Charlie said. "I'll be right outside. Don't worry about me at all."

When the door closed, he slid down the wall again and sat head in hand, ignoring the occasional puzzled glances he received from men passing in the hallway. Thirty minutes later, John found him there wiping his eyes.

Charlie scrambled to his feet and hugged his father. "Mom's here too?" he asked when he drew away.

"Yes, with Stasia. Rick said I would find you here. What's wrong? where's Sara?"

"Inside talking with a psychiatrist. Nothing's wrong with me, but she's in a lot of pain."

"When we arrived, Rick explained how you think you're married now."

"In every way that counts, except legally, she's my wife," Charlie said without hesitation.

"You feel what she does now, like Rick said?"

"Yes, her strong emotions come through, and what she's experiencing right now is horrible," Charlie said, tears coming to his eyes again.

"But, she isn't physically hurt?" John put an arm around his son. Charlie gave him a quick squeeze being careful to not touch his skin.

"No, the magic healed her body. I wish she could cast soothe on herself."

"Couldn't you steal it and cast it on her?"

Charlie laughed and smacked himself on the forehead. "Duh, I'm such an idiot. I never thought of that. When she's done here, I'll try. I'm hoping the doctor can help her."

"I'm sure he can, but not in one hour. Don't expect her to come out cured," John warned.

"No, I know it'll take a long time for her to recover. What happened to her was beyond horrible."

"Rick told me he was there and feels awful about it."

"Neither of them has a thing to be sorry for," Charlie assured his father. "Seeing something bad happen to someone you love, when you can't stop it, is making them both feel guilt they shouldn't."

His father looked relieved. "I was worried he'd failed her somehow."

"Not at all; he did nothing wrong. Neither did she. The circumstances were beyond their control," Charlie said as reassuringly as he could. He made a mental note to speak to his brother. Sara consumed him so much he'd ignored his brother's pain. A headache began to throb behind his right eye, and he rubbed his forehead. If Rick felt half as bad as Sara over what had happened, he needed to get him help too.

"Your mother will be pleased to hear it," his father said, dragging his attention back.

John glanced at his watch. "Liz traveled with us. She's doing well. Will you have time to see her before you go?"

"I'm sure of it. Sara will insist," Charlie said.

"Prince and the kitten were on the plane with us. Prince cried for hours."

"The kitten's still alive?" Charlie asked in amazement. "I hadn't a chance to inquire. That's the luckiest kitten on Earth."

"Yes, it's fine. Liz had them sent to her vet when they took her to the hospital."

"Can you make sure someone takes care of it until we return, please?"

"Sure, it's a cute little thing. We've been told we'll be kept here for a week. People are going over every inch of our house. They said they'd pack and ship our stuff here. Since you called us, we haven't been allowed home. Camila and your mother are a wreck."

"We know who's behind it. We'll find Flores and stop him," Charlie assured his father.

The magic within him surged, and he needed a moment to control it. Eyes closed, and fists clenched, he breathed deeply, promising the magic he would release it soon. Soon, they would have vengeance. He was proud of himself for keeping it contained. So proud, Sara felt a strong sense of curiosity. Then he was angry again that she needed a doctor and had to take slow deep breaths to calm himself.

The puzzled look on his father's face when he opened his eyes made him grin crookedly, but before he could explain, he sensed Sara's rising need for him. Blue magic swirled from him to the doorway. He recalled it quickly and darted a guilty glance around, but no one was in the hallway except him and his father. To keep these displays under control would take practice.

"Sara's coming." Brown eyes implored his father to be kind to her.

"Don't worry; we wouldn't hurt her for the world," his father said.

The door opened, and a pale Sara peered in alarm at Mr. Hayes. Blue eyes wide and fearful, and biting her lip, she glanced from Charlie to his father.

"It's fine, sweetheart, that anger wasn't for Dad but for something we were talking about." Relief filled her beautiful eyes. Charlie laid his hand on her face and gave her some of his magic.

John pulled her into a tight embrace. "I've always wanted a daughter," he said into her hair, and she started to cry.

Charlie rubbed her back, smiling at his father over her shoulder. Her relief at his father's acceptance was enormous, and her guilt eased.

Charlie introduced Doctor Gotlieb to his father and the two men shook hands. The doctor turned to Sara. "Whenever you like, we can talk. My door is always open. Get that blood work done before you go, and eat something small every hour, even if it's just a cracker. The nausea should pass soon on its own. Try not to let it worry either of you. Remember what I said about feedback loops."

Charlie thanked the doctor and assured him

he would look out for her. "Did he help?" He asked as they headed back to the conference room.

A noncommittal shrug was her reply. When she saw Liz and his mother talking in the hallway, her pace slowed, and guilt and worry intensified. Both women noticed them at the same time and smiled. His mother ran to them with tears in her eyes and hugged Sara hard. Sara's relief made Charlie smile.

"I'm so glad they found you. We were so worried," Mary said as she released Sara and hugged Charlie. "Honey, would you mind getting remarried in a church? Dancing at my son's wedding has been a dream of mine."

Sara sobbed on her shoulder and nodded.

Charlie frowned. "Mom, we can do that for you, but we won't live apart meanwhile."

"We accept you're married now and don't want to separate you. I just want to throw a giant party with photographers, flowers, dancing, and wedding photos to show off. Since the day you were born, I looked forward to your wedding."

Charlie smiled. "Yeah, we can do that." With a gentle finger, he traced Sara's brow, smiling into her eyes, happy with her relief and his parent's acceptance. "We can marry again in a church and honeymoon someplace hot. All day long we can sit in the hot sun," he said.

Sara stood on tiptoe and kissed him. Face in the curve of her neck, he breathed deeply. The connection they shared let her know he wasn't thinking about the days, but their nights.

Sara smiled and kissed him again, guilt and

worry subsumed by love and lust. Charlie smiled at his mother over Sara's head, grateful she was so kind.

Liz cleared her throat.

A blush reddened Sara's cheeks as she turned from him and hugged Liz, then stepped back and healed her, followed by a longer hug.

"I need to draw a few blood samples. My kit is inside. It will only take me a minute."

The rest of Team Valor gathered around the conference room table, eating their lunch. Stasia handed Charlie their food. While Liz organized herself, and everyone else exchanged greetings, they both ate. Charlie was pleased and relieved to see Sara eat the soup and crackers with no ill effects.

Liz couldn't withdraw blood from Sara. Even with gloves on, she couldn't stay in contact with Sara's bare skin. "I can do it fast, but that would hurt."

"Let me try." Charlie took the samples under Liz's supervision.

Sara borrowed a pair of the disposable gloves and tried touching people. Everyone reported no discomfort, so she slipped a few pairs into her pocket. "You never know; I might need to touch a Scout or something."

Charlie nodded and grabbed a pair. "Our uniform gloves probably insulate us enough, but we can carry these too."

"We need to head out if we don't want to be late," Hawk said a few minutes later.

Mr. and Mrs. Hayes watched Team Valor leave. "If anyone should feel bad about what's happened to them, it's me," Mary said after they'd left.

"No, you shouldn't," Liz placed a hand on Mary's shoulder. "I know those kids now. There's no way they would've left Rick there no matter what you did. You should be proud of the children you raised."

-12-

PROJECT ERASURE

The president flew to Camp Pendleton to attend an emergency meeting concerning Team Valor.

"Gentlemen," he said in greeting as he surveyed the gathered men. "Thank you for coming on such short notice. Recent events with Team Valor and their raid convinced me to prepare for the total erasure of the magic if at all possible." Drawn and pale, the last few days had obviously taken a toll on him. "This is a matter of national security. Team Valor is cooperating with us at the moment, but as we saw, they can be seized and used without their consent. We can't afford to let that happen." The president gestured to Doctor Elliot.

The doctor stood. "They've proven to be weak against sedatives of almost all types. In this case, perception is working for us. While they can't be harmed by poisons because Sara and Hawk can cure them, a sedative is incurable." A grimace of distaste crossed his face as he continued, "This goes against my oath. I like the children, but I see the necessity of being able to contain the magic. These extreme measures are hard to contemplate, especially as there's no guarantee that killing the host would stop the magic."

Guthrie interrupted. A deep scowl marred his swarthy face. "Not only is there no guarantee, it seems unlikely. If the host dies, the magic is more likely to become angry and uncontrollable."

The president nodded. "It's our belief as well." Dark circles ringed his eyes, and deep furrows lined his brow. "As distasteful as this is, plotting the deaths of five children who've done nothing to deserve it, it is necessary. The security of the American citizens demands it. Project Erasure is a last resort. Everything in our power will be done to keep the magic both contained and friendly to us."

Doctor Elliot tapped the tabletop. "If Sara had remained a captive under the control of people willing to torture her, they could conceivable harm her to the point where her magic took over or escaped her. We can't let that happen. If Charlie gets out of control, if his rage makes him attack innocent people, we need a way to deal with it." The doctor reached into his bag, pulled out a dart gun the size of a nine-millimeter pistol, and laid it on the table. "This gun contains the fastest acting sedative we have. We propose the magic user—"

"You mean the child," Guthrie interrupted.

Doctor Elliot closed his eyes and nodded. "We propose the child be injected and the body be brought to a secure location if possible before being terminated."

"Stop!" Guthrie yelled. "Killed, you mean murdered! Let's call this what it is. Sedate them and take them somewhere to murder them where we think the magic can't escape from. I don't think such a place exists. Do you?"

"We won't have a choice!" The president slammed his hand onto the table. "If the magic gets out of our control by any means, we'll need to stop it. You must stop it! Five, lead-lined boxes and an underground vault to keep them in are being prepared. They would be brought there under sedation and their bodies cremated and sealed in lead. If they had to be killed before being moved, we'll try to destroy the body." The president closed his eyes, rubbing his forehead with two fingers. "I like them too. I pray to God we never need to do this, but I must protect our people. If the magic can enchant, possess, or whatever word you wish to use to describe entering a human host and making that host do its will, we've entered an entirely new realm of danger for us. One we need to be able to counteract."

Major Nelson cleared his throat. "I'm assuming we're being told because it will be our duty?"

The president stared him in the eye. "Yes, you who are closest to them have the best shot at containing them should they run amok. Every effort is to be made to ensure that never happens."

"If we killed one of them, I assure you the other four will instantly be at war with us," Guthrie said.

"Yes." The president rubbed his eyes again and cleared his throat. "If we kill one, we have to kill all five. Arrangements are in place in their quarters at Pendleton to gas them as they sleep. The entire raid would need to be kept away. I think the Scouts would fight to the death to protect them. If we call for Project Erasure, the raid will be sent out of the zone, and Team Valor gathered together and either gassed or tranked."

Doctor Elliot cleared his throat. "A tranquilizer gun like this one should be kept on you or one of your men stationed with them at all times. The sedatives won't kill them, although they might kill a normal human. If they were out of control, you could use it without harming them while decisions were made."

For another hour, they continued to set up their plans, laying out the details and talking about contingencies. At the end of the meeting, Guthrie stood. "I'm a soldier sworn to follow all lawful orders. This is neither lawful nor right. This is not an order I'll follow blindly. I see the necessity for this plan, but I'll only carry it out if in my opinion the situation is irredeemable. I won't murder my children on someone else's say so."

The president nodded and stood. "None of us want to do this horrible thing. If it becomes necessary, it will be clear to all of us. Keep the guns with you and pray to God we never need to use them. Return to Iraq with Major Nelson and deal with this situation. Keep me informed."

The group filed out of the meeting. Major Nelson touched Guthrie on the arm to stop him from leaving. Once they were alone in the room, he spoke.

"This has to be done." Hard eyes met the staff sergeant's. "Hell, I like them too; you know that. You also know Team Valor would agree with precautions being put in place. They aren't unaware of the threat they present."

"I do know." Guthrie took the gun Major Nelson handed him and examined it. "Other plans must be in play we know nothing about. I realize I've been *enchanted* too. " He made air quotes when he said enchanted and rolled his eyes. "I don't feel a whit different. The only difference I've noticed is I can feel the emotions of the others clearer now if I'm standing in magic. Except for you. Yours are still fuzzy and muted. I don't know if I feel sorry for you for not that you were out of the zone."

The major shrugged and Guthrie pursed his lips.

"It would take an absolute catastrophe for me to harm them though," Guthrie continued. "Sure, I could sedate one, but kill one? No." He shook his head. "I love them all; they're good people trying so hard to do the right thing. If they lose control, we need to give them a chance to regain it."

"We will," Major Nelson assured him. "This is an absolute last resort. Honestly, I doubt it would work anyway. No one wants this to happen, believe me, but if it did, we have the best chance of approaching them."

"Because they trust us." Guthrie clenched his teeth and spun away.

Major Nelson nodded. "They do, and they can. Charlie is dangerous. His anger makes him unpredictable, and his magic will make the others follow him if he rampages. Think of the harm they could cause innocent civilians. My mind boggles when I think of what he could do. Do you think they'd want the magic loose to harm people?" He shook his head and answered his own question. "I'm sure they wouldn't. They'd want to be stopped by whatever means possible. I'm sure Sara would've rather died then help those people discover the secrets of the magic. You're sure of that too."

Guthrie nodded unhappily.

Major Nelson slapped him on the back as he left the room.

-13-

THE BRIEFING

Military personnel from all branches filled the plane. Team Valor sat between teams Alpha and Beta. The closest Marines examined them with interest. Team Valor still wore the Army sweats Guthrie had supplied. Blood stained the left leg of Charlie's where he'd wiped his hand after Sara's earlier accident.

The rest of the Scouts wore black armor and spell-bars with only a Scout patch on their left shoulders, no other insignia, not even names. Guthrie boarded and called Team Valor to the back of the plane where their familiar duffel bags waited.

They suited up in the bathrooms, putting on their matte-black armor and headgear to hide their identities and returned to their seats. Those same Marines now frowned in puzzlement.

The plane jittered and lurched before settling

into a smooth cruising altitude. Charlie's ears popped. Beside him, Oz yawned and stretched. Sara's rising anxiety confused him, leaving him undecided on both cause and cure. He spell-stole her Soothe and used it on her.

His shoulders lowered as she relaxed.

Immaculate in his dress uniform, General Campbell rose and clutched a seat back with one hand and a microphone with the other. The men stilled, only the muted roar of the engine competing with the general's authoritative voice.

"This mission is highly classified. Anything you see or hear, keep to yourselves. If you would please turn your attention to the monitors?"

The small screens flickered to life, displaying the presidential seal. Everyone straightened in their seats. A picture formed of President Carmichael sitting behind his desk in the oval office.

"You've been chosen for this mission because you're the best. Despite your different branches of service, I expect you to work together." The president rose, placed his hands on the desk before him, and leaned forward. "This is a classified project. You might see experimental weapons in use. These won't be explained, any mention of them will be denied, and the person mentioning them will be detained indefinitely. The weapons are being deployed prematurely because of the seriousness of this situation. ISIS has acquired the plans for these secret weapons."

The president straightened and spoke in a stern voice. "If the plans are not retrieved, the

United States could suffer catastrophic losses. Millions of innocent American citizens are at risk. I can't emphasize the importance of this retrieval enough."

A picture of the cameras Sergeant Rinto had used, followed by pictures of Sergeant Rinto replaced the image of the president.

"We want this man alive and any equipment or papers he has. Major General Campbell will go over the plan with you, but I wanted to personally say it's imperative to take him alive."

A picture of Brigadier General Flores appeared on the screen.

"If at all possible take this man alive too, but we'll settle for dead. Our tradition is no man gets left behind, and in this case, it's doubly imperative. No evidence can remain that we were ever in Iraq. We do *not* have permission to be there. If we can't maintain complete deniability, the United States will be at war."

The listening men stirred at that.

"General Campbell will introduce you to five of your teammates. Their survival is vital. If they're killed, the retrieval of their bodies becomes our number one priority." Serious and stern, the president faced the camera directly. "The fate of freedom itself rests in your hands." The screens faded to black.

Dead silence reigned in the cabin. General Campbell examined the gathered men.

"We're trusting you with national defense secrets. We'll tell you as little as possible. I'm sure you'll have your own ideas, most of which will be totally wrong. That's fine if you keep them to yourselves. If word of this mission leaks out, I assure you, the leak will be plugged! Am I clear?"

Everyone murmured, "Yes, sir."

"Team Valor, if you would rise and remove your cover?"

Charlie stood and removed his facemask, wondering what the gathered men thought about their obvious youth.

"This team comprises some of our secrets. Never mention meeting any of them! They have operational command. Am I clear?"

A stunned chorus of, "Yes, sir!" answered him.

"Valor, you may take your seats, but remain uncovered to ensure this company can recognize you." The general inclined his head towards Team Valor.

The screens flickered to life again, displaying a panoramic view of a small town. One and two-story buildings of various sizes were jammed together in a barren valley with three narrow roads intersecting into one wider, center street. The picture continued to pan around the village, pausing on a small fleet of ragtag helicopters before moving on to a line of vehicles parked in a neat row. Two real tanks were flanked by ragged technicals, reinforced pickup trucks with mounted weapons.

Armed men patrolled, carrying rocket launchers and M16s. Still pictures of men standing in ragged lines holding rifles wearing black uniforms and headscarves showed next.

Charlie fumbled with his sunglasses to cover his glowing eyes. The magic pressed, but he kept it contained. It wasn't difficult, and he wondered if were because he too wanted The Enemy dead.

General Campbell used a laser pointer on the screen beside him. "As you can see, this is an ISIS training camp with an estimated four thousand men. We'll be jumping in under cover of darkness. Recon Team One, your position will be outside at these coordinates."

Brenda turned and smirked at the recon team General Campbell addressed, the same Marine recon team they'd rescued in Mexico a few months ago. She gave a tiny finger wave to Mike Wallace. He nodded in acknowledgment, but other than the one quick glance didn't take his eyes off the screen.

The general outlined everyone's positions. "My Scouts will be going into that town. The Scouts will bug and chase target one out. Follow him. Any team sighting him will immediately notify me. Don't lose him. If he enters any of these nearby towns, we have units already in place. Mission priority is to see who his contacts are. If target two is spotted, apprehend him, alive if possible.

"The Scouts will take everyone and everything in that town. If you have hostiles heading to your positions, they'll attempt to notify you. Callsign Hawk is to be believed on sightings even if what he says is unlikely. Don't wonder how he knows, or doubt the intel. He'll be using one of our secret weapons. Are there any questions?" The general's steely-eyed gaze passed over the men.

One of the soldiers in the back rose his hand.

"Should we pursue into towns or civilian populations?"

"If you can do so and remain unseen. But, keep in mind, we need complete deniability here. Covert teams are getting in place through the area as we speak, so follow with discretion. Target one must think he got away clean."

"Excuse me, sir, but how will we maintain deniability? Won't our air support give us away?"

"There won't be air support. After the drop, we're on our own. Pickups will be at the assigned rendezvous points. I suggest you don't get lost or be late."

A disbelieving silence filled the cabin. General Campbell cleared his throat. "The Scouts will be using an assortment of our secret weapons and shouldn't require air support." He glanced at his watch. "Major Nelson will talk with every team leader to ensure everyone knows their positions and call signs. Try to get some rest. In six hours, we land and deploy. I expect everyone to be in position in ten hours. Are we good to go?"

"Arghhh Oorah!" The Scouts bellowed.

Charlie grinned. Even Sara's worry couldn't dent his eagerness. He couldn't wait to lead his team against The Enemy.

Major Nelson stood as the general took his seat. "At ease, men."

The gathered soldiers started putting their seats back and talking quietly with each other.

Charlie tried to ignore the stares they received as the men passed on the way to the lavatory. He shook out a blanket, placed it over himself and Sara, and held her hand discreetly.

He tried not to worry about how she was coping with the thought of the upcoming battle, concentrating instead on the feel of her hand in his and how happy it made him. They'd no time to speak privately, and any worry of his would transfer to her. She seemed calm, neither happy nor unhappy. Her guilt had lessened as well, whether from her talk with the doctor or the acceptance of his parents he didn't know. Nothing she felt was strong enough to reach him without effort on his part except for small spikes of lust when he caressed her hand with his thumb. Happy with her emotional stability, he relaxed even more.

She drifted to sleep with her head on his shoulder. A few minutes later, he fell asleep listening to Major Nelson going over the plan with Recon Force One. Hours later, he woke. Stasia and Rick argued beside him in heated whispers. Sara gripped his hand hard in her cold one. Every Scout was probably awake. He wasn't sure if he should give his brother privacy or interrupt them.

When he heard how angry Stasia sounded, he cringed and pretended he was still asleep.

"Fine, I get it, Rick, you aren't interested. Drop it already, you aren't my father," she hissed.

"Stasia, come on, I didn't mean it like that," Rick whispered back in a conciliatory tone.

"How else could you have meant it? 'I'm not interested is pretty clear.' It doesn't matter anyway, but you have no right to lecture me on anything."

"The hell I don't!" Rick shouted in a furious whisper. "You can't proposition me and go sleep with the first man who asks when I turn you down and expect me to just ignore it."

"Get over yourself!" Stasia snapped, her voice rising. "I didn't proposition you! I asked you to keep me company because I didn't want to be alone, not to have sex with me. And yes, I slept with Harrison. We slept together in the same bed. He was willing to keep me company, not that I owe you an explanation. You're the one with their mind in the gutter, not me. I'm not a whore who sleeps around."

"Jesus Christ, Stasia, you know I don't think that!" Rick protested.

"Really? Didn't you just say I'll sleep with the first guy who asks me? It seems real clear what your opinion of me is."

"Stop it! You know that's not what I meant." Rick took a deep breath and was silent a minute. "I care for you a lot. You've always been a good friend to me, and I don't want to see you taken advantage of," he said, keeping his tone light.

"You goddamn...." She trailed off as she sputtered incoherently. "If I have sex with someone, it will be my choice! Am I such a fool I'll fall for any old line, or am I just that easy?"

"Stasia, I didn't mean—"

She interrupted him in a vicious whisper, "I know exactly what you meant. I'm too young and stupid to know what I want, and I'll fall for the first man who shows me the slightest bit of interest. I'm incapable of making a smart decision about sex or love because I'm just a dumb girl."

She turned her furious face away. Oz took her hand. Everyone else pretended they hadn't heard a thing.

Charlie laid his palm against Stasia's hunched back a moment but left her alone. Sara squeezed his hand and kissed his neck.

To hell with it, Charlie thought and kissed her mouth, running his fingers through her hair. He shifted more towards her and the kiss deepened. Desire for him grew, and he reluctantly backed off. A crowded plane was no place to wake the magic.

He slid his hand to her neck beneath her hair. Still not as hot to the touch as she should be, the warmth of her skin heating beneath his hand comforted him. His fingertips brushed the pulse in her neck, relaxing him even more. She was safe and calm. Small spikes of love and happiness grew and echoed between them. A content sigh misted his skin. He fell asleep again with Sara cuddled against him.

Mike Wallace, the man Brenda called Recon, heard the entire argument. A few minutes later, he went to use the lavatory and saw the other two curled up together and frowned. *This was a pretty lax company. The young people must be along as operators of these mystery weapons they would be picking up and using. Probably super geeks recruited right out of high school. One of them looked like he should still be in school.*

The Scouts better have a good secret weapon, he mused as he covertly examined their gear on the way to the restroom. As far as he could tell, it resembled his, maybe a hair more armored, and black instead of desert camouflage, showing only minor signs of wear. His combat gear showed heavy use. To his eyes, except for their officers, the Scouts appeared shiny and new— untested. Team Valor appeared ridiculously young to be on a combat team.

Over three thousand men lived in that encampment in Iraq, all heavily armed with both air and ground support. Fanatics used to killing, ISIS would swat new recruits like bugs. Weapons wouldn't be enough. To kill required mental discipline, a hardness that developed with each mission until you reached a point where you understood the person in your gunsights was an enemy and pulled the trigger without hesitation, knowing in your soul it had to be done.

The Scouts appeared soft to him without the cold eyes and hard faces his team displayed on a mission. Team Valor looked like children who should be protected from violence, not partake in it. Twenty-one Scouts were on this plane, if you counted the five kids; he hoped more were meeting them.

Numerous reports had passed through Mike's hands, and he knew the weapons and manpower the Scouts would face there would be no joke. Twenty people didn't have a hope in hell of taking that village. The Iraqi government was in the process of negotiations with the United States and England for backing to take out the

ISIS training camps. They wanted weapons but weren't willing to give either nation clearance to bring in the necessary manpower. Apparently, Uncle Sam was tired of waiting.

When he returned to his seat, he took out his maps again to make sure all positions were clear in his mind. His team would be right outside the town, hopefully, first contact for target one.

-14-

THE DROP

Immediately upon arrival at Baghdad Base, everyone boarded helicopters. Mike's entire team rode with the Scouts.

Brenda sat beside him. "Still want to buy me that drink, Recon?" She asked as her team took their seats.

"I thought it was two?" he replied but didn't glance at her, busy watching them load up, hoping to catch sight of the secret weapons.

"So, you do remember," she said with a small laugh." It might have to be three after this. It's been a hell of a week."

"True that," the man sitting beside her said sourly.

Brenda reached over and ran her fingertips over the man's left temple.

"We're fine," the man said gruffly and kissed her hand.

Brenda nodded tightly and swallowed convulsively, turning away. Mike was shocked to see tears in her eyes.

"You and he..." Mike whispered.

"Friends; and he was injured. It's nothing." Brenda's lips tightened, and she busied herself with the device on her arm, clearly not wanting to speak of it.

Mike shrugged and checked his gear.

Guthrie boarded the helicopter. "Gimme one last comm check on Sara's mark!"

The girl sitting two down from Brenda stared at the device on her arm, and Mike noticed all the Scouts looked at the cell phone like devices on their arms too.

The girl said, 'Tick' and thirty seconds later, everyone replied 'tock.'

"Okay, we're in sync," Guthrie said. "Stasia, if Oz confirms locate, you find him, and we move on your mark. Oz, you take out all air support. Hawk, you're on protection as always, but keep a sharp eye on transport. No one leaves except target one if we can help it. A little flame to speed him along wouldn't be bad.

"Report in the clear if we catch General Flores. We're hoping Rinto hears and it inspires him to contact his associates. Stasia, you have the bugs to place. Only do so if you're sure to remain unseen. Stasia, Chief, and Hawk, you all have explosives to plant. Place them for maximum damage and chaos when they blow. Remember, they know about our secret weapon program, and while they have none of their own yet, they might be ready to counter ours. We want them to think we're at home licking our wounds from last week. Decoys are on base to foster that illusion."

Mike frowned. Last week there had been a red terror alert, but he'd heard of no engagements.

Major Nelson tapped the device on his arm and small green lights raced along the outer edge, leaving a line of distinct green dots. He stood, clutching a handhold on the ceiling to balance against and turned his back on Mike to address the Scouts.

"Chief will call out targets as always. Sara is positioning. Sara will drop us in, and Stasia will scout it out. Stasia, you'll have the markers for all the vehicles. Get them marked as fast as you can."

"Stasia and I will scout it out," Charlie corrected.

Major Nelson met Charlie's blue-eyed gaze and nodded. "Fine, take the explosives and go with her. Chief, stick to the plan. The plan is for Sara."

Charlie nodded and pulled Sara tightly against his side.

Mike could pick out who was who now. *Chief had two swords and a shield on his back, for Christ's sake.* A black backpack rested against his knee.

Stasia was inspecting a dagger that she sheathed on her leg before opening a pack that emitted a soft yellow light, which she checked rapidly.

Sara was the other young woman. She carried no weapon except a sidearm strapped to her thigh and what looked like a small wooden baton.

A bulletproof cape covered her black armor. White-knuckled fingers gripped the baton. In Mike's opinion, she looked scared to death.

The rest of them seemed thrilled, exchanging cold, excited glances over Sara's bowed head. Oz wore a fancy dagger cinched to his thigh with a flashlight built in that he'd left on, and a cell phone thing on his arm. The light on his dagger died as he snapped the cover down.

Hawk was the only one with a real weapon, a sweet M110 SASS Mike wouldn't mind having himself, customized for a larger clip with a scope that made Mike drool.

A pack sat at Hawk's feet that gave off the same dim light when he opened it. It appeared to be full of standard plastic explosives. But the pack wasn't big. Mike scanned the packs again. None were that big, just average back-pack size. Even if they were full of explosives, there wouldn't be enough to blow up the tanks and technicals. No secret weapons of any sort were in sight except for the weird devices on their arms. The weapons must be in the packs.

A deep frown etched Mike's forehead. The packs weren't big enough to carry any significant amount of ammunition. The Scouts carried no rocket launchers or anything else, except the explosives, to take out the tanks and technicals he knew would be there. How they planned to sneak up and place explosives on the vehicles without being caught, he didn't know, but he assumed they must have a plan.

"We're now in Iraqi airspace," the pilot announced.

"Confirmation, of both targets in the zone," Oz said.

A blue mist abruptly filled the cabin of the helicopter and was just as suddenly gone.

Major Nelson sighed so hard Mike heard him over the growl of the helicopter engine.

Oz snickered and turned it into a cough and then went down a list of names. "All confirmed in the zone."

Every Scout stared at Charlie. He grinned and shrugged. Brenda laughed and punched his arm.

"I got this," Charlie said to Major Nelson and put on a pair of sunglasses.

Major Nelson sighed again.

Mike had no idea what they were talking about.

"Beta, you're with Chief. Alpha, Hawk's your lead." Major Nelson glanced at his watch. "Okay, we get off in one minute. The helo is giving us a spin in the right direction. Link up."

Mike watched bemused as they clicked a cable from their belts to each other. They wore no parachutes and had no lines deployed. How Oz knew where the targets were, he had no idea. He hadn't seen him do a thing. He hadn't seemed like he'd gotten a private com, but he must have, even though Mike hadn't noticed Oz glance at the device on his arm. Memorizing so many names with a glance impressed Mike. He figured Oz had a photographic memory.

Everyone slipped headsets on, and the devices on their wrists beeped, then a line of yellow light raced around the edge. The light turned green one dot at a time. It took less than a minute, and Sara waved her hand.

"Line up, and go on my mark," Guthrie said. The helicopter banked sharply. Guthrie stared at his wristwatch. "Tick" he yelled and jumped. The rest followed him out.

Mike glanced at the altimeter on his watch in disbelief. They were way too high to survive a jump. He gave himself a quick shake. Obviously, they knew what they were doing. He needed to keep his head on his mission.

"In three minutes, we'll be at your departure gate," the pilot warned.

Mike's team hooked themselves to the ropes and prepared to disembark.

"What the hell was that?" one of his men whispered.

"I have no idea," Mike whispered back. "Probably best if we don't speculate."

They jumped from the hovering helicopter using the rappelling lines. Mike led his team south at a fast jog. They had fifteen minutes to cover two miles.

-15-

INFILTRATION

As they jumped, Sara casted Ascension. She had pre-levitated all except the first four jumpers. Those four provided the direction of the jump, their momentum would pull them in the proper trajectory. In six seconds, they floated down at a steep angle. The goal was to land within a quick jog of their assigned position, coming in at a shallow slant.

"Stay near Oz." Charlie kissed Sara, trying to ignore her anxiety. He gripped Oz's shoulder for a moment, leapt after Stasia, and spell-stole her invisible.

Sara stared after them, her rising anxiety an itch Charlie couldn't scratch. He gritted his teeth and followed Stasia.

Charlie, Stasia, and Hawk ran into the small village, slipping past the armed patrols. Their mission was to determine where the targets were and what defenses were in place while teams Alpha and Beta set up.

The two Recon teams should be getting into position ready to supply backup and stop anyone who tried to escape. Further out, two Ranger teams waited. Agents of all types saturated the surrounding towns. The United States' top priority was finding out who and what General Flores had told.

For Sara's sake, Charlie attempted to keep his anger under control. The answering spike of alarm when he let his rage overtake him worried him. She was much too fragile both emotionally and physically to be here, but that wouldn't stop her. He'd given up on convincing her to stay behind. Determined to be there for them, she wouldn't leave no matter what he said, and they did need her. The most he could do for her was keep his emotions as even as possible. It wasn't easy. The need to kill the men who'd hurt her filled him with a burning rage he couldn't wait to release. He'd never hated anyone before. He hated these men with a white-hot passion.

The three of them jumped and grabbed an edge of a roof twelve feet over their heads and swung themselves up. Hawk ran to the northernmost edge, faded into true invisibility, and started calling out positions. Charlie and Stasia hopped to a nearby roof and jumped to another.

She lowered herself with one hand off the edge of the roof and dropped, catching a windowsill and pulling herself up. The window slid open quietly, and she entered, closing it behind her.

Hawk informed her nobody was inside. In ten minutes, she'd checked the entire place, opening drawers and closets and riffling desks to get a feel for what a building contained.

Charlie leapt to the next building, crossing the fifteen-foot gap easily, and laid on the edge of the roof to use binoculars to examine the town. The three men teams patrolling seemed calm but alert with no sign of panic. They either didn't know about them or thought they could handle them. He was betting they didn't know.

Stasia rejoined him a few minutes later. Charlie spell-stole her invisibility spell again; he'd broken it when he'd leapt.

At random, she examined a few more buildings, keeping to ones with few occupants while he scanned the patrols with eager eyes.

"There's no sign they've prepared for us in any of the buildings I've checked. I need to check a house with more people." Stasia reported. She slapped the button to turn off her mic and said to Charlie, "Go set your explosives and come back for mine if you need more."

They used conjured packs from Oz slipped inside black cloth bags that muffled the glowing V on the back. Each bag held hundreds of pounds of explosives with their detonators, but only the person who took the bag from Oz could open it.

"Hawk, where are the most people gathered? Over." Stasia asked as Charlie jumped from the roof, landing lightly and ran still invisible toward the west where the tanks were parked.

"Building nine has over twenty moving around. Buildings seventeen, eighteen, nineteen, twenty, and twenty-one have a hundred or so each in them, but stationary, I assume asleep. The same in buildings twenty-five to thirty-two. Buildings one and two have small groups of less than ten active— out." Hawk crept to the edge of building four's north side.

"I'm heading to building nine— out." Stasia started to roof hop.

She dropped to the window ledge, grabbing and then letting go to slow her descent to the ground. "The window was open; I'm waiting on a door."

Charlie slapped another block of plastic on the ragged helicopter he doubted could fly anyway and inserted the detonator. It wasn't on his list, but it also wasn't near the ones for Oz to destroy and he was taking no chances someone flew away. He ran to the nearby shed being used as a mechanic shop and began setting more explosives.

He had almost emptied his pack before Stasia whispered, "I'm in," ten minutes later.

"This house is prepared for us," she said with satisfaction. "Wait outside for now, Chief."

Stasia snuck down the hallway, avoiding the mines under the floorboards. "The floor is mined, and the windows are alarmed." She used a miniature camera to take pictures of files opened on a desk. The safe her Find-Hidden spell revealed opened easily for her, and she took pictures of every document inside. The writing was incomprehensible to her, but Sara or Oz could read them later.

When she finished, she left everything like she'd found it, and placed a brick of plastic explosive on the underside of the desk before moving to the next rooms. Distract let her pass a guard in the hallway, and she entered another small office. This one was occupied by two men talking. They leaned over a desk on which a map of the compound was spread. Her gaze landed on the candid pictures of she and her brother at home and her eyes narrowed. These men would know about them. Not able to understand them, she turned on her recorder, casted Find-Hidden again, and located the safe.

This safe she didn't open, they would notice, but she used pickpocket on both the men. Wallets in hand, she paused before each closed door and waited for Hawk to tell her how many were inside. Every person she passed she casted Distract on and photographed. Stasia returned to the roof.

Charlie waited outside on the roof burning with impatience, becoming Chief.

Stasia had been in the building almost an hour. The bag holding his explosives was empty now. All that remained was for Stasia to locate the target, and she better do it soon, he couldn't wait much longer.

Mike's team took up position, keeping a clear view of the town in the distance. Hunkered under his ghillie suit, he blended unnoticeably into the rocky hillside. His M4A1 carbine and SOPHIE, his long-range imager lay beside him. In his hands, he carried his baby, an M39 equipped with a night vision scope. An M45 was strapped to his right thigh, and a k-bar lay in his boot. Four other similarly equipped men on his team hid on the hillside.

The tangos and Scouts wore black pants and long-sleeved shirts with black facemasks, making it impossible to distinguish who was who. When they engaged, it would be difficult to tell them apart with only the headgear and weapons they carried to differentiate them. The Scouts carried rifles identical to his M4A1and wore matte-black, advance combat helmets while the enemy carried a mish-mosh of older AK's and few wore helmets of any sort, most just wearing black face masks or turbans.

"Eagle Eyes One, three men coming up to the right of your position. Don't engage unless assured of stealth— out."

Hawk broadcasting his call sign startled Mike from his observations.

Mike eased into deeper cover, and sure enough, a few moments later, three armed men passed. How Hawk had spotted them on the other side of the hill, he didn't know, but he wanted whatever device Hawk used.

Stasia said, "I'm leaving building nine. Where is the closest building with people awake in it?"

Hawk immediately said, "Stasia, three men are in the bottom corner left of the building directly to your right. Six are moving around the bottom floor in the next. The following twenty feet no one, then thirty or more together. I'm on the roof of building four with a clear field of fire. Oz should join me after he takes out the helicopters. Almost all vehicles can be targeted from here— out."

Mike swung his rifle to building four and scanned the rooftop with the scope but didn't spot Hawk. From where Mike laid, the tops of most of the buildings were partially visible. Low parapets edged the rooftops. The bigger buildings contained metal boxes he assumed housed air conditioners. Tin pipes for venting heat from cooking stoves dotted the roofs. The cover on the rooftops seemed sparse, but he never noticed movement even when he knew where to look before they moved.

"Five more vehicles are to your left, Stasia. Cut through that building. I make out five men inside. Eagle Eyes Two, you have a three-man patrol approaching. Only engage if stealth can be maintained— out."

"This hallway is mined," Stasia warned. "Straight down the center is advised. No sign of either target, recommend Oz circles— out."

Mike placed his rifle on the ground, picked up the binoculars and focused on the group Major Nelson headed. Twelve Scouts were tucked tight against the back of building three, hard to spot unless you knew where to look.

"Understood." Major Nelson nodded to the Scout beside him who ran around the back of the building. "Chief, return to Beta— out."

"Fifty or so men are gathered by the

helicopters. I can take them all," Hawk said. "Recommend Beta proceeds to the hanger interior, one hundred or so in there— over."

"Roger that." Major Nelson turned to Sara, identifiable by the staff she carried, who stood beside him. "Sara, help Hawk clear the men at the helicopter. Alpha, stay with Sara. Chief, you clear inside. Beta, give him room to work— out."

"Stasia, more untagged vehicles are further south," Hawk continued calling positions for both Stasia and Oz.

Mike became confused. How the hell Hawk kept track of all the enemy's movements and positions remained a mystery. He was calling targets even infra-red couldn't target in buildings blocked by other buildings and landscape. And he was doing it fast, too fast for it to be relayed satellite images.

That was some seriously amazing new tech, Mike thought in awe.

The Scouts moved from their location in front of Mike, spreading out in two different directions, hugging the walls and running in a crouch. A rapid count showed seventeen of them now, but he hadn't seen where the extra five came from. In moments, he lost sight of all except five who crouched by a corner of a building before him.

"Locate, target two is in front of my position." Oz's voice rang with satisfaction.

"I don't see him," Hawk said. "He must be underground."

"Hold position," Major Nelson said. "Stasia, reconnoiter— out."

"Go back six hundred feet, sis. Oz, is there a tunnel or cave? Over."

"Yeah. Also in front of my position," Oz replied a second later.

"I see ten men split into three small groups. Stay on your toes. If it's the target, he'll have some traps— out," Hawk said in a worried tone.

"Windows are suspiciously open, waiting on a door— out," Stasia said.

Tense silence permeated the airwaves for a few minutes before Hawk spoke. "Someone approaching your position now— out."

"I'm in. Windows have a sensor, or maybe that's just a string with a bell. Hallway is mined left side. Cameras, motion sensors, and what I think are heat sensors line this hall. Target two acquired— out," Stasia said happily.

"Jesus, Stasia!" Hawk said, "You're way too close to that crowd. Get away from them."

"Relax, he's bugged, and I'm looking for the cave entrance now. Hmm, we might want this stuff. They have files in here. Careful with the fire here, Oz. I can't pass into the underground area without killing the sentries— out," Stasia reported a few minutes later.

Major Nelson knelt with a M4A1 resting across his knee as he peered through the scope. "How many vehicles left to bug? Over."

"Four, I believe— out." Hawk replied.

"Stasia, stay there. Oz, after you take out the helos, go to Hawk and get those four first. Stasia, when Oz starts, take out the two guards and check the hallway. If you can hide the bodies, do so. We don't want them alerted to your presence there. Alpha and Sara, proceed to Stasia's position, clearing as you go. Hawk, cover them— out."

Mike frowned. *How the hell did the major expect the girl to kill two sentries without being seen or heard?*

"Must be code," the man beside him whispered.

"Yes, sir," Hawk replied.

"Good to go," Oz said three minutes later.

"Heads up, Eagle Eyes, we'll be engaging the enemy momentarily, stay alert." Major Nelson stood. "Count us down, Oz— out."

"Fire three," Oz said, and three seconds later, all hell broke loose.

Mike lowered his binoculars as giant balls of orange fire spun through the air, and the helicopters exploded.

Rapid shots sounded, so fast it was unclear how many shooters or what type of guns they used. Muzzle flash on the roof of building four showed where the shots originated from, but Mike never saw Hawk or any other Scout there. A minute later Hawk said, "Clear, waiting on Oz."

Sara yelled, 'Tick' and the Scouts yelled 'Arghhh,' and then Mike watched in awe as lightning forked from the clear sky, and impacted a tank. The lightning crawled over the surface of the T-62 tank and branched out in seeking tendrils. Two more bolts hit and then a ball of fire impacted and flipped the tank onto its side.

"T-twelve, T-thirteen, T-b-six, T-b-seven," Hawk said, and four more balls of fire lit the sky.

From Mike's vantage point, he couldn't see

what they hit, but large explosions and billowing black smoke and flames told they'd hit something and that something had exploded. Armed men boiled out of the buildings, yelling in Arabic.

"I'm in," Stasia said. "After a steep flight of stairs, it branches into a complex tunnel system."

"I have no visual," Hawk warned.

"Oz, get to Stasia. Give her a locate. There could be more exits— out," Major Nelson ordered.

When Oz casted the first fireball, Chief started his attack.

"*Arghhh*," he screamed his attack cry, drew his swords, casted Charge, and rushed into the hanger.

The Scouts echoed his attack command and followed through the door behind him, firing their weapons as Chief swung his swords.

Inside, men stood in shock at his sudden appearance, grabbing for their guns. Chief laughed when they fired at him. Valorous Leap took him to the closest group. Invincible made him impervious to anything for thirty seconds, so he attacked in a frenzy with a sword in both hands. Blue magic swirled about him. Small sparks of electricity shining white with blue tendrils raced over his black armor. The smell of ozone competed with the smell of gunpowder and death.

Thirty seconds later, no enemies remained in

sight, everyone inside the building either dead or hiding behind anything they could.

The Scouts had taken out their fair share. Chief's aura forced the men in the hanger to attack him and ignore the Scouts, so the Scouts stood right inside the doorway in plain sight, firing as targets presented themselves.

Chief leapt from one small pocket of cowering men to another, using Waylay on cooldown, not worrying about showing his magic, they wouldn't live long enough to tell anybody. In battle stance, using straight damage spells, he killed as many as he could as fast as he could. In less than five minutes, no live enemies remained in the hanger.

"That building is clear— out," Hawk said as Chief wiped his bloody swords on a dead body.

The magic surrounding him had dissipated. The relief of letting the magic loose made him realize how tense he'd been. Much more relaxed, he followed team Beta from the building, the overwhelming compulsion to protect his team sated for the moment.

"Group on Stasia's position. Eagle Eyes, stay sharp— out," Major Nelson ordered.

Mike had lost sight of the Scouts except for one crouched in a doorway, covering someone he couldn't see.

The rate of fire increased. "Good, they're getting in the technicals now. I make four of them approaching. Sara, you ready? Over," Hawk asked.

"I am." Sara's voice cracked.

"Armed men are exiting your building, Stasia— out," Hawk warned.

"On me," Sara ordered, sounding angry and afraid.

The Scouts raced together, falling back from their firing positions, forming in the road before Mike's location. Mike couldn't make out individual ones. Grouped in a compact bunch, clustered so close, one hit would take them out, they stood directly in front of the oncoming technical. He cringed, anticipating their destruction.

Sara slammed her staff on the ground and a silvery sphere formed over her and the grouped Scouts as the vehicles fired. The missiles raced around the sphere and returned to the technicals, as lightning arced from the sky, followed by fireballs. The rolling thunder of the explosion that followed shook the ground under Mike's feet.

"Technicals are toast," Hawk said happily. "Eagle Eyes One, we're leaving three intact vehicles in your vicinity. Inform us at once if target one shows— out."

"Fire at will, Hawk." Major Nelson stood beside a still smoldering truck, using binoculars to survey the area.

"Which one is Will?" Hawk snickered. "Everyone looks alike to me."

"That joke never gets old, Hawk. Target two is on the move," Stasia said. "He's heading for the tunnels. Oz, what's your ETA? Over."

"Two minutes until I can invis," Oz replied.

"Beta, clear us a path to the house where Stasia located the entrance to the underground facilities, on Sara's mark— out," Major Nelson said.

"I start casting on the first row in three." Forty-five seconds later, she said, "Chief, tick,"

The Scouts yell carried to where Mike hid, a loud *Arghhh Oorah*. Binoculars glued to his eyes, Mike panned the scene before him, wishing he was one of them as the Scouts attacked.

Chief, identified by the sword and shield he carried, led the Scouts in the attack, pushing forward at a run. Enemies converged at the sight of the tank explosions and fired from the cover of the surrounding buildings and vehicles parked on the street. The attacking men fell back from the Scouts furious assault.

Everyone in reach of Chief fell to his blades while the Scouts covered him with their rifles. A group of Scouts surrounded Sara about thirty yards back from the attacking group. The Scouts covered her so closely, Mike lost sight of her. The compact bunch inched forward, keeping within thirty or forty yards of the Scouts standing in a straight line firing their weapons.

For the life of him, Mike couldn't figure out how they weren't mowed down like grass, but no one even seemed like they were getting shot at. All enemy fire was aimed at Chief. Whatever his shield was made from was impressive because none of the fire pounding him slowed him at all. Mike lost sight of him as the road curved, but the

Scouts surrounding Sara kept up their slow advance.

Armed men ran to their location from all over. Alpha kept position by Sara and picked off targets that showed themselves, but most attackers hung back out of sight, firing blindly at them. A group carrying rocket launchers approached, and Hawk called out the targets. Bright explosions rained sparks and fire onto the ground. Somehow the Scouts were destroying the missiles in midair.

Another silvery sphere covered the Scouts surrounding Sara, and then Mike lost sight of them too.

Chief led Beta team to the men holding the rocket launchers firing at his wife. He'd killed four and was chasing the last two when Major Nelson called him back. Indecisive, he stood panting, his swords hanging by his side, dripping blood. With a glare at the two men running away, he turned back and met Sara at the door of the house Stasia had entered.

Major Nelson slapped his shoulder as he stalked by.

Chief snorted a small laugh. "Don't think I'm letting them get away. I'm letting Hawk have them."

Two sharp cracks of gunfire sounded.

"Thanks," Hawk said. "I was starting to feel left out."

Major Nelson rolled his eyes. "Alpha, remain outside. Beta, clear the building— out."

"This is Eagle Eyes Two; we have multiple people leaving. None appear to be either target— out."

"Take them out. Will you need assistance? Over." Major Nelson asked.

"Negative— out," Eagle Eye Two replied.

"A large group is forming, Major," Hawk said, "Over a thousand men, south of your position on the edge of my range— out."

"Oz, report— over," Major Nelson said.

"I'm not underground yet. As we speak, I'm clearing the traps. Major, Hawk could probably tell you more than I can. All I know is target one is in front of me— out." Oz sounded frustrated.

"Hawk, go. Be fast." Major Nelson glanced at his spell bar. "Oz, clear that gathering group. Sara, give him a tick— out."

Hawk jumped from the roof and ran to Alpha team's position. No enemies shot at him or seemed to notice him in any way.

Oz sprinted from the building.

"I'm going with him!" Without waiting for permission, Sara followed Oz towards the assembling men.

"Sara, no! Stay with Alpha!" Chief yelled.

"We'll be right back," Sara said, sounding determined and terrified.

"Damn it, Sara!"

"Invis three." Oz casted, and he and Sara ran together toward the large group.

"A considerable number of people are down here," Hawk reported as he entered the underground chamber. "More than I can separate, a few thousand at least."

"Stasia, where are you? Over." Major Nelson asked.

"Exploring this place, it's huge. Lots of booby traps and sensors everywhere. The first few corridors appear empty. A large armed group is in the third right-hand corridor, but... I think I'm missing something; they seem calm, not panicked as you'd expect. I think they have a plan in place I'm not seeing— out."

The radio crackled with static, then Oz said, "Fire three."

Three seconds later Sara said, "Tick."

Fire lit the sky again. Dark-orange glowing spheres grew in size and brightness as they spun through the air. Fifty fireballs struck in less than five minutes, interspersed with lightning that impacted with sizzling crashes. Gouts of flame and smoke billowed into the night sky.

When the first fireballs landed, men screamed and scattered in different directions. Sara encased Oz in a reflective shield and hunkered down out of sight behind a still smoldering car. Oz picked off the men that lingered with lightning. Blue and white phosphorescent tendrils leaped from man-to-man, covering the corpses in between with glittering arcs of electricity visible even through the thick smoke.

Nine minutes and twenty seconds later, Oz reported he and Sara were returning. Ten seconds after that he said they were making a pit stop.

"We're searching an office," Oz said. "Well,

Sara is searching, I'm guarding her— out."

"I'm returning to my position up top— out," Hawk said.

"Copy," Major Nelson answered.

Ten minutes later, they returned. Sara carried a bulging file box.

"Sara, check the recordings I made earlier, maybe something on them will help," Stasia said.

Moments later Sara wailed, a long, drawn-out scream. "Charrrlliiee!" Blue magic exploded from her as she scrambled to the door.

Brenda grabbed her, and Sara shrieked, lifting glowing blue eyes to Brenda's face. "Everything's fine, Sara. Don't panic." Sara struggled in her grasp. "Chief, you better come," Brenda said unnecessarily.

Charlie was already on his way. Her terror pulled him, making him frantic.

"Let me go! It's them, they're here!" Sara screamed.

Brenda released her, and Sara headed to the door.

"I'm coming. Wait with Brenda," Charlie ordered futilely.

She couldn't wait. The need she had for him wasn't hers alone but her magic's. It sought his protection with desperate strength. Charlie moaned and ran faster, using Valorous Leap on cooldown.

Mike had crawled to his left to get a clearer view

down the road before him and could now see around the curve in the road, but no one was in sight. The vehicles still smoldered, sending an occasional thick cloud of smoke through the air and obscuring vision. He listened as he watched through binoculars.

This is what you got for taking girls into combat—hysterics. That young girl had no business being anywhere near this violence. Mike winced in sympathy as she continued to sob and call for her husband.

The door of one of the buildings before Mike burst open and someone stumbled out, tripping on the stairs and falling headlong into the street on their hands and knees. The cape identified Sara.

Black suited figures followed her out, but before they could reach her, another figure, this one carrying a sword, ran up and grabbed her. Two other black-suited figures raced up, and Mike knew they were Oz and Stasia by the lack of weapons. The girl held a k-bar in one hand.

"Where, Hawk?" Stasia panted.

"One building to your left is where you took a recording. Ten men are inside." Hawk sounded grim and very angry.

Stasia ran to the building, moving faster than Mike had ever seen anyone move in his life.

Chief knelt by Sara who was sick and gasping on the ground, a crumpled black facemask clutched in one hand and her braided blond hair coming loose as her husband rubbed her shoulders.

Mike worried about Stasia going into the building alone armed only with a knife. *Anger was making her reckless. Why didn't anyone stop her? Obviously, Stasia was a spy, carrying no weapon except the knives and would get herself killed while the Scouts did nothing.*

"Stay with Rick and Brenda. Stasia and I will be right back. Oz, guard them."

Without waiting for a reply, Chief rose, and sword in hand, headed to the building Stasia had just entered.

Before he reached it, a man ran out. Stasia appeared out of nowhere directly behind the man, grabbed the man's shoulder, batting the gun he aimed at her away with ease, and before Mike could blink had stabbed him five times across his chest. The dead body fell at her feet, and she ran back into the building followed by Chief.

Maybe she wasn't as defenseless as he thought.

Mike heard the screams from the men inside the building through his headset. *For the headset to transmit, they must be killing them up close and personal. Far from being defenseless, Stasia was a regular Jane Wayne.*

Outside, two black-suited figures knelt beside Sara. Still crying, she pushed herself to her feet. One of the figures hugged her, and the crying stopped. The other helped her replace her headgear, and they returned to the building they'd come from.

The screaming men had quieted. "Sara, Stasia is coming to you. They're dead. You don't have to worry about them ever again." Satisfaction filled Chief's voice.

Mike winced again. Form the level of fear Sara displayed and the violence that met it, something truly horrible had been done to that young girl. His eyes narrowed, and his hand tightened on his gun. For the United States to risk young weapon engineers, ones with severe emotional issues, to retrieve stolen plans, the threat must be extreme indeed.

Stasia ran from the building and entered the one Sara had gone in. Chief exited the building and headed west at a run, back to the buildings Stasia had entered first.

"Two doors down, Chief. Two men are upstairs to the left," Hawk said, and Mike lost sight of him.

"Chief, get those two and then return to position— out," Major Nelson ordered.

"Hawk, don't lose them," Chief said.

"I won't." Rapid gunfire sounded. "The way is clear, but they know I'm out here now, Chief, and there might be a back door, hurry. Both are still to the left in the second room."

The door hit the wall with a thud as Chief ran into the room the men cowered in. Both men babbled at him in Arabic, holding up empty hands. A grim smile lit his face, he was in perfect agreement with his magic.

"I can't understand a word you're saying, but it makes no difference. My wife will sleep better once you're dead," he said, and he casted Waylay, appearing behind his targeted man, he slid his sword between his enemy's ribs before the man had time to turn. The other ran for the door.

Chief leapt and grabbed him. Spinning the man to face him, he pulled him tight to his chest and put his sword against the man's neck. Blue eyes watched with satisfaction as he slowly slitted the man's throat. When the man was dead, he released him, letting the corpse tumble to his feet and yelled his attack cry.

Every Scout echoed him.

Mike shivered.

Filled with violence and satisfaction, the eerie sound carried on the night air, twenty cold-blooded killers announcing joy in their work.

He shivered again.

-16-

CATCH AND RELEASE

Charlie headed back to Sara. Blood dripped from his sword and smeared his face, the wild blue glow in his eyes began to dim. His vision was returning to normal, and the magic that had been surrounding him disappeared.

Stasia pulled Sara into a tight embrace for a moment before speaking. "Sara, it's clear to the third corridor. Get an invis and come and see if they're saying anything good."

"Invis three." Oz casted invisible on Sara. "Go."

Sara ran by Beta team, and followed Stasia, being careful to step where Stasia did, avoiding the mines in the floor. The armed men in the corridor conversed in whispers. Sara's passive magical ability to understand languages let her understand them.

Stasia took Sara's gloved hand and led her

out before invisible failed. The two girls hurried back down the tunnel.

Charlie rejoined Beta team, no longer feeling the overwhelming need to be Chief. Calmer now, his eyes had returned to their regular brown. The magic and he were both sated with the deaths of the men who had terrorized Sara.

The murders didn't trouble him. He'd long ago come to grips with the fact he was a protection warrior, not a human man. The old Charlie Hayes couldn't have killed them and wouldn't have wanted too. He'd have been wracked with guilt. They'd been unarmed and had surrendered, but they remained The Enemy, and a warrior killed its enemies. He was just happy he'd been in control, choosing his actions during the encounter.

Maybe I'd feel guilty if I'd attacked first, he mused as he wiped his sword before sheathing it. *But they'd brought this on themselves by taking Sara.*

Sara gave him a quick hug, ignoring the blood that coated him. Her relief at the sight of him was overwhelming. It literally caused him to stagger a step back. He tightened his grip on her as she turned to Major Nelson.

"No news to report," Sara said. "Sorry, Major. Someone said the plan, but no details, just 'we stick to the plan.'"

"Try again in two minutes."

Sara turned back to Charlie, gripping him tightly, resting her forehead on his chest.

Major Nelson gave Charlie a pointed look, letting his narrowed gaze linger on Charlie's arm around Sara before turning away. Charlie tensed, trying not to let the major anger him. Major Nelson couldn't feel Sara's and his magic's need the way he did. To the major, it must seem as if he was a having a romantic moment when nothing could be further from the truth.

His magic needed Sara. Her fear and worry agitated his magic until it felt as if it would overpower him and force him to attack and keep attacking. Touching her, feeling her pulse eased the magic, letting him remain Charlie. Enough of Charlie Hayes remained in him that he hated the thought of doing violence without control. If hugging Sara on a mission let him keep control that was okay with him.

"Hawk, what's it looking like up there? Over," Major Nelson asked.

Hawk answered immediately. "Small pockets of men spread out, in and around the buildings randomly, except for the five buildings to the left of where you are. Those remain empty— out."

"That would put them over the empty corridors." Major Nelson tapped his chin thoughtfully.

"Invis three." Oz casted invisible again on Sara, and she ran back down the corridor with Stasia.

"We have movement up here," Hawk warned.

"Keep us apprised— out." Major Nelson stepped to the back of the Scouts grouped tightly in the hallway, leaving Charlie at the head of the group.

After a minute of eavesdropping, Sara gave Stasia a thumbs up, and they returned to Alpha team and Major Nelson.

Sara passed Charlie, giving him a nod and tight smile, and stopped at the major. "Two men argued. General Flores is here for sure. One man said, 'the coward hides behind us.' The other one said, 'he's given us the keys to destroy the unbelievers. If you're afraid of the godless invaders, go wait with the coward next door. Even the infidels can't survive the roof falling on them.'"

"They must have another exit, Oz." Major Nelson glanced at Oz, lifting one eyebrow.

"I keep getting this one, sorry." Oz shrugged, looking frustrated, fingers still flicking in Magical Locate pattern.

Charlie narrowed his eyes at Major Nelson before turning his gaze on Oz. "Reword it. Try backdoor, or escape hatch or whatever damn thing they might have called it."

"Okay, I got one," Oz said.

Major Nelson keyed on his mic. "Stasia, can you get by the men in the hallway? Over."

"Affirmative. Out."

The radio crackled, and Hawk came on the line. "This movement is heading to Eagle Eye One, permission to engage? Over."

"Permission granted. Eagle Eye One, back him up— out."

Mike rose the binoculars to his eyes again. A hundred or so enemies were spread out in eight small groups leapfrogging from building-to-building, covering each other with an assortment of weapons.

"Move up, Eagle Eye One, let's get rid of some of this clutter— over," Hawk said.

Mike's team crept closer. Rapid fire sounded, and the enemy started to fall. Muzzle flash lit the roof of building four, but no Scouts were visible on the rooftop. The advancing enemy dissolved into a teaming mass as men ran in every direction, some trying to retreat. The smarter ones entered buildings.

Hawk crouched and peered over the side of the building. "I can't get the group all the way left, they're out of my line-of-sight. Can you see them, Eagle Eyes? Over."

"Affirmative. They're running toward us along the backs of buildings thirty and thirty-one— out."

"I'll regain line-of-sight if they leave those buildings. Scare them out— out."

Outnumbered ten to one, Eagle Eyes One opened fire. The men returned fire, forcing Eagles Eyes to take cover. Two men ran out, making a break for the hills. Hawk dropped them both in seconds before Mike could take aim; he wanted Hawk's rifle. The rest hugged the building and continued to fire into the hillside where Eagle Eyes hide.

"Fall back, Eagle Eyes, I'll get them," Hawk said. "Here come the rats."

A minute later, the men began swatting wildly at themselves and appeared to be shooting at each other. Three men broke cover, running in different directions. Hawk picked them off, impressing Mike with his marksmanship. It wasn't easy to hit a moving target at that distance, and he'd hit three in seconds with no time to aim between shots.

"Hey, Major, you know what likes rats? Snakes!" Hawk snickered and a minute later said, "That group is done. Keep a sharp eye out. I'll be out of range of this side of town while I check the far end— out."

Mike and his teammates exchanged bewildered glances. Hawk had somehow killed those men or gotten them to kill each other. Mike still wasn't clear on what had just happened even though he'd watched it.

"Alpha, move into the building and get us the papers Stasia saw earlier." Major Nelson pointed on his map and nodded at Brenda.

"Wilco." Brenda led Alpha team back outside and into an adjoining building where they ransacked the place. An explosion rocked the building. Smoke and flame billowed from the windows and doors. Charlie began running before he realized he was going too.

"Damn it, we hit a mine. Send Sara— out," Brenda shouted.

Sara didn't wait for orders. Charlie halted before the door and let Sara run past him.

"Careful of the mines," he called after her.

She held up a hand in acknowledgment but

didn't slow.

He headed back to Beta. Sara was calm and focused, and Alpha didn't need him. The Enemy was below him in the tunnels.

"Jesus, that's a lot of blood," Sara said. "Okay hold his leg in place, and now his arm. That's just gross. Better?"

"Drink some water," a woman, Mike thought was Brenda said, but the radio distorted her voice a bit, so he wasn't sure.

"Yeah, thanks, Sara. I'm good to go," A man said. "Not even a scar."

Mike exchanged a bemused glance with his teammate, who crouched behind the rock beside him listening in consternation to the conversation taking place inside a building in front of them.

His teammate snorted a laugh. "They must be speaking in code because it couldn't be what it sounded like."

Mike shrugged, and lifted his rifle, peering through the scope. No live enemies remained in range. Only dead bodies littered the ground before him. Closer examination showed the small bodies of rats and two snakes.

"Rats and Snakes. How the hell did Hawk know they would attack?" Mike glanced over at the man beside him.

His companion shrugged. "Better question, why the hell would they attack men and not run from the gunfire?"

Uneasy, Mike continued to peer through his scope, searching for signs of small wildlife near him.

"Let me see these papers." Sara leaned over the desk and leafed through the documents. "Looks like crap to me." Papers scattered on the floor at her feet as she discarded them after a fast perusal. "Speeches, prayers, more speeches." She held up a thick wad of paper stapled together. "This might be helpful, a file of inventory and this one is names." Sara continued to rummage through the files ending up with one, small, usable box filled with paperwork. "A bunch of nothing, let's go."

Alpha team headed back to the tunnel complex.

"Stasia, Hawk, report— over," Major Nelson said.

"Nothing new here," Hawk said. "They're still skulking around those houses. No one new is moving up— out."

Stasia made no response. "Use your bar, Stasia," Major Nelson ordered. With the spell bar, she could text or use the simple yes-no code. "Give me a yes if you can't speak because you would be overheard."

Charlie pulled Sara closer as she stared at her bar, her body tense until her spell bar lit up with a yes. Sara's fear for Stasia upset him more than Stasia's silence. He trusted Stasia could handle herself. She could sense traps and disarm them. No one could see her, and even if they could, she could use her defensive cooldowns. She would have to be taken by surprise to be injured, and that would be hard to do with glowing blue eyes. When the magic manifested like that all his senses sharpened. The slightest noise or breeze alerted him to the movements of those around him, and he knew without looking what they were doing as if someone shouted the information in his ear.

His skin twitched as he considered that was probably exactly right. The idea of an alien living inside of him was so new it hadn't really sunk in yet.

They'd have to perform a lot more experiments when this was over to see just what this alien could do, and how it affected them.

Sara sighed with relief and stood straighter as Stasia answered Major Nelson. Charlie released her to peer over the major's shoulder to see his spell-bar. Unlike his, the major's bar showed a crude map sent by Hawk. Sara glanced at the map and frowned. Oz and Sara had written the program, but they weren't happy with it.

Charlie laughed to himself as Sara fumbled with her pack, removing a small tablet and began typing. She glanced at him and smiled but she wasn't amused, she was concentrating.

Likely working on the programming right now," Charlie thought and earned another, brighter smile, for his spike of amusement.

"Did you bug target one?" Major Nelson asked as he tapped the map, lighting a square green. "How about target two? Stay on target one, we'll take down target two— out."

Stasia signaled yes again for each question.

"So, this roof is rigged to collapse—" Major Nelson started to say when Charlie interrupted.

"Give them what they came for. Stasia, if Sara *calls* you, can you return to target one safely? Over."

Stasia indicated she could.

"Okay, Sara, cover me. When the roof falls in, call me back here." Charlie ran a hand over Sara's tense shoulder. Fear emanated from her now that you didn't need magic to feel. His magic was making her fear all too noticeable to him. Blue began to creep into his eyes. The magic pushed for him to protect her, to become a protection warrior again, full of rage and deadly dangerous.

"I'll come too," Oz said, "They'll see three members of Team Valor, and I can locate the mines."

Major Nelson grinned at Oz. " Good idea. Hawk, come down and run with them. And, Joy, you go to. Let them think there are four of you. Remove the facemasks and let them see it's you. Oz can disguise Joy. Brenda, take Alpha team and run out looking panicked when the floor comes down. Make this believable. I want you outside the town perimeter going north. The back door is there somewhere— out."

Three minutes later, Sara turned her pale face to Charlie. "My staff is primed. You have one minute on my mark. Please be careful, Charlie. I love you."

"I love you too, Sara. We'll be fine." Charlie

squeezed her hand for a second.

"Okay, lovebirds, we're working now." Major Nelson sounded exasperated.

"Aww, give 'em a break, boss," Hawk said, "they're newlyweds."

"Head in the game, guys," Guthrie barked. His gruff voice instantly stopped the snickers.

"Okay, Oz, Hawk, follow me. Run down each of these corridors on Sara's tick." Charlie ran a gloved hand across his wife's cheek. "I'm stealing your call, Sara, and if you hear us yell now or an explosion, use yours."

Sara nodded and wiped her sweating brow. "Ready?"

"Yes." The outward signs of distress didn't match her inner fear. Without this connection, he wouldn't realize how terrified she was. He had to force himself away from her. Mentally trying to communicate with his magic, he barely noticed Hawk's arrival. Oz disguised Joy as Stasia.

"Tick." Sara casted a shield on each of them followed by her heal-over-times as they ran down the nearest corridor. Small specks of brightness the size of fireflies flowed to them down the hallway, Sara casting heals they didn't need. Charlie frowned but kept running, glad she was limiting herself to her smallest heals.

Beta team stood in the hallway behind Sara.

Upstairs, Alpha team waited by the door to run out.

The ground rumbled as Charlie led his team down the second corridor. "Wait," Charlie said. "Third corridor, Hawk, Oz, cast something." The rumble turned into a roar.

Sara didn't wait for Charlie's order, she summoned. The tunnel to either side of the main hallway crumpled with an angry roar. Billows of dust and debris filled the corridors.

Five buildings fell in, collapsing in graceful folds, sending up clouds of dirt as they settled. Black suited figures raced out. The Scouts ran straight to Mike's position, pretending not to notice them, although one gave a little finger wave.

Mike choked back a laugh. "That had to be Brenda," he murmured.

His teammate snickered. The Scouts continued running over the hill out of sight of the town where they hit the speed and ran twice as fast. Mike watched until they ran from sight. He'd never seen someone sprint so far before. They would exhaust themselves at that pace in no time. He shrugged irritably and turned back to the town. They must know what they were doing, probably some kind of energy drink or some shit.

Sara hugged Charlie when the team appeared, shivering in his embrace. Dirt and small debris fell around them, coating them in dust. Rubble partially blocked the entire hallway. In the distance, men yelled and cheered.

"Okay, keep the razzle-dazzle to a minimum. They think they got you," Major Nelson whispered into his mic. "Beta, this has to look like all you. Sara, stay with Beta. Chief and Oz, pull down the facemasks, conventional weapons only— let's go." Major Nelson climbed over the rubble and was met by gunfire, which he returned.

Beta pushed forward, climbing over the corpses, exchanging fire, using Sara's shields for protection and forcing their attackers back.

"Target one is on the move," Stasia whispered. "Oz, locate the backdoor and then Brenda, line her up— out."

"Brenda, go six-hundred-yards to the left. That will be Eagle Eyes Two position— over," Oz said a few minutes later.

"Eagle Eyes, we have no vision upstairs now. Stay alert— out," Major Nelson warned.

"Damn, you sure we can't fireball them? They're grouped up so tightly down that tunnel Oz could take them all." Hawk sounded disappointed.

"No, let them think he's dead," Guthrie clapped Hawk on the shoulder. "One hundred to one, we got this."

"Mines, middle of the floor," Hawk reported.

"Give 'em some flash bangs," Major Nelson ordered. As soon as the grenades were deployed, five Scouts stepped up to the tunnel entrance, shielded by Sara, and opened fire, decimating the men disorientated by the flashbangs. Before the shields Sara had casted ran out, all five threw live grenades down the tunnel and retreated. Loud explosions and screaming replaced the sounds of gunfire. "Move up. Sara, close your eyes.

Harrison, guide her."

Corpses lay two and three deep in the narrow corridor. Charlie glanced back as Sara hid her face in Harrison's shoulder, blocking out the carnage on either side of her. The sight didn't bother him a bit, but she was horrified.

Harrison swung her into his arms and climbed over the bodies, carrying her. Charlie gave him a grateful smile. He spell-stole Hawk's rapid-fire spell and rounded the next corner.

Hawk moved up until he was in front and turned to the major. "Over two hundred men are around this corner in tight clumps. Target two is mixed in there as well, but they're so tightly jammed I can't pinpoint him exactly."

"Stasia?"

"Target one is packing. Want me to run back and see? Over."

"Can you and still catch our primary target? Over."

"Yes— over."

"Do it— out."

"It will be yes if I see him, no if I don't— out." Stasia sprinted back up the corridor, leaping over the mines she'd already spotted. "Oh, this is almost too convenient. General Flores just crossed the hallway in front of me, alone— out."

"Be careful, he knows— out," Charlie said.

An echo of worry built, Sara's emotion matching his perfectly. The magic amplified their worry until it took an act of will to not charge into the crowd and rush to Stasia.

Stasia made no reply.

"Thirty-six seconds left on my, um, call you

stole. Charlie, don't leave her in there," Sara said.

Charlie didn't reply, but his mouth tightened into a thin line. "Stasia, if you don't answer, I'm calling you in ten seconds— over."

He was counting down when Stasia said, "Keep your knickers on; I got him cuffed to a bed, blindfolded, and gagged. I'm going after target one. Hawk, let them know if anyone else comes for him— out." Stasia sprinted back down the hallway.

Guthrie motioned his team forward. "One more corridor; let's go."

Hawk went first, shielded by Sara, and opened fire with magical speed and precision. Charlie hung back, not wanting his aura to notify the men he was there. They might know of it and be looking for it. His magic hated that he let Hawk lead into gunfire. He didn't think he could hang back much longer.

Men in the tunnel returned fire, the bullets bouncing harmlessly from the shields around the Scouts. The few bullets that got through the shields, causing injuries, Sara healed. The men attacking them had no chance against Sara's magic and the firepower of the Scouts. Narrow, twisting confines of the tunnels kept word of the massacre from spreading because around every corner more men waited, firing futility on them.

Charlie was just about to inform the major he needed to be in front when Hawk said," Got him. He's in the next room. Push this lot back."

Smoke hung heavy in the air tickling the nose and ruining visibility, but Charlie could have navigated the room blindfolded. The acrid stench of gunpowder overlay the meatier scent of fresh blood. Gunfire in the close confines made Charlie's ears ring until he could barely hear the screams and shouts of the wounded.

He took Sara from Harrison. Contact with her eased him, and they didn't need his gun. Hawk was holding them back all on his own. Sara shook in his arms, and he thought she might get sick again.

"Just a few more minutes," he said, not sure she could hear him.

"Package is secure," Major Nelson said in the clear when they had retrieved General Flores.

The Scouts retreated the way they'd come while Major Nelson called headquarters.

"Callsign niner-foer-three actual, requesting pick up— over."

They would make a show of leaving.

"Roger that, niner actual, Mother says sit tight, your bird is on the way— out."

"Armed men are escaping on foot past our location," Mike reported. "No sign of any surveillance tags near us— out."

"Stop as many as you can— out." Major Nelson flipped his mic off and turned to Hawk. "How many more down here, Hawk?"

"A couple hundred enemies spread out in all directions. This tunnel system is huge, Major. Large groups of people are leaving my range," Hawk added a moment later.

"Go assist Eagle Eyes when we leave here," Major Nelson ordered. "I'm setting the charges to blow the hell out of this hallway when target one is clear. When we're good to go, give us a yes, Stasia— over."

Charlie tensed and turned towards the sound of distant gunfire where Eagle Eyes fought. He and his magic agreed that he should be helping them. Sara's need was the only thing keeping him by the major's side. The magical pressure to run to Eagle Eyes eased when the sound of gunfire faded.

Finally, Stasia whispered, "Rinto is twiddling his thumbs by the back door. Either afraid to leave or waiting. Give him incentive in forty-five. Out."

"On my mark, I'm going to blow it. Beta, get out now and give them a show."

Charlie set Sara on her feet outside the door. She lifted her face to the night sky and breathed deeply. An impassive observer would think her calm. Charlie's hands clenched on the hilt of his sword he didn't remember drawing, and he reluctantly sheathed it and casted Spell-Steal to steal Oz's disguise spell and disguise himself.

Major Nelson waited forty-five seconds, said 'mark,' blew the hallway, and then ran up the stairs after his team where they made a production of protecting their captive. Outside, the sounds of gunfire could be heard in the distance where Eagle Eyes fought.

"Hawk, get to Eagle Eyes Two once Eagle Eye's One position is clear. Go with them and help clean up our mess." Major Nelson grabbed

Hawk's arm as he ran by. "Discreetly, Hawk." When Hawk nodded, he released him and turned to Glenn, Beta's leader.

Charlie took two steps to follow Hawk and then returned to Sara. Her fear of the general was extreme. *Hawk doesn't need help*, he told himself firmly. This time he and his magic disagreed, but after repeating Hawk and Eagle Eyes were fine a few times to himself, his magic stopped pushing. He didn't know if it understood him or was more worried for Sara. He waited anxiously for the helicopter to land so he could Spell-Steal her Soothe and use it on her again.

Helicopter rotors kicked up dust and stirred the clothing on the corpses as it settled into the street. Charlie leaned over Sara to block the sand and grit from her. She stood motionless, her glowing eyes focused on General Flores, consumed by terror to a degree that worried Charlie with its intensity.

"He can't hurt you or anyone else," Charlie said.

"My magic is afraid of him."

"Sara, look at me." Charlie had to force her to turn away. "He's harmless now. I swear on my soul, he won't hurt you again."

She nodded jerkily and hugged the files she carried so hard she bent the box.

"Major, get Flores out of sight before I do something we all regret. Sara can't be near him."

"Copy that," Major Nelson said, sounding exasperated. "Let's go, team. That's our ride."

Team Beta jogged to the helicopter, passed their prisoner on board, and headed off at a run to meet Alpha team. Major Nelson slapped a piece of duct tape over the general's mouth, zip tied his hands, feet, ankles, knees, and wrists, wrapped him in a blanket, and strapped him in the farthest corner of the copter before throwing another blanket over him.

"That's the best I can do. Can you board, or should I call for another bird?"

"Charlie shrugged one shoulder and pulled Sara to the helicopter. She followed, pausing a second and shaking her head as if she were going to say something to Flores but changed her mind.

"What?" Charlie asked.

"Nothing. He's so full of greed and hate nothing anyone says will get through to him. And it doesn't matter why he did it."

"You're safe now," Charlie said, willing her to believe it.

To his relief, her wild fear eased, and all he sensed from her was exhaustion. She sat gracelessly beside him and closed her eyes, leaning her head back on the metal wall and clutching the box of files to her chest. Charlie put his arm around her and settled her against his side.

Everyone else boarded, and the helicopter lifted off in pursuit of their quarry. The orange glow of the destroyed outpost faded into the dark night.

-17-

THE CHASE

Mike jumped when Hawk appeared beside him. "Holy crap, you're not even in camo," he said and frowned at Hawk.

"I'm part Indian." Hawk chuckled and gestured to the west. "Twenty or so bad guys are just over this rise. The rest of them are too far away to give you any trouble. I'll clear a safe path out of here for you."

Mike's eyebrow rose. "Just you… against twenty men armed with AK-47s?"

"Well, not all of them have AKs, there's a few M16s in there too." Hawk shrugged and then grinned. "You can help if you want." He raced off before Mike could answer.

Rapid gunfire broke out, and men yelled in Arabic. Mike signaled his team to follow. By the time they'd eased themselves over the small hill only six armed men remained. Crouched with their backs to a boulder, they yelled in Arabic as they formed a semi-circle, weapons pointed out. Dead bodies littered the ground before them. Hawk was nowhere in sight.

Mike called for the men to lay down their weapons. His request was met by gunfire and more yelling. Three black-clad men knelt behind their comrades firing M-16s. Mike's team returned fire, and the men firing on them crouched and ran behind the boulder. They were met with a brilliant flash of light. Their screams petered out into silence in moments, and the light died away.

Mike jumped again when Hawk appeared by him.

"Jesus, stop doing that! You're going to give me a heart attack or get yourself killed." Mike glared at Hawk and lowered his weapon.

"Just popped by to say it's all clear at the moment from here to your extraction point." Hawk gave Mike a two-finger salute and raced off.

"Are you done messing around out there, Hawk?" Major Nelson said, sounding annoyed.

"Mostly." Hawk sounded as if he was stifling a laugh. "I'm headed to Eagle Eyes Two to make sure they're clear to the pickup. Don't wait for me; I'll catch up."

"Where's our target, Stasia?" Major Nelson asked.

"Running out now," she whispered. "I'm following. Eagle Eyes Two, we're at your position. Let him go. Time to throw our surprise party."

"Setting off the farewell package." Major Nelson confirmed and triggered the explosives Hawk, Charlie, and Stasia had planted.

"Jesus Christ!" Mike exclaimed as the sky lit a dark, angry orange. Flames shot hundreds of feet into the air as every building collapsed with a rumbling roar. The ground shook, and clouds of dirt and smoke obscured the sight of the collapsed buildings. "How the hell did they have time to sneak around and rig that? And where did they get the explosives?" Mike whispered to his teammate who just shrugged.

Mike's team took a moment to admire the destruction before jogging away, headed to the extraction point.

"Oz, confirm our dead bodies, please," Guthrie asked.

"We got quite a few of them." Oz closed his eyes while he ran locate. After a moment, his eyes opened. "Only ten left, spread out in all different directions."

Sara handed her box of files to Major Nelson. The slow thwap of the rotors stirred the papers.

After leafing through it, he grinned. "Nice work, Sara. This should help a lot."

"I thought so." Face white under the dust, she leaned back in her seat, closing her eyes again.

Charlie frowned at her, feeling her

exhaustion and a craving, he thought was for sunlight. He recognized it as the same hunger-like need she'd had yesterday at the pool. With his eyes closed, he concentrated on her, trying to distinguish her feelings. Much weaker than it had been just hours before, Sara's glow was now a dull golden light. The connection was too new for him to say with certainty what he sensed, but he knew she was afraid and exhausted. The brightness that should be was tarnished and weak. She needed sun and rest. Her magic was seriously depleted.

"Sara and I need a minute soon," he said to Major Nelson.

"When we can," Major Nelson assured him. Busy coordinating the teams following Sergeant Rinto, he didn't glance up from the maps in his hand. "We're going to pick up Eagle Eyes One, Two, and Alpha. Beta is with Stasia now. The target is moving on foot. Stasia is getting us good intel."

The helicopter landed at the rendezvous and Hawk boarded. "Sara can't wait much longer, Major," Charlie insisted. "She really needs magic."

"Okay, you two go do what you need to when we have them all on board." Major Nelson glanced up and met Charlie's brown eyes.

"We can do it here. It won't take long." Before the major could order him to wait, Charlie removed his gloves and placed his hands on Sara's face.

Major Nelson watched in apparent fascination as Charlie's hands glowed blue. The blue disappeared, absorbed into her skin.

Sara sighed in relief and sat straighter. "I'm okay, thanks."

Charlie ran his hand through her hair, smoothing back the strands that had escaped from her braid and kissed her. "Don't wait so long next time. I don't mind sharing."

When she blushed, he grinned.

Sara slouched, half leaning on him and squirmed as if she couldn't get comfortable. Major Nelson glanced from her to Charlie who was frowning again.

"Sara, if you need more, say something. If that's all it takes, I can order them to close their eyes. I'm sorry I made you wait. I thought there would be an explosion or something."

"This will be good for a while. Some sun, food, water, and rest, and I'll be back too normal," Sara assured him without opening her eyes.

"My control is getting better," Charlie added. "I'm not saying it wouldn't cause an explosion if we waited too long, but there was no danger of that here. The hurry was because the lack of magic hurts her."

"When you're magically depleted it hurts?" Major Nelson asked.

She heaved a sigh and sat straighter. "Yes, it's draining or something. Like a bad flu or you ran a marathon with a cold. You feel tired, and sore, and empty, and a bit alone, which I especially dislike." Sara gave a small shudder while removing her gloves and taking one of Charlie's hand in both of hers.

Major Nelson gestured to their clasped

hands. "We can't afford for you to be weak. If you need his magic, say something right away. Don't let it run you down. Can you transfer it hand-to-hand?"

Charlie nodded. "It just takes longer, the more skin contact, the better."

"Then it's no problem. Use a blanket or shirt to cover your hands if you have to, and if there is nothing available, just do it. Let them wonder what the hell they're seeing." Major Nelson glanced at Oz and then Sara. "You're good to go now?"

"Well, I wouldn't want to hold off a tank attack, but yes," Sara affirmed.

Oz touched her hand in sympathy, then yelped and drew his hand away. "Damn, that's much stronger now!"

Hawk leaned over and touched her quickly. With a wince, he shook his hand and touched Charlie. He kept his hand on Charlie for about thirty seconds before taking it off and shaking it. "Only Sara hurts more, Chief feels the same."

"May I?" Major Nelson asked as he reached for Sara's hand.

"Doesn't bother me, I don't feel it. Go ahead."

He laid a fingertip against the back of her hand and jerked back, and then reached for Charlie and gingerly touched his hand. "Yeah, sorry, Sara, but it's extremely unpleasant to touch you. It's not much better to touch him. I wonder if it's because you just gave it to her. So much research needs to be done. That's a great defense for you. Does it work through gloves?"

"Try it and see," she said with an evil grin and replaced one glove and reached her bare hand to him.

He put one glove on and touched her bare skin. "Oh, yes it still works!" He shook his hand and flexed his fingers.

She reached for his hand with her gloved one.

He cringed in anticipation but felt nothing.

"I can touch you if I'm clothed, but clothes won't work for you. My bare skin will hurt you. Charlie is doing his best to ensure no one touches me again."

"That effect is fascinating." Major Nelson touched them both a few more times.

"Friendlies inc," Hawk said and turned his mic back on. He jumped out of the helicopter and went to lead them in.

Mike started in surprise again when Hawk suddenly appeared.

"This way, Lieutenant. We can go straight in. No one is near us."

Mike nodded and gathered his group.

Hawk ran off into the dark desert and faded from view. A few minutes later, they heard him talking with Eagle Eyes Two over the headsets.

Everyone boarded the helicopter. Powered down, the helicopter parked between two steep-sided gullies. "This spot is secure, so we're going to wait here. Rest if you can." Major Nelson pointed to a carton of supplies. "Rations are in that box there. Help yourself. We're waiting for Beta team to report, so it could be a while."

They passed around the meals-ready-to-eat.

Charlie was glad to see Sara eat one even though she wrinkled her nose. He handed her a bottle of orange juice, which she took gratefully, and then opened meals until he found another for Oz. He made a mental note to stock his pack with food for juice for his team.

Brenda and Mike talked quietly.

Most of the others settled in trying to sleep.

Charlie pulled Sara over until she was lying with her head in his lap. "Sleep if you can. You need the rest." Blond strands of hair sifted through his fingers, his touch relaxing her. A soft smile lit his face, he loved knowing how she felt.

Mike frowned. "What's with that?"

Brenda smiled. "Newlyweds, they're, um, weapon specialists, not in the service, it's fine."

Mike nodded, his hunch confirmed. Supergeeks he was sure. Something was familiar about them as well, especially the girl. He bet he could Google Sara, supergeek, and get a hit, but knew he shouldn't. He wasn't supposed to know.

On the edge of sleep, he placed it; the bar in Mexico and Brenda being upset at the news report. Sara Mitchel. They'd shown her picture on TV, something to do with a divorce. He tried to put it from his mind, he wasn't supposed to be figuring it out.

Two hours later, the helicopter lifted off. "No news, we're just moving closer," Major Nelson said. "Hawk, when you see her, holler out, and we'll wait there."

Mike watched in fascination as Hawk did nothing as far as he could tell.

"Stop, I have her," Hawk said a few minutes later.

"Stasia report." Major Nelson glanced at the device on his arm.

Harrison replied, "She's unable to. She's right on his ass."

"Any ideas yet where he's going?"

Stasia texted, 'Yes.'

"Drop back and inform us."

Moments later Stasia spoke. "Sergeant Rinto is on foot, and I'm trailing him. Right now, he's about three-hundred-yards in front of me. He made a call to this number with a satellite phone." Stasia rattled off a string of numbers. "Someone named Jahmar answered, and Rinto told him to pick him up at the agreed spot. Rinto said he has the money and the proof. They argued, and he said, 'take it or leave it, Colonel Travensky was interested too.' After arguing another few minutes, he said, 'Fine, I keep the money, you get the proof, or you get the money, I get the proof, you choose, but I need a ride to Baghdad airport, and if you cross me, this goes on the web with your names and every location I know.'

"They argued again, and he laughed at the man on the other end of the phone. Told him he didn't give a damn about their cause and if anything happened to him, the report would go out automatically. When he hung up, he said, 'Idiot, how does he think I can reach a computer from here?'"

"Good work. Keep him in sight," Major Nelson said, then made some phone calls and arranged for more tails at the airport. Finally, he called Agent Lewis and gave him the phone number.

Harrison sounded agitated when he spoke next. "Do not get in that car, Stasia. That's an order! Major, we have a problem here. Stasia is going in a vehicle, and we won't be able to catch up to her."

"Stasia, don't get in that car!" Major Nelson yelled.

"Yeah, it's too late; they're headed down the road. She's on top of the damn car." Harrison sounded angry.

"We'll pick you up in a few minutes, Beta," Major Nelson said. "Stasia, for the love of god, don't get caught." A hard smack turned his mic off. "You kids are going to give me an ulcer."

"We can find her, right?" Sara asked.

"At the moment, yes. The bug she planted can be tracked. But, if she's stupid enough to get on the damn plane, we could lose her." With another smack, he turned his mic back on. "So help me god, Stasia, if you get on that plane...."

"Stasia, if you can hear me, don't get on the plane, please." Sara leaned forward and clenched her hands around her staff. "If you're in trouble, hit your panic button."

"Should I call her?" she whispered.

"No, not yet. Oz, give us a locate. If she suddenly changes direction, we will," Major Nelson said after a moment's thought.

Oz pointed. "She's that way, but I don't know how far."

Major Nelson looked around at the Eagle Eyes teams sitting in the helicopter, watching this in perplexity.

"Oh, goddamn it!" he yelled. "This is classified! I'm tempted to drop you all off and make you walk back." Two fingers pinched the bridge of his nose, and he snorted and took a deep breath. "Okay, we proceed as planned," he said in a voice of forced calm when he dropped his hand. "Pick up Beta and go to the airport in a roundabout route. Hawk, go get her. If it's going to hell, call for an, um, *emergency extraction*," he added with a meaningful look in Sara's direction.

"Wilco." Hawk switched seats with Tony, obviously trying to use his aura to calm the angry major.

Major Nelson glared and crossed his arms.

Hawk stifled a laugh.

Stasia reported by text she'd bugged the car and the man inside had taken the money, not the videos.

The helicopter lifted off and stopped for Team Beta.

"Let's get this circus moving," Major Nelson said in disgust.

Sara stifled a laugh, turning it into a cough. Major Nelson glared. Charlie stifled his own laugh. The major transferred the glare to him. Everyone else sat silently.

Hawk jumped from the helicopter as it approached the airport.

"Get this crate to Baghdad base now. Iraqi

air force is seriously pissed at us. Team Valor, wait here, we'll lose radio range. Do not, under any circumstances, get on the damn plane! We have agents for this. Am I clear?"

"Yes sir," Charlie and Oz chorused and jumped.

Sara followed.

Curiosity was killing Mike. *How the hell did they do these things?*

"Well, this is FUBAR," Major Nelson mumbled, "Damn kids never listen. We'll head straight to Baghdad base where the general is busy right now covering our asses. We're on a training exercise, and our pilot is an idiot who went to the wrong airport. We were never outside of this helicopter and didn't see or do a damned thing."

Major Nelson surveyed the men with pursed lips and narrowed eyes. "Sure, they'll believe you guys need training." Sarcasm dripped from his voice as he closed his eyes, leaning back in his seat.

Mike examined the men too. They looked exactly like what they were, a well-trained, heavily armed, special forces unit. He stifled his grin, which was sure to irritate the already annoyed major.

The helicopter flew directly into a bunker.

"Everyone out, move it!" Major Nelson ordered. As they exited, a troop of green privates entered. The pilot also exited, and a new, younger pilot entered the cockpit. Their pilot winced as his replacement took the helicopter back out, swinging around crazily.

"This won't fool them for a goddamn minute, but it'll allow them to save face," Major Nelson said as the helicopter landed with a bounce in front of a big building. He jerked his thumb at the pilot. Captain Sanders is in charge. You'll do whatever the good captain tells you too!" Major Nelson beckoned to his Scouts. "Joy, come with me, civilian clothing, look harmless please, we're going to pick up the kids."

"Hawk, can you see her?" Crouched in a patch of weedy vegetation Charlie held Sara's hand in his.

"Yes, I have her in sight. She can't reply verbally."

A flood of text filled his spell-bar, names of people and places. Charlie memorized it quickly.

"We need to find his computer if he really has one," Sara whispered.

Charlie turned his mic off. "I'm tempted to tell her to get on the plane, but it's so damn risky."

"No, absolutely not! If she steps foot on it, I'm summoning her," Sara said her voice strident.

"If we could all get on it...." Charlie trailed off.

"No!" Her voice had risen too shrill. "We're not doing that. It's way too dangerous."

Charlie rubbed her back. Her fear was very real. "Yes, it is, but we've snuck onto transport before."

"Not of men who want to torture you. No, I won't let you," Sara yelled, almost in a panic.

"Okay, we won't," Charlie said calmly, worried now at how afraid she was.

"Stasia, I mean it, don't even try it! Hawk, if you see her get on, call me!"

"Don't worry, Sara, I will. I don't want her to try either," Hawk said. "She's following him into a building. I can't follow and remain unnoticed."

"Watch her on your radar," Oz said.

Another flood of text crossed the spell bar. Stasia reported Sergeant Rinto believed he'd escaped unseen but was in a hurry to leave the zone. He was headed to Greece. Another text, this one directed to just Sara, promised she would remain in the airport.

"Well, that's completely random," Oz said after he'd read the text.

"That's the point." Sara shrugged, running a finger over the message Stasia had sent her. "He knows you can locate him in the zone. If he picks randomly, it will be hard for you to find him."

"Stasia, confirm he gets on the plane heading there, and we'll get our own ride," Sara said.

'Two hours.' Stasia replied by text. Thirty minutes later she texted a new phone number and a name brand of a disposable cell phone.

"I copy that." Major Nelson passed the information on. Parked outside of the airport his radio was once again in range of them.

"She's waiting to be sure he boards the

plane," Charlie said. "We have another hour and a half to wait. Then we'll need a fast ride to Greece."

"Copy that." Major Nelson made more phone calls. Thirty minutes later, he called back. "Two SEAL teams are on their way there. Our ride will be waiting back at Baghdad base."

Charlie glanced at his blood-splattered black armor. No way could they blend in wearing this. "Some civilian clothes would be helpful."

"Already on it," Major Nelson assured him. "Alpha and Beta will go as regular Army personnel on leave. You'll drop in wearing civilian clothes."

Oz, Hawk, Charlie, and Sara hid beneath Hawk's No-See-Um in a patch of scraggly weeds right outside the fence that encircled the airport.

"He's on board," Stasia finally said. "Where should I meet you?"

"Outside of the airport, down the road from the main gate, go to the right. There's a small shopping complex, meet us behind that."

Charlie practically jittered with impatience to chase The Enemy.

-18-

GREECE

Three hours later, Team Valor jumped from a plane headed to Crete. They'd changed into civilian clothes inside a nearby hangar where Guthrie handed them bags. "I did the best I could, in the time I had, for sizes."

Charlie stood in front of Sara and changed while she took off her armor and put on jeans, a t-shirt, and light-blue windbreaker.

Stasia removed her uniform, and Oz turned bright red.

"Are you blushing?" She grinned at Oz as she buttoned her shirt. As usual in clothes she didn't try on first, the top was too tight. "You've seen me in a bikini a million times."

"But, not in your underwear." Oz turned away.

"What's the difference?" she asked, glancing at her purple, lacy undies.

"I don't know. It just is, jeez." Oz dressed quickly with his back turned.

Stasia and Sara laughed.

"Dude gross; she's my sister." Hawk glared at Oz.

"She isn't my sister," Oz mumbled under his breath and busied himself tying his sneakers.

Charlie moved closer to Sara, scowling at both Hawk and Oz.

Stasia snickered.

They bundled up their gear and passed it to Guthrie. He handed them each a prepaid credit card and fifty dollars in cash. To finish their ad-hoc disguises, he offered them each a pair of sunglasses and three baseball caps.

Aboard the plane, Alpha team waited, wearing Army fatigues. Most of Beta team had stayed behind in Iraq to oversee the clean up there.

Major Nelson greeted them with a distracted nod. "When we arrive, I'll be taking a room in a hotel." The map in his hand crinkled as he glanced up. "Your phones should work there. Radios will be too conspicuous. Call in reports. Target one is code-named Uncle. Say no names in the clear.

"Sara, find something to cover your hair. Use a cap for now. Stasia, bring a throwing star, and everyone take a small knife in an ankle sheath. Oz can summon his dagger if he needs it, but the rest of you go weaponless. Don't attempt to sneak the knives past security though, leave them behind if you need to go through the metal detectors. I suggest splitting up as well. Try to blend in as much as possible."

One thick finger stabbed the map, tapping the icon for the airport. Major Nelson glanced at Hawk before turning his gaze back to the map. "Oz and Hawk, you should have no problem locating him. We know right where the plane will land. Two SEAL teams are standing by. Code word 'Uncle is having a heart attack,' and they'll move in. FBI teams will be there too. If you make them, don't give them away. If at any time you need help, press your panic buttons.

"Once you have him in sight, let Stasia follow him. You can car hop, Stasia. It's an island so we can locate you easily enough. Check in every ten minutes with an emoticon. If you miss two check-ins in a row, Sara summons you."

"I'll summon her," Charlie corrected.

The major nodded a brief acknowledgment. "Fine, Chief will summon you. A small recorder will now be standard gear for you." The major handed her the small device. "Find out who else he told, and we need those recordings back. Under no circumstances do you leave this island— any of you. Keep the razzle-dazzle to a minimum. Stay under the radar. Come to my hotel room at any time. If it goes to hell and you need a safe place, go to the American embassy or Souda Bay Naval Base. Ask for General Campbell and claim you're a niece or nephew. You know his direct line, use it."

Major Nelson paused. "I want to be clear here— crystal clear. This is a fact-finding mission. Stasia will be the only one in sight of him. Everyone else hang back. Frankly, we don't need you on this, just her. Don't compromise her by being seen. Sara can get her out instantly. Hang well back."

He pulled up pictures of the airport and surrounding area on his laptop, and everyone committed the details to memory.

"Sara, convert the money at the first opportunity. If Stasia does car hop, you'll need cab fare. Let Sara do the talking. She can blend in best accent wise."

Major Nelson took a quick phone call. "That was Agent Lewis. He's been in touch with our agents here, and they're slowing the plane. You'll have twenty minutes to reach the airport before he arrives. The plane is going as slow as possible, any slower and Rinto could get suspicious. The Scouts are here for emergency backup. Let's not have one of those, okay?"

As they approached the coast of Greece, their plane slowed, and they jumped out and floated over the water, soaring in fast at a sharp angle toward Crete. As soon as they landed on the water, Stasia casted Sprint and towed them toward the shoreline as they levitated, feet dangling a foot off the ground.

When they got closer to the shore, Hawk ran in front, pulling them.

Stasia unclipped her belt and darted away. To their eyes, Stasia was a misty white outline of a person running atop the water without touching it. To the rest of the world, she was invisible, leaving no wake to mark her passing. At the shore, she gathered herself and leapt, landing lightly on the roof of a passing car, catching hold with both hands below the windshield wipers on the first car heading in the correct direction. The driver never glanced at her.

A brief twitch of his fingers and Charlie stole Oz's invisible spell and used it on himself and Sara.

Oz casted Invisible Duo on himself and Hawk. Now cloudy outlines of people, they ran as fast as they could on top of the water to the shore. A small planting of pine and carob trees, growing to the water's edge, sheltered them from view as invisible ran out. Few people were in sight on the windswept beach.

Charlie didn't think anyone had seen them jump from the plane and fall to earth, and no one on the beach seemed to take any particular notice of them. Once the cooldown was up for invisible, they ran again, putting as much distance as they could between where they'd come ashore before calling for a taxi.

Crouched on top of a metal detector, Stasia watched Sergeant Rinto exit the plane. She carried a recorder and stood behind him as he made a phone call. The rest of her team was spread out in the airport.

Charlie was the only team member in sight. Wearing a disguise he spell-stole from Oz, he appeared as a forty-year-old executive with a potbelly and a balding head to everyone else.

Oz had disguised himself as an old woman

with gray hair and sat on a bench between Charlie and baggage claim. Hawk waited invisibly outside by the taxi stand, while Sara slouched against the wall outside the main entrance, pretending to read a map.

A commotion at the baggage claim entrance made everybody stare. Photoflashes lit in a blinding array, and people yelled as airport security converged and ushered reporters from the building.

Charlie looked for Sara. A blond ponytail under a blue ball cap bobbed around the reporters near the entrance. She was amused and then alarmed. Charlie half rose from his seat.

A reporter grabbed her arm, and then everyone swarmed her shouting questions and taking pictures. Charlie settled back and winced. She was in no danger, but her cover was blown.

Hawk called Charlie on his cell phone, sounding disgusted. "That's Tara's paparazzi, and they just identified Sara. Rinto is bound to see this."

"Damn," Charlie mumbled as he glanced towards baggage and spotted Sara's stepmother and her entourage striding through the airport as if they owned it.

Sergeant Rinto stared after Tara. A commotion at the door drew his attention, and suddenly Sara pushed out of the reporters as airport security held them back. When she broke free, she ran to Tara and hugged her. The reporters shouted questions and took pictures.

"Oh, Mom." Tears filled Sara's wide blue eyes as she wailed. "Phone calls were impossible.

I had to follow you here. I ran away, it was so awful. You'll let me stay with you, won't you?" Tears trailed across Sara's cheek as she clutched Tara's arm dramatically.

Sergeant Rinto backed up and peered over a newspaper at them.

Tara stopped dead and lowered her sunglasses with a manicured hand. The bag she held in her other hand dropped to the floor. One of the women following on her heels snatched it up.

Sara hung from Tara's sleeve. "My friends died horribly. When I found out you were here, I came right away. I knew you would be there for me and not make me return." Not giving Tara a choice, she hugged her as more reporters gathered.

"Sara," one shouted, "why did you come here?"

As another yelled, "How come Tara wasn't expecting you?

What accident?" another asked.

"Why didn't you go to your father?" another shouted.

Sara turned her tear-stained face to the nearest reporter. "I came to be with my mother. My friends were killed, and I need my mother now."

Charlie stifled a laugh. Sara would've been an amazing actress. The tears on her face looked real when Charlie knew she was annoyed, not sad, as she clutched Tara.

Tara rose to the occasion like the Oscar-winning actress she was. "Give us some space, please. My daughter needs me."

Then she turned to Sara, putting an arm around her, kissing her temple, and stroking her hair as she leaned down and murmured something. Charlie laughed as she flinched away, converting it into a wide, open-armed gesture, and waving people back.

Sara's defensive shocks must have got her.

Tara was the picture of a devoted, loving mother comforting a grief-stricken daughter. The flashes almost blinded Charlie.

This was bound to be the cover of a hundred tabloids, he thought as the reporters scurried for good shots and hollered questions.

Tara waved a hand in the air for attention as she stepped in front of Sara. "My daughter will stay with me. Please respect her privacy; she's a minor. I'll set up interviews to answer questions. Give us some space now."

Charlie's phone rang again. "So, I'm watching the local news live, and who do I see?" Major Nelson's voice dripped sarcasm.

"Reporters spotted her." Charlie sighed. "I think he's buying it though," he added as Sergeant Rinto eyed Sara contemplatively, practically rubbing his hands together. As Charlie watched, Rinto headed to a phone booth closer to the baggage claim.

Tara led Sara to a limousine, still comforting her as if they were close. Stasia stayed behind Sergeant Rinto.

Charlie debated following Sara, but she was safe with Tara. The magic within him pulsed hard. It knew he watched The Enemy and wanted him to act. Charlie gritted his teeth and forced himself to sit patiently and tried to convey his intent to kill their enemy later. He almost laughed when he felt the magic pout and withdraw. It was learning.

Sara got in the car with her ex-stepmother. Neither said a word until the driver pulled away from the curb and the privacy shield rose. Tara tapped manicured fingers rhythmically on her knee.

"We both know that was BS." Sara shrugged and gave her a slight smile. "I had no idea you were here. When they saw me, I needed a reason to be here, or we would both look bad. So, I came to my loving and supportive mother in a time of distress."

"Does your father know you're here?" Tara glared at Sara, her blue eyes cold.

Sara laughed. "He never told you I was emancipated from him?"

"No, when?"

"Before you divorced. Good thing you didn't sue for custody, huh?" Sara grinned.

Tara's glare deepened.

"Look," —Sara held both hands up in a placating gesture and heaved a small sigh— "I'm not your enemy. I'll play the devoted, loving daughter. Tell people a few of my friends died suddenly and I came to you for comfort. You look good and get good press. I'll stay out of your way. Tell them I decline all interviews, and you'll speak for me."

Tara nodded, but her eyes were narrowed. "Why are you here?"

Sara shrugged and stared out the window.

Tara frowned. "What about the dead friends?"

Sara shrugged again. "Keep it vague. I've attended so many schools that someone somewhere must have died."

Three deep lines now formed on Tara's forehead.

"Fine, I'll get you a name or two. Just tell everyone I'm too much of a wreck to leave my room."

"Okay, I'll check you in, and you bring me something I can use in an interview," Tara agreed after a moment's thought.

Sara nodded as she texted the major.

Inside the airport terminal, Stasia recorded every call Sergeant Rinto made. Still invisible, she climbed onto the back of the taxi he hailed and rode with him to the hotel.

Hawk, Charlie, and Oz followed as discreetly as they could.

Stasia called Hawk. "Come upstairs and tell me when he's in the bathroom so I can enter the room. I'm afraid he'll notice the door open if I just enter."

Stasia let Hawk into an adjacent room so he

could see the layout. Outside the door of Rinto's room, they hunkered against the wall, both invisible until Rinto entered the bathroom and Stasia could sneak in unseen.

Hawk returned to Charlie and Oz and called the major. "Stasia is inside, and she thinks he believed Sara's act. He called someone named Georgios and arranged a meeting in his room. She forwarded you the conversation. Three possible leaks remain to plug. The computer, if there is one. This Georgios person, and Colonel Travensky. Stasia said the colonel didn't believe him and wanted more proof. She doesn't know what Georgios is meeting him for."

"Okay, good work. Be ready to follow this Georgios guy when he leaves," Major Nelson said.

Charlie grabbed Hawk's phone. "I see where this is headed. No way are we using Sara as bait."

"Too late, Chief, she already put herself out there," the major said matter-of-factly. "I'll get her back up in her room. Not a Scout, he would recognize that, but we could put someone else in the room with her. Scouts will be in the building ready to go. Chief, she'll be safer if we catch these guys, and this is a good way to do that."

"I'm going to her. Oz can disguise me."

Major Nelson sighed heavily. "I need you in the field. Sara will be safe, I promise."

"If I feel for one second she needs me; I'm going to her." Charlie paced in small circles frustrated annoyance clear in every movement.

"If she needs you, she'll summon you," Major Nelson answered, sounding impatient.

"Send my brother to her. Sergeant Rinto would accept that as realistic."

"Yeah, fine." Major Nelson heaved an impatient sigh. "If you died, they would naturally comfort each other."

Charlie handed the phone back to Hawk with an apology for snatching it, and spell-stole Oz's invisible. Oz casted Invisible Duo on himself and Hawk, and they headed into the lobby looking for a good spot to use Hawk's No-See-Um while watching the door.

A corner behind a giant potted palm made a perfect spot, and they settled in to wait.

-19-

RINTO'S PLAN

Three hours later, Stasia texted Hawk that Georgios had arrived in the hotel room. As Georgios left, she texted again, warning her team.

In the lobby of the hotel, Oz's fingers twitched as he casted a new disguise on Charlie and invisible on himself and Hawk. As pale shadows of their former selves, they split up.

Hawk dashed up the emergency stairs and waited by the door for Georgios to leave Rinto's room and followed. After pointing out Georgios to Charlie, Hawk ran out the door to give his passive ability Hidden Nature time to work.

Disguised as an overweight man in a blue jogging suit, Charlie followed Georgios from the building. A newspaper tucked under one arm, Charlie leaned against the front of the hotel.

Georgios wore worn jeans with white paint stains and a faded, black sweatshirt. A red ball cap covered graying brown hair. Otherwise nondescript, of average height, weight, and age, Georgios resembled half the men walking the streets here. Charlie snapped a picture as Georgios hailed a taxi.

Visible now, but hard to see from Hidden Nature, Hawk tracked the taxi on foot, running down the side of the street. Charlie jogged down the sidewalk, staying within sight of Hawk. Few people walked the sidewalk, the dinner hour luring them into the adjacent restaurants.

Inside Sergeant Rinto's hotel room, Stasia crouched in the corner beside his telephone. Rinto paced around the room for a moment before flopping onto the queen-size bed and kicking his shoes off. Stasia settled herself, sitting cross-legged against the wall.

In a busy cafe across the street, Oz waited disguised as a businessman in a blue pin-striped suit, sipping coffee and pretending to read a newspaper. Once an hour he left the building and returned wearing a new disguise.

Sara waited to hear from Stasia in a fancy suite of her own adjoining Tara's rooms. A balcony set off the bedroom and the living area, but she couldn't use it. Each time she stepped a foot out the door flashbulbs announced the lurking reporters. So, she opened the curtains and sat in the weak sunlight with her face lifted to the sun and her eyes closed. Every hour Stasia sent an emoticon. Four hours later, someone knocked. Rick, dressed in civilian clothes, stood at the door.

"I've been sent to support you in your grief

over your loss." Rick grinned and hugged her, kissing her cheek quickly.

Sara laughed as she tugged him into the room. She ordered room service and warned him not to go near the windows, then closed the curtains and turned on every lamp in the room.

Rick watched her turn the lights on, a frown growing on his face.

"I'm sorry," he finally whispered.

Sara glanced up from her phone in surprise as she checked Stasia's latest emoticon. Pale and avoiding eye contact, she nodded. "Me too." The phone in her hand trembled. She took a deep breath and stared him in the eye. "Are you sorry we came for you? That we changed your life?" Unable to maintain eye contact, she turned away and fussed with the table setting.

Rick stood behind her, placing a hand on her shoulder and kissed the top of her head. "No, none of this is your fault. You didn't ask for any of this." He trailed a gentle hand over her bright hair. "Thank you for saving us, both times. We're family now; I'll try not to let you down again."

"You never let me down, or Charlie either. If it wasn't my fault, it certainly wasn't yours." A crooked smile lit her face before it darkened, and she looked away again. "If I hadn't loved you, they wouldn't have shot you."

"If I hadn't been there, they would've picked a different Scout to shoot." Rick gave a small shrug. "It was evil of them to pick who you love the most. It isn't a bad thing to love us. The bad thing is what they did."

Sara stood in front of the closed curtain and

fingered the drapes. "My head knows that, but my heart hurts for you all."

Quiet descended as she rubbed the fine, silk fabric between her fingertips. "I sometimes wonder if the world would be better off if I hadn't casted that first heal," she said barely above a whisper.

Rick put a hand on her shoulder and turned her to face him. "The world is much better off with you in it. Never doubt that. You have a great gift. Bad people will want to steal it, to corrupt it. We'll make sure that doesn't happen."

Rick laughed suddenly and sat on the bed where he stretched out, placing his hands behind his head. "Besides, if you had no magic at all, Charlie would still think you were the most important person on Earth." He patted the bed beside him, and she lay on her side facing him. "Tell me what it's like using the magic."

Sara smiled and tried to explain the unexplainable.

Pressed to the side of a house behind a thick planting of shrubs, Charlie felt the spikes of guilt, fear, and love from Sara. Love overshadowing the guilt relieved him. Whoever she was with made her happy, and that was good enough for him. As soon as he could, he would call and check on her. But, right now, he hid under a No-See-Um beside an open window as Hawk surveyed the area.

The man inside the house spoke on the phone, but Charlie only caught a few words. A dog somewhere inside whined and barked. Georgios yelled at the dog, and a cage rattled as he kicked it. What Charlie heard was enough to reassure him that Sergeant Rinto had, indeed, bought Sara's act.

Right now, Georgios paced by the window, telling whoever was on the other end of the line that he had two more calls to make, and no he didn't know who they were just that Rinto told him the numbers to call and if they wanted in, they had to be ready with their men by midnight tomorrow. Georgios slammed his phone down, rambled the room muttering obscenities, and made more phone calls. Charlie couldn't hear the conversations; Georgios was too far from the window.

Hawk appeared twenty minutes later and gestured for Charlie to follow. Charlie crawled backward away from the open window as quietly as he could. When he was out of view of the window, he stood and sauntered to the street as Hawk kept watch to see if Georgios noticed. A few minutes later, Hawk joined him.

Teeth gritted tight, Hawk stomped down the street. "I heard all his calls," Hawk said without preamble and called the major. "Georgios is setting up a group of men to take Sara tomorrow night. None of them knows a thing about her. They think it's just a rich man's whim to take her. That Rinto's willing to pay a lot for the daughter of Meredith Barlow.

"After setting up a morning meeting,

Georgios called another man and told him Rinto said the prize could still be had if they got here before tomorrow night. Those men will know the real deal. I'm heading back to Stasia. She'll need a break. I'll make sure she gets out of his room unseen."

"Rick is with Sara now," Major Nelson said. "Let's hear what Stasia has to report."

Shoulders stiff and tight, Hawk fumbled in his shirt pocket for his sunglasses to cover his glowing, blue eyes.

Charlie laid a comforting hand on his shoulder. "We won't let them take her again."

Hawk nodded. "So much evil. All these people willing to harm her for no reason. The things they said, well..." He trailed off with a grimace of distaste. "I never think of Sara as a movie stars' daughter, she's just Sara. To them, she isn't even a person. What they said and have planned… well, they were truly disgusting."

"We're you able to get in the house to listen?"

"Sort of, they have a dog in a cage inside. I used the dog's eyes and ears." Hawk kicked a rock into a trash can. The sharp metal ding echoed his angry grunt. "That man is torturing the poor thing."

Ahh, Hawk's bad mood explained. "We'll rescue him too," Charlie said and tightened his grip on Hawk's shoulder a moment before letting go. "When this is done, we'll come back and take him with us. Go tell the dog to be quiet and well-behaved until you return."

Hawk smiled, pulled the blue ball cap down

on his head, and ran back. Charlie kept walking. With his magical endurance and speed Hawk would catch up fast.

When they reached Rinto's hotel, Charlie entered the cafe and took a table near Oz. Hawk snuck upstairs and texted his sister. Twenty minutes later, Stasia and Hawk left the hotel, and he and Oz joined them. Together, they hurried down the street until they found a yard with a small grove of trees where they sat under Hawk's No-See-Um.

Stasia called the major, talking softly to keep from breaking Hawk's No-See-Um. "Rinto doesn't have a computer. I'm almost one hundred percent sure of that. The briefcase contains both the pictures and the video camera. After every call, he laughed at how gullible they were for believing he had a grand backup exposure plan for them. I'll bring you the recordings, but in a nutshell, he arranged for everyone who escaped to come here and take her. The cave in fooled him. He thinks we're dead and she panicked and ran from the government to her mother."

Stasia leaned forward and placed a hand on Charlie's knees as his eyes kindled. "Georgios is getting Rinto men, weapons, and a boat. Rinto plans to double-cross them. He called a Colonel Travensky, and they argued. Travensky didn't believe him, and threats were made. After pacing and swearing for twenty minutes, he called someone else, a Mr. Nadir. Rinto was nervous and sweating. If he had another choice, I really believe he wouldn't have done it. I think this is the original buyer. Rinto talked as if he was anyway. Nadir agreed to meet him tomorrow at three a.m., Rinto's last chance to produce her. Threats flew back and forth for five minutes.

"The meeting will be offshore. I have the coordinates they set up. Right now, Rinto is stone drunk. I can leave him and get some food and rest. Tomorrow, I'll return in the morning and stay with him all day. Can you get me more bugs and new recorders so I can hand them off to Hawk?"

"Great job, Stasia," Major Nelson said. "Yes, I can. Come to my hotel room and eat and sleep. Tomorrow will be a busy day."

"I'm going to Sara," Charlie said.

"Fine," Major Nelson snapped. "Have Oz disguise you as Rick. Bring food, or eat before you go. Oz can get you in the morning and, Chief, try not to let her use summon tonight in her sleep. I want it available."

Charlie turned to Oz after they hung up. "Sorry about that. I'm sure I can get in and out by myself."

Oz laughed and slapped his back. "Don't worry about it." Suddenly, he looked unhappy. "She'll need you. I'm sure of that. I wish we could all be there for her." Red climbed his cheeks, as he looked away. "Sara already had issues about being trapped in dark places. After this week, she'll need serious therapy. Hell, we all will." His expression was sad and angry as he glanced at their faces. "We need to be patient and supportive. She'll need us more than she'll admit."

Stasia looked horrified, and her eyes swam

with tears. "Did they—"

"No!" Charlie interrupted. "No one raped her. Don't ask her about her time there either. If she does want to talk about it someday, we'll all listen and be as sympathetic as possible." Charlie's eyes flared blue, and he took a deep breath. "She feels horrible guilt for what the Scouts went through. So guilty it's making her physically sick. I hope Doctor Gotlieb can help with that."

"We'll keep telling her it wasn't her fault," Stasia said.

Charlie pressed the heels of his hands against his eyes for a moment. When he dropped his hands, his eyes were their normal brown color. "Only if she brings it up. She really hates when anyone mentions it. I mean it; hearing about it really upsets her."

Stasia nodded and took his hand in hers, squeezing tight before letting go. "We'll all be there for her in any way she needs. She seems to be handling things well."

"She is," Charlie paused. "Mostly she's calm but has moments of real terror. If we didn't have this connection now, I wouldn't know. The guilt she feels is oppressive and worries me more than her fear." He stood and dusted off his pants. "Let's get going. I don't want her alone at night, in the dark."

Stasia and Hawk headed to the major while Oz and Charlie grabbed a cab to Sara's hotel. Charlie Spell-Stole Oz's disguise spell and made himself resemble Rick. In the back of the cab, Oz cleared his throat and spoke hesitantly. "I admire what you're doing for Sara, but isn't it unfair to let her depend on you this way? You're giving up so much."

Charlie laughed as he slouched in the corner of the cab. "God no, I wanted this— the connection we have. When I didn't know where she was or how she was… I was going crazy."

Remembering his anger and fear made his magic roil within him, and it took him a second to regain control. The sudden surge had almost hurt and left him slightly dizzy with the influx of new information as all his senses sharpened. The magic settled, his vision returning to normal, his senses lessening until he no longer felt the push of magic as if it would rip through his skin. "I don't regret this at all, Oz." Charlie glanced at Oz then away.

"I sort of took advantage of her here. She's so desperate for comfort, but she does love me. I have no idea if the magic would've connected us this way anyway if we didn't want to be. Is all I know is, I'm happy we're so connected, and I hope we never lose it. I haven't given up anything. She makes me more complete, more...." He trailed off. "Sara is everything to me," he finished.

"If you guys are happy like this, I'm happy for you."

For the rest of the ride, they were quiet. Before they entered the hotel, Oz made himself resemble Marcy with his disguise spell, and they headed to Sara's room without speaking.

-20-

REPLACING GEORGIOS

The real Rick let Charlie and Oz into Sara's hotel room.

Sara ran to Charlie and huddled against him. The feel of her body pressed against him eased him, and he slumped, suddenly exhausted.

"I didn't know what else to do. When the reporters spotted me, I knew we were in trouble. Major Nelson was really mad." Her worried voice was muffled by his shirt.

"Don't worry about it. Rinto believed you." Charlie kissed her brow. "So much so, he's setting up a group to take you."

Outwardly, she remained calm, but her inner fear alarmed Charlie, making muscles that had just relaxed tense.

"That man will never touch you again. I promise you! Oz and I will bring you food tomorrow. Eat nothing we don't give you, okay?"

Black fear filled her now, and she shook in his arms, nodding her understanding against his chest.

"Rick will be with you, and the Scouts are in the building. We haven't worked out a plan yet, but Stasia got the drop site. I swear you'll be safe." Charlie hugged her tighter.

A blue glow formed around his hands in response to her fear. The magic wanted to be with her, for them to be together. He placed his palms on her face and let his magic seep into her.

"Nothing will happen to any of us."

When she was calmer, he sat and pulled her into his lap while he filled the group in on everything he knew.

"So, what's the plan?" Rick asked when Charlie finished.

"No idea," Charlie shrugged. "Oz will be busy sneaking Scouts into the hotel tonight. I'll have him bring us a pizza or something. The major will let us know when —"

A knock on the door interrupted him.

"Tara," Rick whispered after peering through the peephole.

Rick headed to the bathroom with Oz.

Sara opened the door.

Tara looked the disguised Charlie up and down and leered. "So, this is why you're here." A flirtatious smile tilted her lips as she held out a hand.

Charlie shook it, trying not to laugh. Tara had met him a hundred times before.

"Wait, I know who you are. You're the old boyfriend's brother." Tara rose a perfectly plucked eyebrow at Sara.

Sara led her stepmother further into the room, ignoring the inquisitive look. Without making conversation, she went to the bedside table, tore off a sheet of paper from the notebook there, and handed it to Tara.

"If anyone needs names, these kids just died in a car accident in France. Three years ago I attended school there for a month. I have no idea who the kids are, but no one can prove that. I'm sure you can handle these reporters without having to resort to names though. Just make it clear I'm inconsolable and don't want to return."

"I only planned to stay here a week." Tara tucked the note into her Gucci bag. "Where should I tell people you'll be after that?"

"Tell them I'll be privately tutored now." Sara shrugged. "Say anything you like."

"Where will you go?"

"California, but not to school."

"You're not thinking of acting, are you?" Tara's voice rose, and lines appeared beside her mouth.

"No, I'll never do that. He's stationed in California." Sara smiled in Charlie's direction.

"I see. Isn't he a bit old for you?"

Sara grinned at Charlie. "I'm sixteen now, and he doesn't care. I can legally do what I want."

Tara rolled her eyes. "Try to stay out of the tabloids… A little while, anyway."

"I'll do my best," Sara promised.

Tara shrugged and left.

Sara laughed and sat with Charlie, cuddling into his lap. "She's the shallowest person on

Earth."

Soft, warm lips touched his, deepening into a long lingering kiss before she went to tell Oz and Rick the coast was clear. She left his head spinning, dizzy with desire and the need to protect her. His magic urged him to follow her. He was proud of himself for realizing it was the magic urging him to act, so proud she glanced back at him. He waved her on and mentally told it to wait, promising it they would touch her again shortly. It subsided instantly, and he felt nothing from it. He was able to remain seated and calm when the others reappeared.

The major called, and Oz left to start sneaking Scouts into the hotel. Two hours later, Oz delivered a few bags of food and brought Hawk and Stasia.

"I brought a lot in case more Scouts come to this room. They're still working on a plan. Major Nelson has recon teams on the way here as well as two Navy SEAL units and a submarine. No one will get away, Sara."

"Be careful. They want you too, or they would if they didn't think you were dead." Hands rubbing her shoulders as if she were cold, she circled the room. "We need to work on better security devices. I have some ideas. When this settles down, we need to work on that."

Oz glanced at Sara for a moment before returning his attention to the bag of food. "When this settles, we need to work on a lot of things."

Charlie said, "As soon as this all settles down; I'm taking my wife to the hottest tropical island I can find. All day long we'll sit in the sun and not think about any of this." Charlie grinned at Sara. The thought made her happy, and to his surprise, aroused.

Sara blushed and averted her face. His grin widened. On her next circuit of the room, he grabbed her hand and pulled her close for a kiss. The desire she felt grew, and he chuckled against her hair, aroused now himself. Blue magic covered her with surprising suddenness.

Charlie took her hands and kissed them, trying to dampen his response to her. This would take getting used to, for both of them. With his eyes closed, he could see embarrassment tinge her energy pink but didn't know if it was because he knew how she felt or because they weren't alone. He moved away to let her regain her composure.

The blue on her hands faded, absorbed into her as she got her feelings under control.

"After this, we could all use a vacation," she agreed. "I'd love to just sit in the hot sun with nowhere to be and do whatever we wanted."

Charlie turned red in embarrassment as magic swirled around him when he envisioned what they could do alone on a beach.

A sympathetic grimace crossed her face as she met his eyes. "This is awkward," she murmured as she put his glowing hands on her cheeks and absorbed his magic with a happy sigh. "We need to learn to control this better."

Their friends gave them privacy by opening the bags of food and spreading the contents out on the table beside the windows.

"I'm willing to practice all you want," Charlie

said in a deep, husky voice. When he kissed her neck, she made a low moaning sound and flared up blue all over.

The magic flickered wildly until she reabsorbed it. Flushed, she moved away from him, and he felt her embarrassment.

He hadn't meant to cause that reaction but wasn't upset he had. His smugness must of have come through to her because she narrowed her eyes at him. He held out both hands in a placating gesture.

"Sorry," he said quickly and laughed when she glared.

A sudden smile covered her face as she drew one finger around the V-neck of her T-shirt and snickered when his skin turned blue.

"Stop. You win," he conceded as he fought back the blue. Eyes closed and a frown of concentration on his face, he forced his magic to retreat, promising it he would let it touch Sara soon.

"What the heck are you two doing?" Stasia eyed them both and rose an eyebrow.

"Learning," Sara said.

Charlie mumbled, "Nothing."

Stasia returned to unpacking the food. "If you're done learning nothing, we can get back to work. Major Nelson just texted me the plan, and the first part is tonight. Well, this morning," she corrected, setting the last bottle of soda on the table with more force than necessary. "Georgios is meeting his men early today at his house. We'll take them all out discreetly and replace them with our own. Oz will disguise himself as Georgios and attend the meeting with Rinto.

"The Scouts disguised as Georgios's men will take Sara. Sara can pretend to be unconscious when we bring her to Rinto's boat. Hopefully, all Rinto's men will be there. We'll take everyone on the boat, and then Oz can disguise himself as Rinto, and we'll meet Rinto's buyers. Back up will be standing by if we need it. I doubt we will."

Charlie frowned. "I hate that she has to see Rinto again."

Sara clutched his hand hard. All her early happiness had vanished into fear.

"You're going to hate this idea at first, Sara." Stasia put an arm around her. "But, consider it, okay? What if we do sedate you? We'll be there the entire time. If you were sedated, it would be much more realistic. I don't think you could act relaxed enough otherwise."

"No!" Charlie said instantly as his wife's fear spiked to new highs. "No," he repeated in a calmer voice and patted her hand. "How about if we disguise Joy as her? I can steal Oz's disguise, and he can make Joy resemble Sara. Does it work if she's sedated?"

"No idea." Oz glanced up from the sandwich makings on the table. "We can test it though. Let me call the major and try it."

Sara turned to Stasia, her expression anxious. "Use a super small dose on her."

"We'll be careful." Oz gave her a reassuring smile.

"Don't think you're leaving me behind." Sara faced Charlie with narrowed eyes. "I'll need a regular disguise."

Rick laughed, cutting it off abruptly when Charlie glowered at him.

"Sara, there's no way you'll pass as a man." Rick's gaze flicked to Stasia and traveled her. "Neither of you could pass as male."

Stasia rolled her eyes. "I'll be invisible and won't need a disguise, and Sara could be an overweight man. I'm sure the guys Georgios is getting won't be pros. A fat man would be okay. Brenda could disguise her if she had supplies."

Rick pursed his lips as he eyed Sara. "A really fat man, I guess," he finally said.

Stasia glanced at Rick then Charlie and snickered. "You'll see. She won't be hugely fat, just not so…" She used her hands and made an hourglass shape and laughed again when Sara snorted.

Stasia took the phone from Oz and told the major they needed Brenda and supplies.

"I'm on it already," Major Nelson assured her. "All the Scouts will wear regular disguises and so will our recon teams. Oz will bring in the disguise kit and knows what to do. You get some rest. Tomorrow will be busy. After we take Georgios's group, I want you to stick to Rinto like glue. Oz should have his deliveries done in an hour or so. Brenda will be at Sara's room at five a.m. Be ready to go by then."

Stasia relayed the information. Hawk pulled out the sofa bed while Stasia made another spot to sleep on the floor. Sara and Charlie took the bedroom but gave them the blankets and pillows.

"Alone at last." He smiled as he locked the door behind them.

Sara was already glowing blue. Without answering, she reached for him.

At four forty-five, Rick woke Oz, finding him groggy and hard to wake. The events of the last week had left the entire team exhausted, and they still had to catch the man with the bounty on Team Valor.

Oz made a quick trip to the bathroom and then left to get Brenda.

Rick shook Stasia's shoulder. She clutched her pillow tighter and groaned. He used one finger to brush the hair from her face.

She made a contented sound and opened her eyes. The brown eyes that met his held a clear invitation.

Rick stared as if transfixed before swallowing heavily and turning away. With more force than necessary, he ripped open the packet of coffee.

Stasia heaved a disappointed sigh and went to take a shower.

"I wonder if I could bribe the major to keep him too busy to date anyone else," she mumbled and then gave a snort of laughter.

After her shower, she had to put her dirty clothes back on. Brenda was already busy with her makeup bag when Stasia rejoined the group.

A loud peal of laughter rang through the room when she saw Sara sitting cross-legged on the floor in a patch of weak morning sunlight with her eyes closed and face lifted to the light.

Otherwise unrecognizable, she was disguised as an older, balding man with thinning, blackish-gray hair and a matching light beard. A blue baseball cap almost covered the fake bald scalp. Dirty khakis with brown work boots, a big beer belly held in by an old brown leather belt, and a faded blue flannel shirt tucked into her pants finished her disguise. Sara opened her eyes when Stasia laughed, revealing they were now brown.

Sara smiled and rose to show off the outfit, lifting her worn, black leather vest to display the gun in the holster on her side. Her white teeth had been yellowed. The only weak link in the disguise was her hands. Her fingers were still graceful despite nails cut and filed into square tips.

Sara glanced down at them as Stasia did. "Brenda says she can make them manlier with grease after we eat. Wait until you see Charlie and Rick."

Stasia turned and inspected Oz who was disguised by a mustache, slicked-back hair, darkened skin tone, and the same type of clothes Sara wore.

"Oz doesn't need much," Brenda said as she packed the makeup kit away. "He'll be using disguise spell most of the time. Oz and I will finish the Scouts. Be ready to go in thirty-five minutes."

She and Oz left together.

Hawk entered from the bedroom, wearing a blue plaid shirt over stuffing that made him appear fatter and less fit. A wig of long, gnarly brown hair in a ponytail and a scraggly beard finished the costume.

Hawk poured himself another coffee and grinned. "Wait until you see them. I helped."

Stasia stood in the bedroom doorway and burst out laughing.

Charlie turned from the mirror where he stood beside his brother adjusting his tinted eyeglasses and grinned at her as he smoothed his stringy goatee. Black, slicked back hair now hung to their shoulders, and both wore heavy bronzer and fake tattoos. Rick hadn't shaved in two days, leaving his face covered in stubble, and Brenda had somehow changed the shape of his cheeks. Flannel shirts over T-shirts, which covered small beer bellies, and short black vests that almost concealed shoulder holsters bulked them up even more.

"You two look like forty-year-old has been bikers." Stasia laughed again.

Charlie gave her a shark grin, showing off his newly yellowed teeth.

Everyone gathered around the table where Oz had left the bags of food.

On her way to the bathroom, Sara stopped to kiss Charlie and Stasia groaned. "Oh, that's just awful. I wish I could take a picture."

When Brenda returned, they were ready to go. Brenda now looked like a man too. A receding hairline and thick glasses matched her old clothes and boots, leaving her unrecognizable.

"Okay, let's blow this pop stand." She handed out Bluetooth headsets and walkie-talkies. "Hawk will tell us positioning as always. The plan is to be in place inside Georgios's house before his men arrive. Take them as they enter, silently, with no visible razzle-dazzle."

Brenda handed Stasia another small recorder. "Stasia, enter first and see if anything's changed. If Georgios isn't making or receiving calls, we'll take him out. If he is, wait until he's finished. Cubs go in pre-shielded by Sara. Drew and I will accompany you. Oz will invis himself and Sara. All the guns have silencers. Give them one chance to come along quietly." Brenda shrugged. "I expect they won't come silently, so be fast. I don't expect everyone to arrive at the same time either and we can't afford for word of a firefight to get out. Do this quick and quiet. Don't let anyone get a shot off."

At five after eight in the morning, Brenda ordered them into action. Stasia entered through the backdoor, the lock not slowing her, and reported Georgios sat on his couch watching television and drinking beer. Brenda gave the go-ahead, so Stasia sapped Georgios and the team walked into the house.

Eyes wide, with a shocked look on his face, Georgios didn't struggle when Rick grabbed him, breaking the sap. Brenda used zip-ties and gagged and blindfolded him.

Charlie carried Georgios into the cellar and dropped him on the floor. He crouched over him, debating murder. He didn't fool himself. He knew it would be murder to kill this man. Georgios hadn't done a thing to Sara, or anyone else as far as Charlie knew, but he'd planned too. If Charlie's team had really been killed, this man would have willingly given Sara to men who would torture and abuse her. The magic didn't press him. It felt no fear of this man. This was all Charlie's decision.

Georgios cowered on the floor before him, straining against his ties, his wide, terrified eyes locked on Charlie. Charlie nudged him with the toe of his boot. "Go near her again, even think about her, and I'll come back and kill you."

Georgios nodded frantically.

Charlie hesitated. He really wanted this man dead. It must have shown on his face because the sharp scent of urine laced the air.

"You disgust me. But it wasn't your idea, was it?"

Georgios nodded again.

"Rinto is a dead man, and I'm not Sara's only protector."

Georgios nodded again, his terrified gaze darting about the room.

Charlie leaned down until his face was inches from Georgios. "I'm also not a murderer, but if I think for one minute you haven't given up this plan, I'll be back."

Georgios whimpered and tried to scoot away. Charlie watched him for another minute before striding for the stairs. By the time he returned upstairs, Oz had casted disguise to look like Georgios.

Hawk knelt beside an open cage door where a half-starved, mangy dog crouched. The dog slunk from the cage and into Hawk's lap. Hawk petted the animal, then rose and filled a bowl with water. After he poured water, he opened the refrigerator and grinned at the dog as he unwrapped a steak and gave it to him.

"Why would anyone bother to get a dog and keep it like this?" Hawk asked as the dog ate the steak with slobbering enthusiasm.

Sara pointed to a picture on the refrigerator of a pretty, thirty-five-year-old or so woman holding a puppy. "I bet the dog was hers." The woman in the picture grinned as a small black puppy licked her face.

"Well, he's my dog now." Hawk knelt and rubbed the dog's ears. The dog licked his hand and then resumed gnawing on the steak bone. Hawk's eyes turned blue as he stared into the dog's eyes. The dog stopped eating and met Hawk's gaze, both remained unmoving. The smell of ozone filled the air and static sparked off anyone who moved.

Slowly, the dog's eyes turned the exact same color as Sara's, a brilliant, periwinkle blue.

Hawk glanced up at Sara, his eyes their usual dark brown color. "Can you heal him? He's in pain."

A clear yellow ball of light traveled from Sara's hands to the dog, causing him to glow translucently for a moment. "He really is your dog."

Hawk rubbed the dog's ears. "He doesn't like people much. Let me introduce everyone to him one at a time."

Sara approached, moving slow and easy and held out her hand for the dog to sniff.

Hawk sat beside the dog with his eyes closed. The dog's ears were back but perked forward after a moment.

Sara rubbed his ears and crooned to him, telling him he was a good boy. The dog's tail thumped the ground as his body relaxed.

Charlie squatted by Sara, ruffled the dog's ears, and patted his side. The dog licked his hand before returning to his bone.

"Sweet, he likes you." Hawk opened his eyes and smiled. "I'm telling him we're friends, and he believes me. Keep being nice to him. No yelling at him or anything. I'm sure he'll do bad stuff, but I'll teach him not to. He's been in this small cage his entire life and has a lot to learn."

Sara and Charlie made way for Stasia and Oz. The dog loved Stasia. Perked ears and happy wriggling made his feelings clear as she rubbed his stomach and scratched his ears. Stasia sat on the floor beside Hawk, and they both petted the dog. Hawk introduced the rest of the Scouts while they waited for Georgios's men to show up.

Brenda was busy searching the house. Stasia casted find-hidden and located a small safe, which she opened. Without bothering to read the papers inside, she handed them to Sara and then sat beside Hawk again.

Papers littered the floor at Sara's feet as she glanced at each one, then tossed it aside. "It's crap, his bank accounts, a divorce decree, the deed to the house, insurance papers and this." She handed the envelope to Hawk.

"If these are his papers" —Sara gestured at the dog who was still gnawing the steak bone— "then he's a worse mess than I thought. The papers say he's supposed to be an all-black Blue

Bay Shepard. Not this weird brown-gray color."

Hawk examined the pages, shrugged, and handed them back to Sara. "If you say so; I can't read a word of that. What is that, French? He's filthy, and I'll have to shave him to get these snarls out. He's still a puppy really. When he's full grown, he'll be a tank, look at his paws."

"He needs a vet and a groomer." Sara leaned down and ran a palm over the dog's head. "And sunshine, fresh air, and dog toys." She rubbed the dog's ears again. "Don't you, Tank?"

Hawk grinned. "His name is Tank." The dog and Hawk stared at each other a moment and Tank wagged his tail.

Sara laughed. "He likes his name. Don't you, Tank?" The dog sneezed at her and thumped his tail on the floor.

"Okay, everyone." Brenda waved a small notebook and smirked.

The Scouts glanced over from their positions by the doors and windows.

"Georgios was kind enough to leave us a list of men right by his phone with notes. Milo will be bringing four men. His men aren't individually named, which probably means Georgios didn't know them personally. They're unlikely to know every person he called. Get out a few beers, look relaxed, let them in, and take them quietly when they arrive."

Brenda turned to Sara. "Stand by the door. If anyone speaks Greek to Oz, you translate."

She swung to Oz. "Just repeat what Sara tells you to. If they speak English, keep the talk general and get them inside as soon as you can."

Brenda turned to Drew. "You answer the phone; you sound the most like Georgios. Sara will listen for you too if they don't speak English." She checked her watch. "Look sharp, people. Hawk, keep an eye out. Stasia, go invisible at the first hint of someone coming." She pursed her lips and eyed Charlie thoughtfully. "You better wait as far from the front door as you can get. You're aura might scare them away."

Charlie heaved an exasperated sigh and stepped back.

The first group of men arrived twenty minutes later. Oz opened the door disguised as Georgios and let them in. When they were inside with the door closed, Stasia sapped one and Sara hypnotized one. Both men stopped moving. While the sapped man swayed, the hypnotized one raised his hands to cover his eyes.

Charlie zip tied them as Tony and Marcus held their weapons on them. His aura made them cower, and they offered no resitence. Rick and Drew each had a man pushed face down hard against the wall with a gun to their heads. Charlie carried the bound men downstairs one-by-one after gagging and blindfolding them.

"We don't care about you." Cold and emotionless, Charlie stopped on the basement stairs and spoke. "Give us no trouble, and we'll let you go later. Cause any problems, and we'll kill you."

He left them tied in the dark, straining against their bonds to get away from him, and returned upstairs, not feeling the least bit bad. They were willing to do the same and worse to

Sara. The thought of his sun-priest tied in the dark made his magic roil within him. He recognized the sensation of too taut skin and knew his eyes would be glowing.

Soon, he promised the magic, and the glow in his eyes dwindled. When the internal magical pressure receded, he returned upstairs.

The next group of people arrived a few minutes later. The Scouts were still subduing them when the next group arrived. Rick crouched by the captives lying on the living room floor.

"Make one sound, and I'll kill you," he warned, waving his silenced gun in front of them.

Oz, disguised as Georgios, was opening the door to admit the new people when one of the men on the floor yelled. Rick shot him. Tank started barking.

"Shut up, dog," Oz yelled and gestured the men to come in. "Damn dog. I need to shoot that mutt." He continued to grumble and complain about the dog and strangers until everyone was inside. As soon as the door closed, the Scouts leaped into action.

Stasia sapped one as Sara casted hypnotize. Drew and Charlie each took one to the floor as Brenda covered the last one with her pistol pressed to the head she had jammed against a wall.

"Tie up Rick's guys first," Brenda ordered Oz.

"A man is still in the car," Hawk said as he passed Brenda headed to Rick.

"I got it." Stasia ran out the back door and headed to the car.

The man spoke on a cell phone, apologizing to someone for missing their date that night and making big promises to make it up. When he finished his call, Stasia casted Distract, jerked the door open and used her Knockout-Punch as the magic forced the man to look away.

After zip-tying him, she pushed him under the dashboard and crouched down in the passenger seat as he thrashed. "I don't want to kill you, but I will if you don't stop moving," she whispered. "All your friends are already tied. Your kidnapping plan is busted. That target is ours. Am I clear?"

The man stilled. "That's our mark."

Stasia kicked him in the head hard enough to get her point across, but not hard enough to do permanent damage. "Shut up and don't move." Stasia spoke on her headset. "Bro, can I bring him in the house yet?"

"Give us a few more minutes. Oz will escort him in. I'll warn you if the next group is arriving."

Stasia waited in the car for Oz, invisibly sitting on the man's bound form. When Oz exited the house, Stasia cut the man loose and pushed him out the door. "I'm right behind you." A sharp knife tip emphasized her point. "Give him any trouble, and I'll kill you right here."

Brenda checked people off the list. "One more group, guys."

The last group arrived and entered the house. The Scouts tied, gagged, and added them to their collection in the basement. "Drew and Rick, make sure they aren't getting away anytime soon. They should be grateful. We just saved their useless lives. Oz and Sara, wait by the phone. Stasia, head to Rinto. Hit the panic button if he sees you or you get in trouble."

"Send me emoticons every thirty minutes, please." Sara hugged Stasia, letting her go reluctantly. "Please be careful. He's very dangerous. If they catch you, they won't be kind."

"Don't worry about me. Rinto will never see me. Every half hour I'll send you a text or emote. This is almost over, Sara." Stasia gave her a quick, hard hug and sprinted from the room.

Charlie's blue-eyed gaze followed her.

-21-

ON A BOAT

Brenda opened her pack and handed out protein bars. "Now we wait. Use the bathroom while we have the chance. I'll report to the major." Brenda called Major Nelson to fill him in.

The major answered on the first ring. "Eagle Eyes One and Two are at the hotel watching Sara's room. Joy is there already waiting to go. When you leave the hotel, they'll follow discreetly. How are the cubs holding up?"

"Fine," Brenda said. "Charlie and Sara are glowing blue randomly, but it disappears quickly. We'll need to keep them away from people until they get a handle on that if they can."

Major Nelson sighed. "One damn thing after another. I'll make arrangements for them to be somewhere private a while so they can work that out."

Brenda moved away from the others and

turned her back. "Sara is exhausted. She needs rest, not more prodding and poking. Everyone needs rest."

"After we handle this mess, we'll make sure she gets a break. We need to know what's happening to the magic. They need undistracted time to figure that out. I'll see that they get it. She's more of a liability than an asset now." The major cleared his throat. "If the magic gets out of control, sedate them, don't wait."

"Right now, it isn't necessary." Brenda glanced over her shoulder. "It's manifesting, but they control it quickly. It isn't doing anything except showing itself. If it does do anything else, I'll sedate them."

"Make sure you do." Major Nelson hung up.

A few hours later, Rinto called Georgios. Drew answered the phone. "Your people are in place?" Rinto asked.

"Yes," Drew said in his best Georgios impersonation.

"The guy you have at the hotel can get the sedatives into her food? Don't even try to take her if she isn't sedated."

"You've made that very clear," Drew said.

"The deal is off if she doesn't arrive sedated. She must fall asleep in that hotel room and wake on the boat with no idea where she is. Anything else is unacceptable. Call me when you have her." Rinto slammed down the phone.

"These idiots have no idea how dangerous Sara is," Brenda said in disgust.

Drew shrugged. "Doesn't matter. Let's go. Take the keys. Milo was supposed to be getting the ambulance and Stevens's group was inside the hotel. Our own ambulance is waiting, so let's go get Joy. Oz, go upstairs invisible and disguise Joy. Charlie can be Georgios in the ambulance. Drew and Rick stay in the back and keep your heads down. Even disguised Rinto might recognize you. Manny, he's never seen you, so you do the talking and keep his attention."

"I just got a text from Stasia." Brenda held up her cell phone. "Rinto is on the move now. Make sure he sees nothing to give us away if he's coming here." Brenda split them into small groups, and they got in the cars and left for the hotel. An ambulance waited in the underground garage of the hotel. Drew and Rick entered the ambulance and emerged wearing paramedic uniforms, carrying a stretcher.

The pickup went easily. Joy was already lightly sedated. Charlie casted Spell-Steal and stole Oz's disguise to make himself look like Georgios wearing a paramedic uniform, and got into the driver side of the ambulance. Drew and Rick carried Joy out using a back entrance and loaded her into the ambulance. Oz casted a disguise on himself, making himself resemble one of the men they'd left bound in Georgios house and yanked the back door closed. Charlie drove while Drew and Rick stayed in back with Joy.

"Rinto is outside of the hotel now," Brenda reported.

"I'll make the call," Drew said and called Rinto. "We have her."

"Meet me on Harbor Road. I'll text you the address. Make sure you bring all your guys. We might have to liberate a boat," Rinto said and hung up.

Brenda sent the information to the major as they received it.

Charlie drove slowly after taking a few minutes to conspicuously examine a map. He and Oz pretended to argue over the route while Rinto watched from his car.

"Eagle Eyes One is heading there now. Go nice and easy and let them get in place," Major Nelson ordered. Take Rinto alive if you can. Both recon teams are outside the warehouse. On your mark, they'll come in, Sergeant."

"Roger that," Brenda said.

Her car followed the ambulance into the warehouse. Everyone exited the cars and surrounded the ambulance, trying to look disorganized and unaware of the armed men deeper in the warehouse. Charlie as Georgios stood beside Joy who wore a fresh disguise and slept on the stretcher when Rinto arrived. A smug grin covered Rinto's face when he saw Joy.

"What's the big deal? All this bullshit to take one little girl," Manny said in an angry voice. "My grandmother could've done this."

Rinto raised his gun and pointed it at Manny, who held up his hands and backed up. "We do exactly what I say if you want to be paid. Give her another shot."

Charlie made a production of getting the

sedative out and measuring the dose then pretending to inject her.

Rinto gestured them to follow and sauntered to the back of the warehouse. "I have more men I want you to meet."

The men waiting inside the warehouse were heavily armed and armored. They surrounded the disguised Scouts while Rinto gloated. Sara stood behind Charlie, using his body to hide her hands as she casted shields on everyone.

Her emotions were all over the place and hard for him to pin down. One moment she felt terror, the next anger, followed by worry, guilt, and sadness in a confusing cacophony.

Tense, and poised to spring, Charlie waited for the command to attack. These men had harmed Sara. He had no mercy for them. Behind his tinted glasses, his eyes sparked blue, colors brightened, and detail came into sharper focus. The magic was as eager as he to kill The Enemy.

"So, a double cross?" Manny's hard gaze flicked from one armed man to another.

"Kill them," Rinto replied as he smiled at Manny.

His men fired and Stasia sapped Rinto and casted Waylay, appearing behind a man firing at them. One quick slash and the man slumped to the floor, bleeding from a severed jugular. Blood sprayed through the air as she leapt to the next man while men screamed and tried to shoot her while running for cover.

"Shit!" someone yelled. "Get the girl!"

Hawk pulled his gun, and people started dropping.

Muffled gunshots and the smell of gunpowder filled the air. Charlie wasn't standing still waiting. Within seconds, the k-bar in his hand dripped blood as he used Waylay while casting Drop Weapon. Loud curses met the clatter of weapons to concrete, the spell making every armed enemy within thirty yards drop their weapons.

The man Charlie attacked tried to grab his gun from the floor but didn't get a shot off before Charlie slit his throat. The man next to him screamed and held out his empty hands. Charlie grabbed one flailing arm and yanked the man close enough to stab, and then threw the dying man from him and leapt to the next man.

Rinto's comrade screamed obscenities and grappled for the knife in Charlie's hand. Moving inhumanly fast, Charlie grabbed his arm and twisted, breaking it with a sickening crack, then pulled the man into a tight embrace, and stabbed upwards under his chin, watching the light in his eyes die. The body thumped to the ground, and Charlie crouched, scanning for his next victim but none remained.

When the fight had started, the rest of the Scouts had pulled their sidearms and added their fire to the mix.

In less than a minute, it was over with Rinto the only man left alive. Currently a sheep, he wandered aimlessly. Tank still growled savagely from inside the car.

Sara casted a heal on everyone and went to Joy. Soft sobs filled the silence as she laid her face against Joy's chest and cried.

Hawk let Tank out of the car and sat beside Sara. His presence calmed both her and the dog, He remained there while Brenda called the major.

"The warehouse is clear. Send recon teams to the next position. Rinto is subdued, and his men are dead," Brenda reported.

"Give him to one of the recon teams. We'll take him off your hands. I'll send a man to the door for him," Major Nelson said.

Brenda used zip-ties and handcuffed Rinto as Drew held his arms.

A deep scowl covered Rinto's face, and he glared at him. "Damn it, I can't believe I didn't recognize you, Drew. Shit man, why the hell are you still working with them? There's so much money to be made—"

Rick grabbed his arm and punched him in the stomach. "If I shoot you, there will be no healer to fix it," he whispered, his voice thick with hatred.

Brenda held her gun to Rinto's head. "Let's see how chipper you feel after I pull this trigger." A smile filled her voice. Rinto's eyes widen, and he paled, just then recognizing her. She cocked her gun, and Drew laid a hand on her arm.

"Don't," he said. "That's too kind. Let the major have him. Major Nelson can handle this traitor, and it's only right that he gets too." Drew pulled her away as she nodded jerkily.

Rinto laughed at her, his expression twisted into a sneer. "Your secret is done. I'll tell everyone I see what I know. Someone, somewhere, will believe it enough to investigate; you can count on that."

Rick hit him in the face as hard as he could and smiled when Rinto's jaw cracked. Rinto spat broken, bloody teeth onto the pavement.

"You do that," Rick smirked. "Talk all you want."

Brenda returned, grabbed Rinto's bound arms, and hauled him to the door.

Mike waited outside the door, and Brenda grinned when she saw him.

"Ah, Recon, we have your package. Don't take any lip from him," she said and laughed.

Mike took in Brenda's disguise and chuckled. "Scout." He took Rinto by the arm. "I hope you plan on cleaning up before our date."

Brenda's eyes lit, and she laughed. "I expect to be off duty by tomorrow." An evil grin lit her face as she stared into Rinto's furious eyes. "By five after three this morning, we'll have all this trash wrapped up, and I'll be sure to mention who gave them up." Her grin widened as Rinto paled. She gave Mike a little finger wave as he left with his prisoner.

Brenda went to check on Sara, who was now leaning on Hawk with Tank in her lap. Tears had tracked through her makeup, leaving streaks behind. Brenda squatted in front of them. "Are you guys okay?" Brenda asked as she ruffled Tank's ears.

Sara nodded yes, and Hawk shook his head no and tightened his grip on her.

Brenda frowned and stood, looking for Charlie. He was having a heated debate in the corner with his brother. Brenda whistled and called them in. "Let's head out of here," she said with a meaningful glance at Sara who still clutched Hawk.

"Hawk, take Tank and Sara in the ambulance with Joy. Oz, you drive as Rinto. Rick, you be the passenger. Charlie and I will ride in back so I can fix the makeup. The rest of you go with Drew." She waited to make sure everyone went where she sent them and called the major.

"Sara isn't doing too well here. I don't know if she can handle this." Brenda strode away from the back of the open ambulance.

"Her magic," the major asked anxiously.

"No, her. She's clinging to Hawk and still crying," Brenda said in concern. "Hawk's calming aura isn't enough. This is too much, too soon, after what she's been through. Seeing Rinto and his men have really upset her."

"We need her, Brenda," Major Nelson said in a clipped, harsh tone. "Just a few more hours and they can take a break."

"We're going to break her, Major. She's giving us her all here, but there isn't a lot left for her to give. I don't think we should bring her with us.

The major snorted. "No way will she'll stay behind if everyone goes."

"Send her away. Send them all away. We can do this without the cubs."

"They're going."

Brenda was silent a moment. "Have you been shot? I mean since you got the buffs?"

"No." The major sounded confused.

"It hurts, not as much as pre-buff, but it does hurt. Wounds are still painful, broken bones hurt.

With Sara healing us, the pain is fleeting. We feel it but go on, knowing it will vanish in seconds. She felt those shots and broken bones for three days, Major. Tied to a table, naked in the dark, in agony, not knowing what would happen next. She's petrified now and trying to be brave for us so we won't feel pain. Send her away from this. She can heal us after if we need it."

"I hear what you're saying, Brenda, but I think it would be more traumatic for her to heal you afterward. Keep her with Hawk; keep them both in the back. Finish this as quick as you can."

A deep frown on her face, Brenda hung up and climbed into the back of the crowded ambulance where Joy was starting to stir a bit on the stretcher.

Sara sat in Charlie's lap, clutching his hand. Hawk leaned against her, holding Tank.

Brenda checked Joy's pulse, finding it nice and steady. "She's fine guys. Let me fix everyone's makeup." She grabbed her bag out of the closet and checked Charlie and Hawk, leaving Sara for last.

"Sara, if you want to wait at the hotel, you can," she whispered as she reapplied the makeup.

"I'm fine," Sara said in a calm voice.

Charlie winced, knowing the calmness was a lie.

"This should be over soon. We get on board and confirm Nadir is there. They take Joy—don't worry," she said quickly as Sara inhaled sharply. "Stasia will be with her. We want to know what Rinto's men say when they think they have her. They'll not keep her, I promise you. We'll capture them; dead or alive. We have tons of backup waiting to be called in if we need it."

"Sara," Charlie whispered. "You really don't have to come at all. You can wait..." His wife's fear stopped his words, a roiling blackness on her aura he could see with his eyes closed and feel with them open. The magic within him sought her and pushed at him to act, to ease her fear. An overwhelming compulsion to protect made every muscle in his body feel tight. Hands clenched at his sides, he breathed deeply in an effort to control it. The magic didn't understand no enemies were present, a memory scared her.

She said, "I'm a member of Team Valor same as you. We fight as a team."

Charlie kissed her brow and turned worried eyes on Brenda. "Tell Tony and Rick to make sure Sara is never alone there. One of us is with her at all times."

"And Joy," Sara said, clenching Joy's hand tighter in her gloved one. "Never leave Joy alone with them."

"We won't," Brenda agreed.

Brenda called the drivers, and they were on their way. "I'm going to give Joy a bit more sedative. I don't want her stirring while we transfer her. We don't want them to use their crap on her." Brenda gave Joy another small dose and took her pulse to monitor the effects. "Oz can redo her disguise when we stop."

Sara leaned over and kissed Joy's cheek. "I'm so sorry, Joy."

"She's fine." Charlie pulled Sara away. "Joy volunteered for this, and we won't let her be hurt." Guilt rippled along his consciousness. Sara's guilt, heavy and thick, the second-hand sensation so unpleasant he cringed.

"I'm such a coward, letting her do that in my place." Both hands covered Sara's face, muffling her voice.

"No, we need you for heals. Joy is a decoy. You couldn't heal us if you were sedated." Hawk leaned over, pulled her hands down, and patted them quickly. "This will be over soon, and you can rest. Joy will be fine."

Lips compressed and face pale, Sara nodded and then rested her forehead on Charlie's shoulder.

One hand on the pulse of his wife's neck, Charlie closed his eyes again, trying to concentrate on his love for her to give her comfort and satisfy his magic.

Brenda exchanged steely-eyed nods with Hawk. Everyone remained quiet until they arrived at the wharf.

The ambulance stopped and Charlie spell-stole Oz's disguise spell, using it to make himself resemble Rinto, then Oz reapplied it to Joy. Charlie took Sara's hand and pulled her away. "Stay with Rick and do your rotation. We'll be fine."

Sara nodded jerkily, climbed from the back of the ambulance, and stood stiffly by his brother.

Charlie didn't dare hug her in case someone watched them get into Georgios's boat. Petrified and riddled with guilt, it was hard for him to let her go. He helped Drew carry the stretcher holding Joy onto the boat and place it in the small cabin.

Everyone boarded, and Manny drove the boat.

Once at sea, Brenda motioned her team to gather. "This will be tricky, Chief. "We don't know if Rinto knows Nadir personally or not. Be as vague as you can."

Three hours later, they reached the coordinates and waited. Brenda handed out more protein bars and Drew handed out water bottles.

"You need to at least drink some water, Sara," Brenda whispered after she refused a protein bar.

Sara took a bottle but didn't open it.

Brenda put her hands on her hips, narrowed her eyes, and pursed her lips.

"I can't," Sara whispered. "I'll be fine. It's just a few more hours." She swallowed convulsively. "I'm seasick," she lied.

Brenda nodded, left her, and went to Hawk. "Go sit by Sara," she ordered, keeping her voice low. "Stay near her. We have five hours to kill here. Take a nap if you like. I'll be on watch." After one last glance at Sara, she left to check Joy.

Drew and Stasia sat with Joy, keeping her company. Since no one except them could see her now, they had let her wake. "Give her more sedative at two-thirty. Stasia, take a nap, we'll wake you."

She returned on deck and found Charlie, Sara, and Hawk, sitting together along a low bench that lined the port side.

"Marcus, Rick, Harrison, Sam, you get some rest too, Manny and I will watch. You can use the bathroom, but don't touch the food. Only eat what we brought with us. There's a stack of HOOAH bars and some MREs in my bag; help yourselves."

Brenda and Manny kept watch over their team as they settled in to sleep. The occasional blue flicker lit the gathering dusk as the magic passed between Charlie and Sara's clasped hands. Like a static shock, it happened quickly and disappeared before it was really noticeable.

Brenda kept tabs on everyone, most still dozed, catching up on lost sleep although some talked quietly or played cards. Clearly, Sara didn't want to talk as she turned her face into Charlie's neck and closed her eyes when Brenda approached. Another flicker of blue raced from her hands to Charlie's. Brenda shrugged and headed back to her card game.

At two-thirty, Brenda woke everyone.

Everyone took turns using the bathroom, and Brenda fixed makeup and disguises. She gave Joy another small injection and waited to be contacted.

"Twenty people, port side," Hawk reported forty minutes later.

Tank picked his head up and growled low in his throat as the tension on board rose.

-22-

WELL HERE I AM

"Okay people, we know what to do." Brenda motioned her teammates into position.

Charlie stole disguise from Oz again, then Oz reapplied it to Joy. On the stretcher, Joy's form shimmered for a moment the solidified into Sara's image.

A blue-white flicker passed over Charlie as he applied disguise to himself, applying the likeness of Rinto. On deck, beside Manny at the helm, he waited eagerly. Manny returned his eager grin and fingered the knife at his waist. Charlie bit back his attack cry. His teams eagerness fed his own. He could hardly wait to attack.

The boat they'd been waiting for pulled up and tied off. Armed men lined the railings of a seventy-foot yacht with three levels, dwarfing the smaller forty-foot boat they were on.

Charlie counted thirty men, but Hawk would

know how many and where they stood. No one would be able to hide from Hawk. Five, black-clad men jumped aboard their boat, talking together in Arabic. Their arrival caused a surge of fear from Sara that morphed into furious anger. Her anger echoed with his, making it very hard for him to hold in his magic. Every muscle felt tense and the pressure beneath his skin grew too painful proportions.

Sara stared at him now, no longer angry but very worried. He gave her a quick, reassuring smile that didn't ease her one whit and tried to communicate with his magic that it needed merely to wait a few minutes.

A man in a black business suit stood at the rail, examining them with a smirk on his face.

"Fallen on hard times?" he asked in accented, but understandable English as he peered at the disguised Scouts.

"Whatever— they got the job done," Charlie replied, hoping this man didn't know Rinto well enough to recognize his voice.

The man turned and snapped his fingers. Another man dressed in a similar suit, but carrying an AK-47, approached and jumped the rail. "Amr will check."

Charlie gestured to the cabin. "The girl's sedated below deck."

Amr went below. A few minutes later, he returned and nodded.

"So, you bring her to my boat." Nadir waved more men over to their ship.

"The money!" Charlie crossed his arms and glared, resisting the urge to rub the painful tingles that wracked them.

The Scouts pointed the weapons they'd stolen from Rinto's men at the armed men boarding their boat.

Nadir snapped his fingers again and another man, carrying a briefcase, appeared. Awkwardly, he climbed over the rail onto the smaller boat and passed the case to Charlie. "The agreed amount. As we discussed, once we learn how she does it, you'll be notified."

Charlie opened the case and made a production of counting the money before handing the briefcase to Brenda.

"Get her!" He jutted his chin toward Joy's disguised form and pointed at Rick.

The Scouts lowered their weapons but kept them handy.

Charlie gestured to Rick, and they brought Joy on deck. Rick clambered onto the other boat. Harrison and Charlie handed the handles of the stretcher over. Charlie's lips compressed when Sara, disguised as the fat man, scrambled over the rail.

That wasn't part of the plan.

Sara and Rick carried the stretcher below deck.

Invisible to others, Stasia trailed them.

Three men spoke Arabic in heated tones inside the cabin. Sara's knuckles whitened as she scanned the room, her gaze lingering on the hammer and pile of nails on the nightstand. Bandages and medical tape spilled onto the floor.

One man sneered and pointed at the bed where a body-bag lay open, gesturing for them to leave the stretcher, but didn't stop his argument with the other two.

Sara took her time releasing the handles of the stretcher, pretending awkwardness. "T-three hypno three," she muttered and started to cast.

Rick tackled the center man, slamming his hand over the man's mouth and forcing him to the deck as Stasia sapped her target.

Stasia used Knockout Punch on Rick's target, stunning him for ten seconds, and tied and gagged him. In moments, they did the same to Stasia and Sara's targets.

When Sara's target was bound, she called Brenda. "A helicopter or something is waiting in the area. Any minute, it will send a missile at us. These three in here are contained." Sara rifled through the tied men's clothing, removing a wallet, which she searched. "Rick, tell the guy outside Omar wants him in here."

Rick nodded and left, returning in a few seconds with another man.

Sara used hypnosis when he entered line-of-sight, and they tied and gagged him while he stood still unable to move, firmly under Sara's control. Rick used the sedatives he found on the small nightstand on the secured men.

"Rick, grab Joy, and let's go." Sara ran from the room without waiting to see if he did. Stasia shadowed her still invisible. Once on deck, Sara casted a shield on herself and Stasia. Blue magic appeared on her exposed skin as she drew her sidearm and pointed at Nadir.

"On the ground right now; I won't ask again!" she shrieked, startling everyone.

Charlie leapt to nadir's boat.

Nadir's men turned their weapons on her, weapons that without their willing it aimed at Charlie. His aura forced them to attack him, and she laughed and then screamed her fear spell.

Nadir's men shrieked and ran, blundering into each other in their haste to escape. The men near her ran, and she shot Nadir as he grabbed for his weapon.

"Sara," Charlie called as he jumped from the railing in time to see Nadir fall to the deck clutching his wounded leg. Sara dropped her gun and started smiting.

Charlie casted Waylay and appeared before Sara, his sword in hand.

Men on the top deck unaffected by Sara's fear spell began firing on them.

Brilliant white lightning flickered, impacting between two men so hard it blew through the decking. Glowing white tendrils latched onto the men who screamed and dropped their weapons. Oz had entered the fight. Their corpses began to burn as more bolts crashed into the rails and roof of the cockpit.

Men screamed directions and curses as more gunfire rent the air.

Thunder rumbled overhead, and Charlie didn't know if it were Sara or Oz causing it. Charlie stood before his wife, blocking the bullets aimed at her with his body. Sara was making no attempt to heal or cast shields. All her attention was on the screaming men. She was so furious he hesitated to leave her side.

A shrill whistle from a rocket launcher was

immediately drowned by an explosion that rocked both boats. Hawk had shot the rocket out of the air. His next shot took out the man holding the launcher.

Stasia flitted around the boat appearing and disappearing before anyone could target her, leaving dead men in her wake.

Lightning lit the dark night in brilliant flashes of blue and white. Long, thin tendrils of phosphorescent white crawled across the deck, seeking targets and latching onto the men it touched, electrocuting them and scorching the deck they stood on.

The smell of burnt hair and wood smoke filled the air, covering the odor of voided bowels and blood. Men screamed and sprinted for cover, firing blindly as they ran.

The Scouts stood unharmed by the lightning crawling over them and impacting their foes.

Sara ran by Charlie and slammed a booted foot on Nadir's hand. "Hurts, doesn't it," she said and laughed.

The gunfire petered out. Most of the men on Georgios's boat had dropped their weapons and fallen to the deck, placing their hands behind their backs.

Sara kicked Nadir's gun away from his now broken hand and squatted by him. "You have no idea what you're messing with."

A black ball of light formed between her hands. Nadir's eyes widened. Sara rose and threw the ball at his men on her boat that the Scouts had pinned down. The black ball broke into little balls when it landed, causing the people that touched them to scream in terror. Commands were yelled from both sides, and guns fired again.

"Drop your weapons. This is your last warning," Charlie bellowed.

Sara ignored everything and squatted again beside Nadir. "You're going to tell me who knows you're here!"

Nadir whispered in Arabic.

Sara laughed again, a dark, shrill laugh. "If I'm a demon, you created me. Call for the missile."

Another black ball formed in her hands; she drew back her arm and threw it. While the survivors on Georgios's boat screamed, she removed the contacts and rubbed her face hard, smearing her makeup beyond repair, and dropped her wig on the deck. Her eyes glowed blue; the blue darkened as she stared at the man at her feet.

"Are you mad?" Nadir babbled. "It will destroy both boats."

She laughed shrilly, then gasped and panted, leaning over to clutch her stomach as if it hurt. When Nadir stopped trembling, she yelled, "Call it in!" When he started to pray, she kicked him. "God can't hear you! Call it in!"

Charlie stood behind her, unsure if he should pull her away or not. The magic inside him wanted him to destroy these men utterly. The magic didn't care that they'd surrendered or that they should be questioned. It was afraid and wanted The Enemy dead. Sweat beaded Charlie's brow with the effort to hold back. Teeth clenched in a grimace, he pitted his will against his magic's in a silent, unseen battle.

Rick jumped down to the deck of Georgios's boat carrying Joy and handed her to Drew.

"Search the ship," Brenda called.

The Scouts clambered over the rail. Charlie stepped away from Sara to peer over the side. Manny was guarding the prisoners on their deck while Harrison tied them. The sight eased him.

His magic firmly under control, Charlie took two steps towards Sara and stopped. The wildness of her emotions alarmed him, fear, anger, and a deep hatred roiled, pushing every other emotion out.

"Sara? Sweetheart, calm down, okay? You're freaking me out a little."

Charlie held a hand to her, but she didn't acknowledge him. All her attention remained on the man at her feet. Another feeling he didn't have a word suffused the hatred as she continued to scream in Arabic. He reached towards her with closed eyes and his head cocked to the side, straining for understanding.

"Sara! Stop this right now!" Sara's usual golden glow contained dark sludgy edges. Edges that pulsed with a black fire that Charlie just knew would destroy her brightness forever if allowed to remain.

Stasia grabbed Charlie's arm as he gasped and moaned. "Jesus Christ, Sara, stop!"

Brenda's glance darted over them, and she yelled, "Nadir is a bad man, yes, but he isn't responsible for hurting you. There's no need to kill him. Let us arrest him. Stop whatever it is you're doing. You're scaring everyone."

Sara didn't respond to Brenda. She grabbed Nadir and shook him, laughing as she said something in Arabic.

"Chief, what's she doing?" Brenda pointed the tranquilizer gun at Sara.

Charlie moaned again and staggered forward with his eyes closed.

"Someone, answer me right now, damn it, or I'm sedating her… and you! I'm not kidding here, Charlie."

"Don't," Charlie begged.

Brenda lowered her arm. "Are you talking to her or me?" Brenda backed away until she hit the railing, getting as far away from them as she could.

"Give me a minute here, Brenda. Don't do anything until I tell you."

Sara wasn't afraid anymore she was terrorizing Nadir and enjoying it. The feeling he couldn't name he now had a name for, it was madness. Terrified now himself, he grabbed her arm, and she turned to face him, a snarl on her face. No longer shining blue, eyes of solid black glared at him, no whites, no pupil, only shining blackness. His terror surged, and her answering surge caused the sludgy black to further dim her brightness.

"No!" he shouted and pulled her from Nadir's side, dragging her against her will as she struggled. "Stay back!" he yelled as Stasia reached for Sara and he forced his wife against his chest as she screamed shrilly. "Calm down! I swear, he can't hurt you! No one will hurt you."

"Let me go, and I can stop him!" Deep and

low, her voice grated, an inhuman growl that made his palms sweat.

With his eyes closed, Charlie watched the blackness within her pulse, blocking more of her brightness, his fear and terror were causing it to pulse faster. "Oz, what do I do?" Charlie yelled, panting now with fear.

"What's happening?" Oz jumped from the railing to the deck but didn't touch them.

"This… whatever this is she's doing, is changing her, destroying her! How do we stop it? Oh God, please stop, Sara!" In his arms, Sara struggled to get free.

Nadir sat, cradling his broken hand, and laughing. "She's a demon. To stop her, kill her!"

"Shut the hell up!" Charlie snarled, and anger replaced his fear for a moment. That moment of anger lightened the blackness. Intentionally, Charlie thought of the men who'd hurt her and escaped, and rage filled him, replacing terror. The familiar feel of his rage seemed to comfort her, or maybe it was just that he wasn't afraid now, but angry. Whatever it was, it worked, the sludgy black receded.

"I'll kill them for you, Sara. Calm down, and trust that I'll protect you." Letting his rage build, enjoying it, becoming Chief, a grim smile lit his face and the blackness within her retreated, the fire of rage blazing through it. When he kissed her neck, it receded more. With his eyes closed, he saw bright sparks break through the darkness and kissed her lips, deepening the kiss, his love, and desire feeding the light that was Sara.

She kissed him back and stopped struggling

to get away from him. His heart still beat wildly. Adrenaline caused his hands to shake as he smoothed the wild blond hair that hung in a knotted mess on her shoulders.

"That's better," he murmured as she kissed his neck, resting her lips on his pounding pulse. "Together we can stop them. Let me help you. What do you need me to do?"

"Make him talk." Sara kissed him again and then leaned back to meet his eyes. Charlie was relieved to see they were blue once more. Beautiful Barlow Blue eyes now rimmed in black stared back at him.

Charlie ran a hand through her hair again, nodded, and then held out his hand to Stasia while pressing his wife tightly against him. The wild emotional storm had smoothed into anxiety, the sludgy blackness almost gone. Charlie felt like crying he was so relieved. "Can I borrow your knife please?" To keep his wife sane, he would happily kill a thousand men.

Stasia grinned, slapped the knife hilt into his palm, and then squatted before Nadir. The brown of her eyes now shining a sapphire blue, she glanced over at Sara and pulled her other K-Bar from the sheath on her thigh. "Oh, he'll talk, Sara."

"Stay here!" Charlie said and kissed her before leaping to Stasia's side and squatting beside her, his brown eyes also glowed. He knew it by the clarity and depth of vision and hearing. Magic swirled around him, small sparks forming thin strands of lightning that jumped from him to Stasia.

Face grim, he leaned forward and in a voice of terrifying calmness said, "Tell my wife what she needs to hear, or I'll let her destroy you, and when she's finished with you, I'll go and annihilate every person you've ever met. Your country will become a desolate graveyard, your people destroyed utterly. No one will harm her again."

"Your wife? That is a demon!" Nadir glared from Charlie to Sara and then paled and ducked his head when thunder boomed. The thunder rumbled as it faded away. Ozone filled the air as arcs of static flickered between Team Valor.

Charlie reached down and grabbed Nadir by the throat. "Face the fear you caused. This is what your evil has wrought. Sara is a healer, but your cruelty has twisted her. Decide right now! Do you wish to loose us on your nation? Or will you let her rest and become a healer again?"

Nadir licked his lips and glanced between them and then at the Scouts who stood back, staring. His gaze traveled the scorched decking and dead bodies littering his boat.

Oz climbed onto the broken railing, balancing easily on the narrow surface, and casted lightning on the water behind Nadir. Motes of light danced between his outstretched hands, which he flicked into the air, forming the lightning that crashed and sizzled into the ocean, lighting the night sky in a dazzling display of power. Fireballs arced over the water impacting with loud smacks and billows of steam. The men cowering at the Scouts feet began to pray.

Nadir licked his lips and nodded.

Sara squatted beside Charlie. Without turning, she called to the Scouts. "Stay on deck," and grabbed Charlie's hand. "If he doesn't make a phone call in ten seconds, kill him." Eyes glowing almost white she turned back to Nadir. "Do you think you could stop us? That all your people with all their weapons could stop us? You brought this on yourself by trying to take us and force our secrets from us. We came to your country to retrieve what was ours. It wasn't personal. I didn't hate your people or intend them harm. I just wanted my own people back."

In a voice that shook with anger, she screamed, "I hate you now! I'll do everything in my power to destroy you and every man who stands with you. You call upon Allah to destroy the infidels, well here I am!" Shrill and wild her voice shook with rage. "I will destroy every last one of you!"

Wild-eyed she reached over and yanked a piece of the railing with all her strength. Gasping and panting, she pulled again. In a moment, Charlie was beside her and pulling with her. A five-foot section of wooden railing broke free with a grinding crack.

Nadir babbled in Arabic. The white of Sara's eyes dimmed until they were only slightly brighter than her normal blue. When he stopped talking, she stood and took a deep breath and then wiped her sweating face on her shirt, further smearing the makeup.

Charlie watched tensely, knife gripped in his hand. If the blackness threatened his wife again, he would kill this man before fear could take her from him.

No longer angry or anxious, Sara was now determined. Her glance traveled over the silent Scouts, and she seemed to realize for the first time that the fight was over, and her team needed healing. Light balls flew from her fingertips.

Small golden spheres sought out the wounded Scouts and healed them as Nadir and his men watched in awe. When she was satisfied that none of the Scouts remained injured, she glared down at the man at her feet in contempt. "Call in the air strike," she said.

Nadir lifted a shaking hand to his pocket and called it in. Sara laughed a sarcastic mocking sound and slammed her rail section into the decking. A swirling blue mist surrounded her. She reached out a hand to Stasia, calling her magic out. The magic surrounding her grew darker, and small sparks of static crawled over it.

Stasia rubbed her arms and backed away.

She pulled Oz to her side and tore his magic from him. Hawk didn't wait for her to ask or force him, he leapt to her. The smile she gave Hawk deteriorated to a muffled sob as she spun away. Thunder boomed, and the magic darkened. The small sparks were now tendrils of lightning that arced between Team Valor. Sara began casting Reflective Shields on everyone and dispelling them.

From the roof of the wheelhouse, Brenda spoke on the radio with the major. "Sara says he called in an air strike on our position. She's preparing to deflect it, but she's, um… a bit overwrought here. I'm not sure she can."

"Damn it, Brenda. I should have fucking put Harrison in charge. You weren't supposed to let her lose control!" The major cleared his throat and when he spoke again, was calmer. "Can you sedate her?"

"Well, I could, but I don't think I should. Right now, she has control, but if I sedate her, is all we'll have is loose magic."

"Brenda… next time stop her before she's out of hand. Damn it… there's no use arguing over this now. Let her cast or do whatever the hell she's going to do. We'll talk about this later. The captain of the sub assures me he's tracking on radar and I'm coming to your location. Don't let her blow me up. I'll handle the mop up here. Get Valor and Alpha team on the boat and back to base. Leave me the garbage. A plane is waiting to take Valor home. Get her out of here before you debrief her, but I want full reports ASAP."

"The major is on his way here, Sara!" Brenda yelled and turned to her team. "Throw all the bodies on their boat and make sure the survivors are securely tied. We leave in five minutes."

Major Nelson called Brenda back. "Radar shows a fast-moving jet that'll be in range of you within six minutes. We've scrambled our own jets, but they won't arrive in time to intercept."

Brenda lowered the radio to her side and called to Sara, "Your missile is incoming in five minutes. We need to get out of here, Sara."

Sara ignored her and kept casting shield spells. "Stasia, do a precog for me. I need a three-minute warning." Thunder rumbled and the lightning crawling between Team Valor flickered in wild, scintillating patterns. The magic formed a tornado around Sara, whipping her hair, lighting each strand in blue phosphorescence.

Charlie watched in awe as small mirrored-shields materialized and disappeared before they could really be seen she was casting so fast.

Stasia channeled her precog spell. For a moment her stare became glassy and distant. "Sara, a big hit is incoming. I see it destroying both vessels."

"When?" Sara asked.

"Four minutes and six seconds."

"Tick," Sara said and kept casting shields. Forty-five seconds later, she began channeling a Reflective Shield. She held out her make-shift staff and rose a hand over her head. The magical storm she created swirled around her, a whirlwind of magic. A phosphorescent blue glow coated her— outlining her hair and leaving a glowing trail after her every movement.

The silver, mirror-like shield grew until it covered both boats, cutting out the starlight under the shield, and still she casted. For three minutes, she funneled magic into the Reflective shield, making one bigger than she ever had before until they stood in almost pitch blackness. Only the sparks of static and tendrils of lightning lit the dark.

The magic dimmed as her hand lowered, the wild swirling magic slowed and absorbed into Team Valor. Eyes still closed, she clasped her staff with both hands and waited.

"Tock."

The countdown arrived, and nothing

appeared to happen. Three seconds later a blinding flash illuminated the shield.

With a wave of her hand, Sara dispelled the shield, reabsorbing the unused magic. Everyone stared up at the jet that had sent the missiles and watched it disintegrate and fall into the sea in burning pieces.

Sara turned to Charlie and placed a hand on his cheek. A blue glow traveled from the staff through her into him.

Charlie examined her brightness. All that remained of the sludge was a hair-thin line of black. With dismay, he wondered if she would always have that now, a lurking potential for madness. He smoothed her wild hair and pulled her against him, resting his cheek on hers.

Brenda left them alone as she called the major and made another report. "She held off the warheads with no problem. It didn't even dent her shield."

"I'll be there in less than five minutes. Recon Team Two might beat me there. Get them home, Brenda," Major Nelson said. "Captain Sanders will be waiting at the base in Crete for you."

Brenda jumped onto the other boat, zip-tied Nadir's hand, and legs, checked his gunshot wound, and threw a quick dressing on it.

"I want him dead." Sara glared at the man Brenda was helping.

"I know," Brenda said and smiled. "But, if it's any consolation, he'll wish he was dead for a long time."

Sara nodded and climbed back onto Georgios' boat. "I'm sorry I didn't follow the plan, but I heard them talking on deck and needed to get closer to hear better," she whispered to Charlie as he sat beside her, fuming with anger. "I'm a full member of this team, and we take care of each other."

His anger lessened but didn't abate.

"I love you," she whispered, and his anger diminished even more.

"Stop manipulating me!" Charlie growled, and she laughed and kissed his neck. He sighed and kissed her back, anger gone. "I love you too," he said. "But, don't do that again."

She shrugged and knotted her fingers in her lap. "No promises. If I hadn't, that missile might have hit. I don't think my regular Reflective Shield would have held, do you?"

"I don't think the jet would have sent it if you hadn't made him call it in."

She shrugged again and stretched her fingers out, examining and then clenching them. "Nobody is left who knows or at least no one who actively wants us. I'll sleep better knowing that, won't you?"

"Yes," he admitted, thinking about his earlier discussion with his brother when they'd killed Rinto's men. Not everyone who knew was accounted for. Sergeant Guthrie was in Iraq right now with Beta team, searching for the last four—overseeing the agents left there. Charlie wanted those four men dead. Sara wouldn't be safe until they were dead or contained. He preferred dead. He tightened his grip on her.

The rest of Team Valor gathered around. "I need a shower," Stasia said. "And Tank needs two showers. Holy Christ that dog is rank." With a disgusted look at the dog, she moved away.

"He can't help it. The sea air is making him worse." Hawk rubbed his dog's ears. "First chance I get, I'll wash him."

Captain Sanders had fresh clothing and food waiting when they reached the base.

Everyone showered and changed before heading to the cafeteria for a meal. Hawk washed Tank, revealing skinny sides with large bald patches. A quick shave with a borrowed razor gave Tank a more even appearance.

Captain Sanders joined them in the cafeteria. "Major Nelson will be staying behind and overseeing the prisoners debriefing and transport. Major Harris is waiting at Pendleton. Guthrie and I will be with Major Nelson." He turned to Brenda and indicated Team Valor. "Stay on high alert and keep them under surveillance."

"No," Charlie said. "Sara and I need privacy." He interrupted the captain as he started to speak. "I'm not asking. I'm telling you. My wife and I are going someplace warm where we can be alone, and I'll ensure she's safe." He flicked a glance at Sara who watched anxiously.

She was puzzled by his guilt and he let himself get angrier to hide it. He had no intention of going anywhere except after the remaining men. She was going to freak when he left her behind but he couldn't risk her, he just couldn't.

He firmed his shoulders and glared at Captain Sanders. He'd take her someplace warm when he was certain she was safe.

The captain cleared his throat before he spoke. "Security is our paramount concern right now. You'll have to compromise with us on this. We'll arrange for you all to go somewhere warm." He held his hand up as Charlie started to speak. "I understand you want time alone, that's fine, but Brenda will need to know where you are at all times for your own safety."

"I'll compromise," Charlie agreed. "But no one watches us, or runs tests, or any other damn thing. We'll tell you what we want you to know about our relationship. It's no one's business except ours."

"Give me an hour or two to find somewhere secure to send you. I'll ensure it's hot enough to make Sara happy," he said and smiled at Sara and gestured for Brenda to accompany him.

"It isn't like Charlie to be uncooperative, of course, he never had a wife before either," Brenda said, frowning at Charlie. "Keep in mind he's a protection warrior, and his magic will be pushing him. And, remember her emotions will affect him now, and she's really on edge, and they're both exhausted."

"Believe me, we never forget he's a warrior. Both recon teams will accompany you; I want the area kept secure. Have someone on watch at all times."

Brenda's frown deepened.

"Give them privacy, but make sure no one can reach them either," Captain Sanders clarified.

"Send daily reports on Sara's mental state. If it deteriorates any more, I'll send Doctor Gotlieb to her. I know Charlie thinks he can handle this, but it might be too much for him; they're so damn young."

"I'll keep an eye on her," Brenda promised and glanced at the table where the rest of the kids sat. "They're all so damn young... I forget that sometimes. I think they're all doing really well considering this week's changes and stress."

"They are," Captain Sanders agreed. "Keep the Scouts informed on what we find out, but don't pass it on to Valor until Doctor Gotlieb okay's it. We want their stress at a minimum."

"Roger that." Brenda saluted and returned to the table.

-23-

RETURN TO IRAQ

Charlie called Oz away from the table with a subtle nod of his head. "Watch after Sara for me, I'm going back to Iraq," he whispered.

"What, why?" Oz glanced back at the table with his eyes narrowed.

"Four men you located there are still at large. Sergeant Guthrie is there now, searching and tying up loose ends." Charlie laughed bitterly. "I made Rick call him. They won't tell me anything. If I let them escape, she'll never be safe— none of us will be."

"Fine, I'm going with you," Oz said.

"You can't. I'm going to steal Stasia's invisible and sneak on the first plane going back."

"I can, and I am. How are you going to find them without me? Don't be stupid. With disguise and invisible I can get in the baggage compartment." Oz glanced at the table where the rest of Team Valor sat. "If we leave them behind, they'll be seriously angry."

"Sara can't come. The fear she feels is killing me, and it almost destroyed her." The memory of how close she'd been to madness shook him.

Sara glanced over, and he smiled and motioned her to stay with Stasia. She frowned but turned away. Charlie took a deep breath and let it out slowly, reigning in his fear and anxiety.

"Stasia and Hawk will protect her, and she'll be safe here with them. Everyone will be. I know she'll be angry, but I would rather have her irritated with me than them at large or have her going crazy from fear."

Charlie glanced at his watch. "If I want to get out of the zone before she notices, I need to go now."

Oz glanced over his shoulder again and nodded. He casted Decoy, leaving a motionless copy of himself in the hallway leaning against the wall and disguised himself as a soldier. Charlie stole Stasia's invisible. When they were out of sight, they ran.

When they weren't back in ten minutes, Sara asked Rick to check the restrooms. A red flush covered her cheeks, and she bit her lip.

"Nothing here to worry about, Sara, but I'll go check the bathroom," Rick said. In ten minutes, he'd checked both bathrooms, tried calling Charlie's cell phone, and got no answer. He frowned and called the major. "Charlie's missing." He peered around the doorway to the cafeteria. "Oz isn't here either. Are they with you?"

"No," Major Nelson said in alarm. "You're sure they're missing? They're not in the bathroom or something?"

"Damn, I thought Sara was just being a little paranoid when she asked me to check. That was twenty minutes ago now, and they aren't in any of the bathrooms or main rooms. Sara is really nervous; he must feel it, and I can't believe he wouldn't go to her— if he could. Charlie isn't answering his cell, but I didn't try Oz."

"Let me call you right back," Major Nelson said.

Rick paced the hallway while running a hand through his hair. The phone barely rang once before he answered it.

"Oz isn't answering either. Get the rest of them somewhere secure right now," Major Nelson said, his voice grim.

Rick swallowed heavily and headed back to Sara. She took one look at his face and gasped. All color fled her face, and she took two tries to stand and had to lean on the table to support herself. "They're gone?"

Rick nodded.

She casted Call-For-Help. When only Stasia and Hawk appeared by her, she moaned, and her eyes flared blue. A frown of concentration formed shallow wrinkles in her brow and her eyes closed. "Charlie isn't frightened, he's... determined, worried, sad..." She trailed off. "Mostly he's sorry," she finally said. "Nobody took him; he left me on purpose and is blocking me as hard as he can." Tears trailed down her cheeks.

Hawk squatted, examining the ground and followed a trail no one could see except him. "No way would he leave you or us. I'm following them. They went this way."

The Scouts surrounded them with drawn weapons as Hawk led them to a deserted runway. "No one was near them. I can't believe it, but they must have left together on purpose," Hawk said in puzzlement. Sara sobbed, and Hawk hugged her. "You know he'll come back."

She nodded jerkily and glanced at Rick.

"For you, Sara, he'll come back for you!" Hawk said.

"He doesn't want to. I can feel it. As hard as he can, he's pushing me away." Brightly glowing blue eyes turned to Stasia. "I need him," Sara said pitifully.

Her phone rang.

"I *will* come back. Don't feel abandoned. I'm not deserting you. I need you as much as you need me. But I also need to be sure you're safe. Please, trust me." Charlie's voice was gruff with emotion. "Stay there, where you're protected. Oz and I will make sure you're safe— that we all are."

Sara didn't answer. Tears trickled across her cheeks.

"I'll always love you," he whispered and hung up, gritting his teeth against her emotions and trying to block them out again. Not angry she was desolate.

Oz cleared his throat. "Your eyes are glowing."

Charlie closed his eyes and turned his face

away.

They sat quietly in the cargo bay for the rest of the trip.

Rick called Major Nelson. "They weren't taken, they left on purpose, and I know where they're headed." He gave Sara a small apologetic shrug. "He's headed to Iraq."

"I'm going too!" Sara said.

"No, you're not," Rick said and grabbed her shoulder as she turned away. "You're not," he repeated and shook her. "We'll bring them both back, and so help me God, if he ever pulls a stunt like this again, I'll kill him myself."

Sara turned her blazing eyes on Rick. "I have to go! I need him!" The blue in her eyes brightened as she yelled, and her hands flared up bright blue.

Rick released her, stepped away, and tried to call his brother. When he didn't answer, he tried Oz. Neither would answer, so he texted them both. 'Sara needs Charlie.'

He called the major. "Sara has to go too. She's glowing and needs him." He lowered his voice and moved away from Sara. "We'll have to fight her to make her stay here."

"Girls in combat positions is a fucking bad idea." Major Nelson took a deep breath and said in a calmer voice, "Bring Valor to Iraq and keep them on the base there. Is she safe to go on a plane?"

Rick turned to Sara. "Can you keep your magic under control to travel there?"

She bit her lip and shrugged.

Rick gave her a quick hug. "She doesn't

know."

"Trank her. Don't let her see it coming," Major Nelson whispered. "Get her to him as fast as we can. If the damn idiot will answer his damn phone…"

Rick hung up and lightly pulled one of Sara's damp curls. "The major's getting us a ride there now, all of us. Try not to worry so much, okay?"

A bleak smile crossed her pale face, and her hands settled down, but her eyes still glowed. Rick handed her his sunglasses. Only a slight blue glow was noticeable around them.

Rick motioned Sara to precede him and gave Brenda a sign he needed to speak privately with her. When Sara couldn't overhear them, he passed on the order.

Brenda nodded and fingered the tranquilizer gun.

As soon as Sara sat in an aisle seat, Brenda shot her. Before she could do more than look surprised, she slumped over.

Stasia jumped to her feet.

Tank growled, a low, menacing hum deep in his throat.

"We needed to," Rick said. "If the magic got loose, she could crash the plane. You know that. The sedative won't hurt her. She'll just sleep until we reach Iraq. You know I would never hurt her." Rick held his hand out to Stasia, and she jerked away, settling into a defensive crouch.

Tank snarled.

Everyone quieted. A gun cocked behind Rick, the small sound loud in the tense silence. Sweat beaded on Rick's brow, and he held his empty hands out to Stasia. "I would never harm you, any of you, you know that. She's just asleep for the ride there."

Stasia laid her fingers against Sara's pulse, her blue-eyed glare scanning the watching Scouts. The blue faded from her gaze, and she made eye contact with someone behind Rick and nodded. The gun was uncocked, and Tank's low growl moved away.

Rick took a deep breath, releasing it in a long exhalation and leaned down to buckle Sara's seatbelt.

Stasia leapt between them, crouching on the seat back. "Don't touch her."

Eyes blazing blue again, she glared around her. "I'll take care of her. Sit down and buckle yourselves in. I don't trust any of you! I need you to back the hell up now!" Tank snarled again as she yelled.

Rick backed away, holding his hands out.

Her narrowed blue eyes followed their movements, and her hand rested on the knife sheathed on her thigh as the Scouts sat and buckled their seatbelts. Again, she made eye contact, signaling Hawk.

In the rear of the plane, as far as he could get, Hawk stood with his gun drawn. Tank crouched before him with a snarl on his face, white canines gleaming and hackles raised.

Rick held his empty hands out to her again. "Stasia, honey, we had to tranquilize her. You know you can trust me."

"I'm not your honey; I'm not your anything," Stasia snapped. "Obviously, we can't trust you."

"Loose magic is dangerous; you know that."

"You could've asked her. She isn't unreasonable. Trust is a two-way street."

"I'm sorry," Rick said. "You're right; despite orders I should've asked first." His voice lowered. "There's one thing you're wrong about though. You aren't nothing to me. You're my very good friend."

Brenda interrupted, "You're right; we should've asked. Sara wasn't out of control. Next time we will, but, Stasia, if she's out of control, if the magic gets away from her, or any of you, we won't ask. That doesn't mean we want to harm you. We need to be cautious."

"You're asking for a lot of trust here, for us to put ourselves at your mercy." She nodded towards Sara's limp form. "She's defenseless now. You've proved you're willing to shoot us with no warning. You say you'll protect us and intend us no harm, but that's a lot to ask— to be at your complete mercy on your whims. Rinto was one of you."

"You're right, but I haven't shot you though, have I?" Brenda licked her lips and showed her empty palms.

Stasia snorted and held up Brenda's tranquilizer gun. "Because you can't."

Brenda reached to her belt and sighed. "I didn't try. Doesn't that prove I meant what I said about trusting you? In the future, we'll ask if we can. I promise you that."

After a tense moment, Stasia nodded and threw the gun to Brenda and signaled to Hawk. Hawk lowered his gun, took a seat in the back, and rubbed Tank's laid-back ears while Stasia slid into her seat and buckled the seatbelt. Periodically during the flight Stasia felt for Sara's pulse as her blue-eyed gazed flickered over the Scouts.

-24-

CHIEF

Charlie stopped sensing Sara abruptly. Still hidden in the cargo hold of the airplane, he and Oz rode without speaking much. He was sure something had happened to her. Cellphone in hand, he paused. Maybe she had fallen asleep. If he phoned, he would wake her. After another minute of internal debate, he called his brother.

"Is Sara with you?" He asked without preamble.

"If you ignore my calls again, I'll beat you with the damned phone!" his brother sounded angrier with him than he ever had. "Yes, the wife you're traumatizing is with me. Don't you dare hang up! I know you're headed back to Iraq. Charlie, we can handle them. She needs you. You can't just disappear like that, it's cruel. It freaked her out so bad we had to tranquilize her. "

"Rick, I need her safe. I have to make sure

they can't hurt her, to see for myself what they know and who they told. I can't leave the threat we face to anyone else."

"Well, you don't have to do it alone either. I'll call the major and call you back. Answer your damn phone!"

Rick called Major Nelson. "We have a situation, several of them. Stasia freaked when we shot Sara. She wasn't wrong, it was a sneak attack, and she showed remarkable restraint in not attacking us. For all she knew, we had switched sides and were working for Rinto. If we want them to trust us, we have to trust them. In the future, we'll ask before we sedate them if possible." Rick ran a hand through his hair and rubbed his eyes. "As to our other situation, Chief is a protection warrior, a prot tank; his main job is to protect his group, specifically the healer. This healer is his wife. I'm one hundred percent sure his magic is pushing him to protect her. Before they were even dating, it pushed him to her side on his deathbed. There's no way in hell we'll stop him. He'll fight anyone who stands in the way of his protecting her. Stasia was a hair breath from quitting the raid to attack us. This situation could ruin rep with Team Valor if we aren't careful."

Major Nelson was quiet a moment. "Can you get him to check in?"

"Yeah, he'll accept help to ensure Sara is safe; I'm sure of that. The nature of a protection warrior is to protect. The angrier he grows, the more powerful his magic will become, and the stronger that urge will be. Don't fight his nature— work with him. Let him go find the men who hurt her and stop them."

"Rick, as much as we want to preserve rep with Team Valor, we can't have them running around killing whoever they wish."

Rick snorted. "So far, he's only killed people who attacked him. Feel free to ask him to come back, but there's no way he will, not without checking for himself. Order him to return, and you force him to take the rest of his team and go off on their own and good luck stopping them."

Major Nelson grimaced. "It would be better to capture those men so we can question them."

"We can try, but he'll be full of rage and very dangerous."

"Tell them to start the search. Ask them to wait for us to engage and to please accept all calls."

Rick called his brother. "Leave your phone on and answer our calls. Major Nelson says to start the search, but wait for us to engage them. Take them alive so the major can question them."

"How long will the sedative last?" Charlie asked.

"Three hours or so."

"Sedate her again. Keep her under longer. Give me time to find them."

"Chief, she isn't a toy you can take out when you want too. You can't just sedate your wife so you don't have to deal with her."

"I know that, and I'm not avoiding her, I'm trying to help her. Oz and I will be going in stealthed. She can't. Therefore, she can't come. When she wakes, and I'm not there, she'll be frightened and worried. Spare her that, Rick. Sedate her."

"Talk to Stasia first." Rick handed his phone to Stasia.

"Are you sure that's a good idea?" Not speaking, Stasia nodded and then said, "Fine," and handed the phone back to Rick. "While I understand his point, I don't like it even though we know she can be sedated for days with no lasting effects. Put her in a sunny spot and make her comfortable. When she wakes, she's going to be so angry— at all of us."

"Let her wake and see if she'll stay on the base while we look. If she won't, then we'll sedate her," Rick said.

Stasia nodded unhappily and ran her hand over Sara's hair before crossing her arms and turning away.

Major Nelson had arranged for transport on their arrival.

Oz grinned when he saw the dirt bike.

Charlie grinned when he saw the Bowie knife.

Oz drove them down the road and straight across the landscape following his locate. All four men were in the same direction.

Still invisible, Charlie rode on the back of the bike.

Oz stopped for gas, bought a small tank to take with them, and again followed locate. In six hours, they had tracked them down.

Dusk shaded the hillside where a lone farmhouse stood on barren fields. Oz circled the house on foot, confirming the quarry was inside, and then called Major Nelson. One look at Charlie's furious face and Oz placed a hand on his arm. "Take prisoners. Dead men tell no tales, and we need intel."

Charlie turned his blue-eyed glower onto Oz. "These men will get what they deserve. Wait out here for the major. I'm going in. My phone will be on with your end muted," Charlie said.

Oz disguised himself as a tree as Charlie climb the side of the building, forced a window open and disappeared inside.

"This room is empty, but I can hear people talking; they sound like they're downstairs," Charlie whispered as he crept down the stairs and into the dirty kitchen. Knife in hand, he stood behind the men at the table, listening to The Enemy talk. His magic hummed eagerly but didn't press. He was easily able to keep it contained within him. It knew he would protect Sara, that he longed to protect her and his team.

"Nadir isn't coming back. We would've heard by now. Either he crossed us or was crossed himself, but either way, it's bad news for us," one man said.

"The damn mage needs to die! We should have done it before we took the bitch. That dude is too damn dangerous."

"At the end there, she wasn't so dangerous," the man in front of Charlie said with a leer.

The man next to him went to a cooler beside

the front door and grabbed a beer. "You're an idiot. She killed eight of us."

"And we know how to control her now. Break her hands— hell, we can cut them off. We don't want her to cast. We want her." The man in front of Charlie rose and grabbed a beer, then plunked back down in his seat and put his booted feet on the table.

Charlie simmered with rage.

The man sitting across from him rolled his eyes. "Man, you're so retarded. Seriously, you're an idiot. We don't want her to cast, but our buyer will. What good is she if she can't heal?"

"So, break her goddam fingers into tiny pieces; she'll heal eventually. We need to kill the mage first."

"Shut up, both of you!" the last man snarled. "First, we need a buyer. Travensky isn't interested. He doesn't believe a word, and we have no real proof. Nadir was our only buyer, and he isn't answering his damn phone. Only five of us are left. Yeah, she's worth a fortune if we can sell her, but we have the general's money." The man shrugged. "I say we cut our losses, take the money, and split."

The man on the right slammed his beer bottle to the table and snarled, "And I say we don't! The money is the least of it. Don't you want to be able to do what they do? Well, that will never happen unless we capture them and make them talk. We have to kill the goddamn mage, or he'll track us all down."

"We killed him already. All four of them died in that cave in, and she ran to her mommy."

"You're a bigger fool than he is. If they're all dead, where's Nadir? They planned that shit. Rinto ran right into their arms."

Charlie listened as they argued about whether Sara's performance in Greece was real or staged.

The man in front of Charlie threw his beer bottle against the wall where it shattered and landed in tinkling shards on a pile of broken bottles. "Fine, we get the hell out of here. Split the money up when Marco returns. If we hear they're alive, we go kill the goddamn mage. If we can find a buyer, we take her. I don't know how the hell we'll find one. The general looked for months and only found two, one of which doesn't believe us anymore. None of us has the kind of contacts we need for this."

"So, we make contacts. I'll follow her and make sure she doesn't disappear. If the mage or any of them surface, we meet and make a plan. One of you stay here and see if we can line up another buyer. Someone will take Nadir's place, talk to him. All the people the general lined up aren't necessary. Jesus, we can take her ourselves and break her fingers; deliver her, collect our money, and go. That other plan was way too complicated. We don't need all of them. The general was too greedy."

Charlie listened while they argued about who was going where.

"Marco will be back in an hour or so, give me my share; I want to get the hell out of this shit hole." The man in front of Charlie put his booted feet back on the floor.

"I'll give you your share," Charlie said softly

from behind him. Before the man could do more than start in surprise, Charlie grabbed his arm and broke it as the man reached for his holstered gun.

Charlie stabbed him in the neck and used his body as a shield as the other men opened fire. The dead body thumped to the floor as Charlie jumped across the table, yelling his Berserk cry. The men screamed and swore. Charlie picked the second man up, and broke his back over his knee then threw him into the man beside him, knocking him onto the floor. The fourth man had run out the door. Charlie ignored him for the moment, intent on the enemy on the floor before him. Magic pulsed hard beneath his skin, and he knew his eyes would be blazing blue from his fury.

The man he'd thrown was unconscious. The other man skittered backward, using his hands to pull himself along the floor, trying desperately to get away from the death approaching him.

Charlie stalked him, ignoring the shots the man fired at his chest. The bullets ripped through his shirt and left shallow wounds that stopped bleeding and healed as the next shot connected. He didn't even feel it.

He kicked the man's gun from his hand. With a savage smile, he stamped on the hand as hard as he could. The man screamed shrilly. Charlie's smile widened, and he stamped on his hand again.

"I believe you said we should break my wife's fingers into pieces." Charlie squatted in front of the sobbing man, grabbed his other hand, and squeezed it as tightly as he could. The man shrieked as bones broke.

"Tell me about Marco." The man on the floor screamed and thrashed as Charlie tightened his grip, using two hands to crush the hand in his grasp until blood trickled from between his fingers.

He told Charlie everything he wanted to know.

Charlie left the man sobbing on the ground and went outside where he found Oz standing by a fluffy, black sheep. Without speaking, they stood and waited for the spell to end.

When the sheep transformed back into a man, he dropped to his knees and raised his hands over his head, his terrified gaze resting on Charlie's blood-soaked clothes and impassive face.

"The major is on the way here?" Charlie asked.

"Yeah, he'll be here in an hour," Oz said, "Marco too."

Charlie nodded and prodded the cowering man with a sneakered foot. "Tell the major to come in quietly. We don't want Marco to run and miss our party." Charlie pulled the man up by his shirt and punched him in the face, not holding back.

Oz looked away from the crunch as blood sprayed. "I think you killed him."

Charlie smiled. "Not yet." He grabbed the man's shirt collar, dragged him into the house, and dropped him on his still whimpering friend. "Your colleague isn't dead yet. I'm betting he dies when I cut off his hands, but I'll wait until he's awake for that." A satisfied smile on his face, he kicked the sobbing man lightly in the leg. "Shut up," he said in a conversational tone. "I won't ask again." Once the room was silent, he strolled outside where Oz spoke on the phone with the major.

"Charlie's, um, handled these guys. Three are alive, and one is on his way here." Oz told the major what Charlie had overheard. "Hang back. We can handle one guy. Don't let him see you."

"Fine, we'll hang back, and I'll call the base and tell them to stop the sedatives on Sara."

"Did she cooperate with you?" Oz asked.

"No, she did not," Major Nelson said. "She woke furious. That was my fault, I should've asked first. I know that now, but I thought it would be less stressful if we just sedated her." He sighed heavily. "We asked her to wait on base, told her Charlie wanted her to. Stasia and Hawk both tried to convince her. She was adamant about getting to him." He was quiet a moment. "So adamant, it took five of us to hold her back until Brenda could shoot her with the tranquilizer. Tell Charlie she's going to be seriously pissed."

Oz winced. "Where is she now?"

"The middle of Baghdad base, asleep on the top floor of a secured building she's locked in. Five stories of reinforced concrete surrounded by twenty Marines armed with tranquilizer guns. She's untied in the sunshine, well, dark now, but I'm sure Hawk will turn on some lights for her; we're trying to limit her stress when she wakes.

When she first woke, she was severely frightened. Hawk is with her. Stasia is with me."

"I need a vacation," Oz said wearily.

Major Nelson snorted back a laugh. "Don't we all. I'm glad we got this cleaned up, but I hate how we're doing it. The way we handle a crisis needs work. I can't have any of you going off on your own like this."

"I know, he knows too," Oz said in frustration. "But, Charlie isn't a regular man, not anymore, and you can't treat him like one. He's a protection warrior. All of us have changed from what we were, and you can't treat us as if it hadn't happened. Trying to stop him from coming here is pointless."

"If this fiasco has shown us anything, it's that," Major Nelson assured him. "Have you changed? I haven't noticed a change."

Oz gave a strangled laugh. "How can you miss the changes? Hawk craves the forest and Sara the sun. Hawk loves the animals, and they love him and not in a normal human way. Sara and I both have a need for books and knowledge. We read incessantly about everything with total recall. We need it." Oz's voice rose. "We don't want it— we need it! I can't explain it to you, it isn't like I want an ice cream, it's I need air, I can't breathe!"

Oz took a deep breath and continued more calmly. "When Chief says he needs to come here and do this, he means it. When Sara says she needs him, she really needs him. A magical need isn't a human one. I can feel the magical push when they say it. When Hawk says, 'I need to take a walk' or Sara says, 'I need to go the library' or Charlie says, 'I need to kill those men.'" He was quiet, they both were.

Major Nelson cleared his throat. "I see," he said finally and was quiet again. "What does Stasia need?" he finally asked.

"I don't know. Hell, I don't know if she even knows. I haven't heard her say it about anything." Oz was quiet a moment before saying very softly, "If she does say it, give her whatever it is instantly. Stasia is very, very dangerous. If her eyes are glowing blue when she says it... you'll have to be very fast to stop her, and I don't think anyone could be that fast. She could kill anyone in two seconds."

"Are you all that, um, desperate when you need something?"

"The more we deny the need, the more we feel it. You know this. You've seen for yourself Charlie and Sara's need to touch each other and what happens when they deny the need."

The major swallowed so heavily Oz heard him.

"What?" he asked in a dread-laced voice.

"Sara has been saying she needs him." He paused. "A lot. Her eyes and hands are blue."

"Then we need her to have him. I'll tell him," Oz said. "As soon as we get Marco, we'll head back to her."

Oz spoke to Charlie who was squatting and glaring before the men he'd stacked together. "Sara needs you."

"I know. I felt her need, but she knows I need to do this. When we're done here, I'll go to her," Charlie said unhappily.

"She'll be very angry."

"I know that too."

Oz frowned, but dropped it and dragged Charlie outside, away from the terrified men as they waited for Marco.

A rusty old car finally pulled in, and Charlie tensed eagerly.

Oz put his hand on his arm. "That might not be him. You don't want to kill someone asking for directions or something. Let me get him."

Oz casted disguise, making himself resemble the dead man, and then went outside where he shaded his eyes and squinted. "Marco, is that you?" he called as if he couldn't make out who was in the car.

"Who the hell else would it be?" The man yelled back irritably as he opened the car door.

Charlie leapt past Oz and grabbed the car door before Oz could say another word. With a tearing shriek of metal, Charlie ripped the door off and threw it across the yard. He grabbed Marco and dragged him from the car. Marco went for his gun, and Charlie let him, snarling in Marco's face as he pointed the gun.

Marco dropped the gun.

Charlie snarled again and shook him. "She's mine! Mine!" He shook him again and then lifted and threw him at the house. Marco hit with a thud and slid down the wall— out cold.

Oz called the major. "Well, we have Marco… mostly intact." With an exasperated sigh, he glanced at Charlie, and then rolled his eyes and huffed a small laugh. Charlie couldn't help his response to the magic.

Charlie flexed his fingers, smiling in triumph, his need sated. Now, he needed to return to his sure to be furious wife.

-25-

THE BEST OF INTENTIONS

Major Nelson arrived, and the Scouts jumped from the helicopter. Some loaded the men on board while others ransacked the house.

"Burn it!" Major Nelson finally ordered Oz who complied with a grin. Once the fire was blazing, everyone jumped back into the helicopter and headed back to base.

Charlie suddenly straightened in his seat. "Damn it, she's awake and afraid. Where did you put her she's in such a panic?"

The major took a call before he answered. While Charlie glared at him, Major Nelson spoke on the phone. "Sedate her again then," he said then swore and made another phone call, fumbling with the phone in his haste.

"Come on, answer, damn it," he snapped and

practically yelled Brenda's name when she answered on the second ring. "Brenda, get back to the office building ASAP! Sara's awake and not responding to Hawk. Sedate her until Charlie gets there. No, I don't know why she didn't summon him, but Hawk says her eyes are pure black and she didn't appear to recognize him or know where she was when she woke and she's destroying the building to escape."

Charlie reached over to grab the phone when he, Stasia, and Oz disappeared.

A cold, hard surface pushed its way into Sara's muzzy consciousness, and she fought to open her eyes. Vomit burned the back of her throat. She recognized this feeling. She'd been drugged. Panic grew as she realized she lay on a metal table.

'No,' she tried to moan, but couldn't manage to make a sound.

Her eyelids felt heavy, too heavy for her to open, and she couldn't force her hands to lift. A man spoke, but her drugged-hazed mind couldn't form the sounds into words. The magic within her surged. It felt as if it would rip through her skin to escape, exploding her from the inside out. For the briefest moment, she attempted to hold it back but its wild need to be safe matched hers to well.

"Get us out," she gasped and let her magic have its way.

Sara half-sat and rolled off the table.

"Jeez, you okay?" Hawk asked as he tried to help her rise.

She didn't answer. Her limbs flailed, and she repeatedly fell as she tried to stand.

On her hands and knees, she crawled into the hallway.

Hawk squatted beside her, telling her she was safe and with him and tried again to help her stand. Pure black eyes met his, and he gasped. "Sara?" When she didn't respond, he shook her. "Sara!" he yelled, and she ignored him, struggling to her feet. Hawk released her and called the major.

While he spoke on the phone, Sara took a step forward, fell, and crawled to the wall in front of her. She slowly pulled herself up, leaning her face against the wall. A dark orange Smite formed in her hands. She threw it at the wall and fell through the person-sized hole she'd created. Another ball of orange light formed in her hands, and she threw it at the wall before her. She threw three more in quick succession, blasting the entire wall down. The lights flickered and went out, and a siren sounded, muffled by the walls. Dust billowed in choking clouds.

Hawk dropped the phone, grabbed her arm, and swung her to face him. He had to release her. The pain from touching her seared his hands. He tried again, grabbing her by the tank top Stasia had put on her so she could absorb more sunlight. The thin material ripped in his hand she pulled away so hard.

Still not acknowledging him in any way, she casted again and blew out the wall behind him. While he shook her and pleaded, she smote the walls. He yanked her back by her ripped shirt, knocking her down, and held her down while she thrashed. Thunder crashed, and something shook the building.

"Jeez, Sara, stop. How the hell will we explain this?" Thunder rumbled again, a long drawn out peel and lightning flashed outside the windows bright enough to read by. Her black eyes focused on him, and a smite began to form in her hands. Hawk let her go.

She pushed herself to her knees and crawled towards the hole she'd made.

"Come this way. There's no need to make holes. We can take the stairs or jump from the damned windows."

Hawk tried to talk her into turning, but she continued to crawl forward and casted as if she couldn't hear him. The building vibrated, a distant rumble turned into a roaring crash as the room behind them caved in. The holes she'd made were destroying the integrity of the building. With a resounding roar, the floor above them settled, and load creaks and cracks warned this floor would be next and soon.

"You're going to kill us!" Hawk shouted as the entire building rumbled.

Hawk charged forward, grabbed her, and ran down the hallway. They both screamed, him with pain and her in fury. He was too late. The building fell with a horrendous crash, sliding to earth in slow motion. A weight hit his back, knocking him to the floor.

Sara woke again in agony, having no idea where she was. Rocks and dust were crushing her. The pain of it made her cry out. After straining uselessly for a moment against the weight trapping her, she casted Call-For-Help.

Charlie, Stasia, and Oz appeared on a pile of wreckage. Immediately, Charlie knew Sara was in the pile somewhere, trapped, he felt her pain. He bellowed her name and then his berserk cry and started throwing chunks of rubble from beneath his feet.

"Stop," Stasia yelled. "Shut up!" She screamed Sara's name. "This way," she scrambled over the broken concrete to where the sound of muffled screaming was clearer.

Charlie threw rubble again.

"Is Hawk with you?" Stasia hollered.

Oz casted locate and winced. "Both are beneath us, Stasia."

Sara groped around in the dark, pinned from the chest down unable to move. Hand-of-Sun illuminated the pocket of debris enough to show broken, cracked cement inches from her face. Unable to turn her head, she felt around with her free hand. Something softer and smoother than broken concrete lay beneath her.

A sharp sob tore from her throat when her shield ran out, and she panted and moaned until she could cast it again. Her questing hand located someone else's hand and trailed the arm back to the body trapped under her. Two heals later, Hawk moaned and then screamed shrilly. Sara casted a shield on him and healed him completely.

Hawk began coughing.

"Can you move?" Sara asked.

Hawk groaned as he struggled to move and coughed hard over the dust he stirred up.

"Sara, hold on we're coming!" Charlie yelled.

Sara didn't reply, busy casting heals as fast she could as the weight of the building crushed them.

"You better hurry, she can't do this much longer," Hawk shouted as he rested in her shield. "Get us out of here!"

"We're trying, Hawk, hang on," Oz shouted back.

Sara bit back her scream and tried futilely to block Charlie from her, not wanting him to feel her pain. His fear made her feel sick and terrified her magic, leaving her dizzy from the panting breaths she couldn't control.

"Don't die, Hawk," she whispered and casted another heal-over-time on him. Automatically, she began counting out the timer in her head. She tried to heal him just enough to keep him alive and leave him unconscious, but it was impossible to judge, and she kept bringing him back from the edge into crushing pain.

His strangled moans made her shake with horror that only eased when she'd healed him completely, and he lay beneath her shield unharmed. It became harder to cast anything. All her magic swirled about her as if it sought to escape. She was so weak and dizzy she could barely keep her timers straight.

"Please, don't die," she whimpered as she casted on Hawk again and couldn't hold back her scream as her shield ran out and the rubble crushed her legs.

Stasia had sprinted off to find a machine to move the rubble to reach them. Oz winced as Hawk screamed and a few seconds later Sara screamed.

Charlie moaned every time her shield ran out and the rubble crushed them, sharing her spikes of pain, taking half her damage. The pain didn't slow his frantic digging.

Oz straightened, panting, his bloody hands clenched into fists at his side. "Sara, use a small heal-over-time on Hawk. You'll run out of magic using full heals. Heal yourself and use a shield on both of you every cooldown. I'm sorry, Hawk."

Tears filled Oz's eyes as Hawk screamed again. The screams stopped, but Sara was crying, telling Hawk to hold on for ten more seconds.

Both remained quiet as Charlie and Oz frantically threw rubble.

"I need to heal him more, or he'll die." Sara's voice was surprisingly calm. "I can do this for approximately thirteen more minutes. Charlie, try to send me your magic; I love you." A stifled scream and crying dissolved into silence as Oz and Charlie continued to try to dig them out with their bare hands.

Charlie's magic swirled around him. "The magic can't reach her, I have no line-of-sight," he sobbed. "We need a hole."

"Sara, heal Hawk completely and have him use Tank to find a hole for us," Oz yelled.

"Tank's locked up somewhere," Hawk hollered a minute later, his voice hoarse.

Oz winked to the bottom of the rubble pile and grabbed the first man he saw. "Get us the black dog now. It's a rescue dog and might be able to find a way to them. Hurry, there isn't much time left!"

The man nodded and ran off.

Oz climbed back up.

Charlie had moved. He'd hit solid concrete and couldn't budge it.

Stasia returned. "Brenda is getting machinery. I brought this." A small brown finch fluttered in her cupped hands.

"Hawk, she has a finch. Can you lead it to you?"

Sara yelled, "Eight seconds."

Charlie grimaced, knowing Hawk was being crushed and wouldn't be able to speak until Sara shielded him again.

Stasia released the bird when Hawk yelled now. It disappeared into a crevice and then reappeared and entered another one. Hawk sobbed as his shield collapsed again. The bird kept searching, disappearing into the rubble for minutes at a time.

"Is it alive?" Oz yelled.

Neither of them answered.

Stasia cried as she helped Charlie throw rocks.

Oz casted locate and found the bird off to the side. "Clear here!" he yelled and started throwing rocks as well.

"The bird reached us!" Sara yelled, her voice hoarse and cracked. "I can't do this much longer. I'm so sorry, oh God, Hawk!"

"Hang on, we're coming!" Charlie sobbed and yelled his battle cry and threw rocks faster. His magic left him in a rush. "It reached her."

Oz straightened. "No way can we move this off them before she goes through his magic. That leaves us two choices," he said grimly. "We let them die, and Chief tries to rez Sara, and she attempts to rez Hawk. That might not work. Chief might not have enough line-of-sight and Sara might not have magic when she rezs. Or, I try to blast them out until they can reach a portal. My fireball won't hurt them, but it will make the rubble around them hot."

Oz looked at his friend's stricken faces and made the decision himself. "Are your hands free?"

"Yes!" Sara shouted back.

"I'm going to blow a hole to you. Hawk put

down a frost field if you can, and maybe the rubble won't get so hot. If I can, I'll set my portal down. I'll do my best not to hurt you getting there, but..." He gestured for Charlie and Stasia to step back.

Charlie wiped his sweating brow with a hand that shook, his eyes beseeching Oz, and stepped behind him. Stasia hugged Charlie. He held her tightly as they watched Oz cast fireballs, trying to knock a hole they could reach through. Rubble disintegrated as the fireballs impacted and broke the large chunks into smaller, more manageable piece. Clouds of dust obscured the area. Small pieces of rock flew like shrapnel, leaving bloody patches behind. Stasia crouched behind Charlie, using his body to block most of the small stones as he heaved the large cement chunks, not caring where they landed.

Stasia grasped and threw debris as fast as she could, ignoring her bleeding hands. Oz kept casting, the orange glow of his fireballs lighting the dust cloud with an eerie umber light.

Every time one of them screamed Oz winced and Charlie moaned. Debris shifted and moved and the building settling with a long groaning crash. Charlie had never been more terrified in his life. Every moment he expected to stop sensing her. The hot rocks and rough edges of broken concrete barely registered as pain through the sharp stings beneath his skin. The magic within him was frantic, it too wanted Sara; it needed her and buzzed beneath his skin like a horde of angry bees, furious with him for not going to her.

"I'm trying," he moaned.

Oz and Stasia's fear and horror echoed to him, growing stronger by the moment. Unable to help himself he screamed his attack cry again.

Overhead, thunder rumbled, and lightning flickered through the dust surrounding them.

Charlie wondered fleetingly what the men below them thought of the fireballs lighting the night sky and why they hadn't tried to come up, and then shrugged, he didn't really care.

Oz cried when he saw their clenched hands and then shrieked in frustration when his portal couldn't reach them.

"I need to make it bigger. Move your hands!" Oz yelled.

"We can't. Just do it!" Sara yelled back.

His lips set in a hard line, Oz casted again and again.

Charlie scooped the rubble up as it filled the hole. Oz's fireballs had no effect at all on him but the rock he blasted left bleeding gashes that healed as the next group impacted him. His hands shook as he shared the agony of hands burning and reforming with heals. Stasia and Oz's magic surrounded him, and he knew they shared his agony. Oz spells didn't hurt them, but hot rocks seared the skin touching them. The smell of burning flesh competed with the stink of exploding masonry. The debris glowed red from the heat, causing the air to shimmer.

"Move," Oz yelled, and Charlie jumped away.

Oz casted another portal. Hawk's hand disappeared. Sara's disappeared a moment after, and Oz slid to the ground and rested his sweating forehead in his hands. "They're out, I think."

On hands and knees on the edge of the hole, Stasia hollered for them as the heat began to dissipate. The cement faded from angry red to orange to soot-streaked gray. Sweat trickled down her cheeks and her shirt stuck to her skin. Blistered and burned, her hands oozed blood and pus.

Charlie jumped to the portal and stretched out his hand. He fell a short distance, landing with a thud on the floor of Oz's room in Florida. Hawk lay beside him, pushing himself weakly from the floor. Sara wasn't there.

Charlie fumbled for his cell phone with hands that trembled badly and called Oz. "She isn't here! Keep clearing!"

Oz pushed himself up and casted as Stasia hugged her knees crying.

"She's here!" Hawk said without opening his eyes. "I see her on my radar."

"Where Hawk?" Charlie knelt beside Hawk.

"Right here; she's right on us."

"Sara!" Charlie jumped to his feet and screamed her name.

Stasia grabbed Oz's phone.

"Hawk, check the downstairs. Charlie, check the roof!" Stasia muffled the phone with one hand and turned to Oz. "Dear God, don't let her be falling through the Earth."

Oz's horrified gaze met hers as he sat limply beside her and began to conjure bandages.

Charlie screamed in rage and fear when Sara's pain and panic ceased with horrifying suddenness. He dropped his phone, raced from

Oz's room, and pulled down the ladder leading to the attic. Stacks of boxes in neat rows filled the narrow space. The cartons tumbled into half-hazard piles as he searched frantically, hoping she was behind or under them. "She isn't here!" he bellowed and ran back to Oz's room where he jumped through the window without opening it. He leapt upward, grabbed the edge of the roof, and dragged himself over.

On the edge of the roof, Sara lay face down, her body twisted at an odd angle. A blood trail marked the spot where she'd landed as if she'd rolled when she hit the peak and slid. Blood covered her, forming a growing pool beneath her. On his knees beside her, Charlie stole her strongest heal and casted it. His hands shook as he ripped his shirt off and wrapped it around her left leg, hoping to staunch the blood that still oozed from deep gouge where the bone had punctured skin. He screamed for Hawk as he pulled her away from the edge and straightened her body. Bones ground and moved in unnatural ways as he adjusted her. He spared a second to be grateful Oz's father had moved them from his apartment into a small house when he began receiving money from the government for Oz's room and board. No one appeared to have noticed them arrive.

Hawk climbed weakly out of Oz's window, and Charlie heaved him onto the roof.

Pale and shaky, Hawk sat as close as he could to Sara. Charlie knelt beside her, two fingers on the pulse of her neck as he waited to Spell-Steal again. On the next heal, she moaned, and Charlie sobbed in relief. While waiting to cast again sweat covered him although he shivered. After three major heals, she struggled into a sitting position and healed herself.

A weak blue glow flitted from Charlie to her, and she healed Hawk.

"I'm fine, Sara, thank you. Use it on yourself." Hawk flopped back onto the roof.

Charlie picked her up and placed her in his lap, cringing at the sticky blood covering her. Magically depleted, she had to wait to cast again. Charlie's magic regenerated faster, he stole her heal and used it on her again.

Small shivers wracked her as she leaned her head on Charlie's shoulder with her eyes closed. "I'm okay just worn-out. What happened?"

"No idea, I wasn't there. You summoned us." Charlie ran his hands over her, stopping on her pulse. Relief made him shiver. The warm caress of her breath on his neck calmed him, easing the shivers and comforting his magic. While she spoke, he breathed on her neck, hoping it would ease her.

"Did someone grab us? I remember waking up on a table."

A shudder traveled her, and Charlie stroked her bloody hair. He didn't have enough magic to sense her clearly, but he knew she was terrified.

"Somebody had me again, but I couldn't focus I was so scared and confused. I just ran away. The next thing I remember is waking under the rubble. Did we trigger a trap?"

"No," Hawk said. "No one had you. You ran from me. When you wouldn't wait on base, Major

Nelson had you sedated. That wasn't a table, but a desk. We thought if you woke in the sun with me, you would be okay. But, it was night time by then, and we didn't consider how the drugs confuse you."

"How did we end up in the rubble?"

"You were trying to get away and blew through the walls." Hawk stopped speaking as her face whitened.

"I'm okay, and it was our fault for trying to keep you from him," Hawk said.

Charlie held her tighter. "I'm so sorry. God, Sara, if I thought for a second this would happen, I would never…" To choked up to continue, Charlie rocked her in his arms. This time his guilt overpowered hers. Guilt echoed between them growing stronger by the second.

"I better find the phone and call Oz. They must be freaking out," Hawk pushed himself to his feet and then leaned down and kissed Sara on the head. He slapped Charlie's shoulder before climbing off the roof.

Charlie mumbled, "Thanks," as Hawk left.

Oz answered on the first ring.

"Sorry it took so long for me to call. We found her on the roof. Everyone is okay now, but I really need a nap."

Oz bit back a sharp laugh.

Stasia grabbed his phone. "I love you. Find somewhere safe until we arrive. Don't nap there."

Hawk grumbled and agreed, and she handed the phone back to Oz. "How the hell are we going to explain this?"

Oz shrugged. "No idea." While Stasia peered over the side of the collapsed building, Oz called Major Nelson.

"So, yeah, the next time Sara says she needs Charlie, get him!" he hollered into the phone. "She knocked down the building you had her in and almost killed herself and Hawk. They're in my room at home with Charlie right now. Stasia and I are on top of the pile of rubble that used to be an office building. This will take fast talking to explain because we blew the hell out of the top with fireballs trying to reach them. Tank is missing somewhere. We're exhausted and not moving from here until you return." Before the major could answer, Oz hung up and sat down hard.

Stasia laughed and sat beside him. "Good plan. Let him handle his mess." Chunks of concrete tumbled down the side of the ruined building as she kicked to make a level spot to sit on beside Oz. He put his arm around her.

Forty minutes later, the helicopter carrying the Scouts and Major Nelson hovered over them. Rick jumped down, dislodging another small pile of debris when he landed, and offered them a hand up. "A ride is waiting to take us back to the states. After we pick them up, it's off to the tropics."

"How will they explain all of this?" Stasia asked, gesturing around.

"Does it matter?" Rick glanced over the

devastated building and shrugged.

"Not at all." Stasia accepted the hand Rick offered and rose wearily to her feet. She pulled Oz up, and they half-slid, half-climbed down in a cloud of dust as loose chunks of concrete tumbled around them.

Charlie buried his face in Sara's filthy hair. "I'm sorry," he mumbled.

"Don't ever, ever do that again! If you need something, tell me. If I don't agree, don't lock me up."

Horror filled her at that, and he swallowed heavily.

"I didn't mean for you to be locked up. I wanted to save you pain, not cause it."

Muffled anger lit the gray aura of her exhaustion in bright sparks of red.

"Neither of us knew that would happen. And, I know you're sorry and guilty, but it wasn't your fault." The anger receded as she kissed his cheek. "The anger isn't over what happened, but why it happened."

His eyes were scrunched tight, and he saw her anger flare as she said that. He squirmed uncomfortably, wishing he could turn off the connection to her so he didn't have to feel how angry she was. Guilt colored his own aura black whenever he touched the drying blood coating her. No matter what she said, he knew that was his fault. His decision had placed her there.

Whether he had good intentions or not, he'd almost gotten her and Hawk killed.

"You're lucky I'm so tired I can hardly sit up."

Shivers wracked her, and Charlie was relieved her aura wasn't the sludgy black of madness, but only the dimness of exhaustion. For the first time in a year, he felt weak, magically depleted and more exhausted than he could ever remember being. With a groan, he laid back on the roof, bringing her with him.

After a few minutes, she kissed his cheek again and sat. "I forgive you. Will you promise you'll never have me sedated again to do something you know I won't like?"

The anger sparking along her aura was fading. When he nodded, and mumbled, "Yes," the anger faded away into the gray of her exhaustion.

She was silent again and then said in a small worried voice. "Will they forgive us?" Then in rising horror, "Did I kill other people in that building?"

Charlie turned white and sat. "No, I don't think so. We heard no one else. If anyone died, it was my fault, not yours!" Black despair darkened her dimness, growing as she began to cry. He picked her up and jumped to the ground, landing heavily without his usual grace. The darkness thickened as he ran into Oz's house, begging her to stop, found his phone, and called his brother.

After a short conversation, he sighed in relief. "No one was seriously injured. A few scrapes are all. Nobody was even hospitalized."

He rubbed her back, trying to stop her crying. "Please, stop, you don't need to feel guilty. No one was hurt."

Voice thick with tears Sara wailed into his chest, "Hawk was hurt. He was hurt badly. I could've killed him."

"It would have been my fault, not yours, and he's fine now."

"I'm fine, and I forgive you both," Hawk said unexpectedly, making them jump. "Let's get out of here, and stop crying, you're freaking me out!" Hawk gave her a quick hug, giving Charlie a pointed look over her shoulder.

Charlie sighed, rolled his eyes, and mouthed, 'I'm trying.'

Sara snorted a small shaky laugh and wiped her face with her shirt as she grimaced. "Give me five minutes to clean up, and we can go."

Hawk threw Charlie the keys to Oz's father truck.

Charlie stole a shirt from Oz's father's room while Sara and Hawk took sweatshirts from Oz's dresser. Everyone washed their faces but kept on their filthy pants. Too weak and tired to do more than wash her face, Charlie helped her rinse her hair in the kitchen sink and borrowed a quilt from Oz's bed, in which he wrapped her in an attempt to stop her shivering while Hawk searched for orange juice.

"Don't bother, Hawk." Charlie held out his hand for the keys. "It wouldn't be safe to drink anyway."

Hawk glared and slammed the refrigerator door. "Fuckers," he muttered.

Charlie kissed Sara's neck, hoping it would soothe her sudden terror. "You're perfectly safe," he said.

She gave him a wan smile and her feelings dimned. She was trying to block them from him. He said nothing, letting her think she'd succeeded.

Charlie drove them to the Air Force base. Covered with dried blood and dust they were sure to attract unwanted attention if they entered, so they waited outside the fence under a No-See-Um. Oz would have to come get them.

-26-

VACATION

A military aircraft landed in the states, picked up Charlie, Sara, and Hawk, and they were on the way to St. Vincent's in the Grenadines. Brenda had the resort layout on her laptop and was setting up guard patrols. She met with both team leaders of the recon teams who accompanied them.

"You've already met our secret weapon specialists. As you can see, they're very young. The last week has been extremely stressful for them, and Uncle Sam is sending them on a vacation. It's our job to make sure no one tries to snatch them or kill them or even sneezes on them."

Mike glanced at the kids in question. When he'd last seen them, they'd been jumping from a helicopter dressed in black combat gear. Now they wore bad fitting, ripped up clothes covered in dirt, and dried blood, and oddly, they all wore sunglasses. Sara's hands shook as she drank water and Mike could see her shiver from here. Charlie covered her in his blanket and put her in his lap. Stasia wrapped her blanket around her as well. His glance flicked to Hawk who slept peacefully beside his sister. If he hadn't seen Hawk fight, he would never believe he killed as easily as he did. He shrugged uncomfortably.

"Brenda," Charlie called. "Is there orange juice anywhere? Sara really needs some."

Brenda rose as Mike asked, "Diabetic?"

Brenda didn't reply as she hurried to the back of the plane and rummaged in the black bags containing the dirty armor and weapons, emerging in a moment with three small cans of orange juice, which she handed to Charlie.

Charlie nodded his thanks and opened a can that he passed to Sara.

Brenda hovered over them a moment before resuming her seat.

"Diabetic shock is nothing to take lightly," Mike said when Brenda sat again. "Do you have insulin on the plan for her?"

"Sara isn't diabetic." Brenda opened her laptop again. "The problem isn't medical."

Mike glanced back at Charlie who was opening another juice and offering it to Sara. Brenda followed his gaze and her brow furrowed. The lines on her brow smoothed out as she watched Sara decline the juice and yawn.

Brenda tapped her screen and cleared her throat.

Mike turned his attention to the laptop

screen showing the resort layout.

"Guard patrols will be here and here," she said and pointed at the map. "Three-hour shifts twice a day, but you'll be on call the entire time, so stay within fifteen minutes of the hotel. What you do when you're not on active guard duty is up to you. Try to blend in. Even when you're off shift, if anything seems hinky, contact me, Joy, Glen, or Guthrie. Those kids are extremely important to the safety and defense of our nation. If they go hiking or to town, the guards go too, as subtly as you can. They're supposed to tell me where they'll be at all times, but they're teenagers, so don't count on my list being accurate. If you aren't sure where they are, report it immediately. Never leave them unguarded. If your shift replacement is late, wait with them."

Mike examined the resort layout. "How many guards will be on duty at a time?"

"Five." Brenda pointed to the resort grounds as she spoke. "Two patrolling on the grounds, one on Charlie and Sara, and two for Oz, Hawk, and Stasia. If they split up for some reason, we'll get another one. None of them are to go anywhere alone, ever. I don't expect them to split up. They usually stick together. The rest of the Scouts will be hanging out with them, so they'll have more protection than just the guards on them too. When guarding, you're checking in every ten minutes."

Brenda paused a moment and continued in a very soft voice. "Sara has had a very hard time. We need to keep her secure, but not frighten her or upset Charlie." Brenda's glance flitted over them. "Don't startle her or try to touch her. When you guard Charlie and her, give them privacy. If you need to verify their whereabouts, announce yourself before approaching. We aren't spying on them, we're making sure no one gets near them. The Scouts will be their guards as much as possible, but keep it in mind if anything comes up— never touch her if you can help it."

Brenda packed up her laptop after she finished the briefing and handed out their assignments. "While this shouldn't be a hard job, more like a working vacation, there's always the possibility of someone attempting to abduct them for the secrets they possess. The last men guarding them were killed, which is why we had to travel to Iraq to reclaim the, um, plans. So, stay alert." Brenda stood to return to her seat.

Mike followed and placed a hand on her arm as they exited earshot of his men. "We'll be off duty together sometimes," he said and smiled. Brenda smiled back. "I still want to buy you those drinks," he finished.

"We're up to four drinks now," Brenda said and grinned, which he returned.

The plane landed, and they took another smaller, commercial flight to the island. No baggage accompanied them except for the armor and weapons, so Stasia insisted they stop at a store when they arrived, and everyone bought new clothes.

Charlie and Sara had a top floor room with a private balcony overlooking the ocean. Sara stood on the balcony, her face lifted to the setting sun as Charlie showered. Orange juice and a long hot shower had cured her shivering, but an occasional tremor still racked her.

Charlie's guilt had eased as she slept in his arms on the plane, and her small spikes of guilt weren't enough to begin the echo again, for which he was grateful. He never wanted to feel that bad again. Just remembering it made the magic within him roil uncomfortably, and he hastily concentrated on his anticipation of sun-filled days instead. His magic settled, and he felt Sara ease.

When he joined her fifteen minutes later, she still stood in the dying light with damp hair wetting Oz's quilt that was still draped over her although clean shorts and t-shirt had replaced her dirty clothing. Charlie stood behind her, resting his chin on her head. "I love you," he whispered as he wrapped his arms around her and kissed her neck.

"I love you too," she replied and leaned harder against him.

When the soft tropical night replaced the orange sunset, she turned in his arms and kissed him. Filled with sadness and determination, she led him inside and pushed him into a chair, taking a seat across from him at the small table.

"Let's talk, and clear the air." She took both his hands and smiled crookedly. "Don't be afraid. It's nothing bad.

"Okay…" he said. "Why are you so sad?"

She stared at the table and cleared her throat, her determination surged, and she met his eyes. "This isn't what you expected, what either of us expected for our lives." She held up a hand when he started to speak. "I can't tell you what it means to me to know how you feel, how much I love the connection we have." They shared a bright smile. She didn't need to tell him, he felt how much she loved him. " But, I want you to have everything you thought you would for your life, college, a military career, living with your parents— whatever it is you want."

"I want you, Sara," Charlie said, his throat dry, not liking how this conversation was going at all.

A sad smile pulled up a corner of her mouth, and her eyes shone with unshed tears. "You know I want you too, Charlie, but I'm a mess, and nowhere in your life plans was a wife as messed up as I am."

"Too late for you." Charlie grinned at her, making her laugh despite herself. "We're as married as two people can be, and I'll never divorce you."

Sara smiled more sincerely. "I know, and I don't want you to either. That isn't what I meant. What I meant was, I could work on my issues myself. You don't need to deal with it. I'll always be yours. I can wait until you're ready, until I'm better, until we're older."

Charlie laughed. "No, you and I will handle our problems together. I agree, you need some help, but you're not a mess. Yes, we're young, and neither of us expected the magic to marry us like this, but I'm glad it did. More than glad!" His thumb traced her hand. "Every time we exchange magic it makes us closer. What you feel comes clearer, and I understand it better. My magic goes to you eagerly. The stronger your feelings, the more my magic wants yours. Is it the same for you?"

Sara nodded.

"I appreciate what you're saying here, sweetheart. That we rushed into this and you don't want to take advantage. We did rush, that's for sure, but our love is real. The problems we have we'll handle one at a time. This one is easy. We stay together forever. The little things like you being afraid of the dark now and closed rooms, we'll deal with. Lights can remain on, and doors open until you're better. The bigger things— your nightmares and misguided guilt— we'll handle as we need to. When bad dreams haunt you, I'll wake you and keep telling you it wasn't your fault until you believe it. Doctor Gotlieb will help you get better."

"And if I'm never better?" Again, she looked away as she clutched his hands.

"You'll get better. I'll help you, but no matter what happens, you'll never be alone again," Charlie promised.

"And our future? What do you want to do, where do you want to live?" Sara nervously bit her lip as she met his eyes again.

Charlie was relieved her sadness had been replaced by a low-level anxiety he experienced as well. It was so low level he probably wouldn't be able to feel it unless he was touching her like he was. "Well, I always wanted a military career. I still do, but only if it's something we can both do. What did you want for your future?"

"I used to want to learn to make video games, to be a professional gamer like we were. Now, I want to kill every single one of those terrorists."

Shocked, Charlie jerked backward. Her feelings had given him no warning. No hate or fear infused her now. Just a slight nervousness he shared.

"I want to study the magic and learn everything about it to make Americans everywhere safe from them. If you join the service, I'll go wherever they send you, but I don't want to join, I want to study. I want to heal those sick children and be able to teach others how to. Magical healing is such a great gift I want to share it. But, most of all, I want us to be safe. A Marine base sounds safe to me. I would be happy being a Marine's wife."

Charlie sighed in relief. For a moment, he'd thought he would have to talk her out of sneaking back to Iraq and hunting terrorists on her own. "So, we both need to go to school. To become an officer, I'll need a degree, and you'll need to study a lot of different things, but that's for later."

Her Barlow Blue eyes brightened, and she grinned at him, sharing his desire. His voice was low and deep as he pulled her into an embrace. "This week is just for us. Don't worry about anything. Enjoy the sun and heat. We'll work on controlling the magic so I don't embarrass you again."

Sara laughed and laid her head on his shoulder. "It is embarrassing that everyone can see how much I want you."

Charlie chuckled. "Nobody knows what we're feeling, but we do need to control it. We can't glow blue in public because I think you look beautiful or you smile at me." The echo of their shared emotions grew as they held each other in the shadowy bedroom. "We'll take our time and figure this out together. No one is here except us, and we can touch each other as much as we like," Charlie whispered.

Sara pulled his T-shirt off and then her own. He made a contented sound when their bare chests touched. "That's a good start," Charlie murmured huskily.

The next morning, Charlie carried Sara to the balcony. "Stay here in the sun. I'm going to go get us food, towels, and toothbrushes, and then we'll find a deserted stretch of beach and go on a picnic, just us. All day long we can lie in the sun. Call Brenda or Glen if you need anything. I'll be back in an hour or two."

When he left his room, he found Harrison in the hallway. Dressed in Bermuda shorts and a white T-shirt with a flowered shirt covering the holstered gun at his side, he leaned against the wall outside the door, holding a newspaper. "You aren't coming with us today."

Charlie called Brenda. "We don't need this much security. I'm taking Sara on a picnic, a private picnic. If you have us followed this closely, I'm going to be really annoyed."

"Chief, you can't just wander off. I'll set up somewhere you can be alone that we can secure. Give me an hour or so, and one of us will escort you there and leave you alone. I'll make sure you have food and towels."

"Brenda... I appreciate you want to keep us safe, but we don't want company. We want to be totally alone," Charlie insisted.

"I'm sorry, Chief, this is the best I can do."

"Fine," Charlie growled in exasperation and glanced at his watch. "I'm going to town, and I assume I need an escort?"

"I can get you whatever you want," Brenda assured him.

"No, you can't," Charlie snapped and then took a moment to get his temper under control. *Brenda was trying to help him and Sara,* he reminded himself, and he did need help to keep her safe. This last week had proved that. And if he'd learned anything from this fiasico it was he needed to keep his temper under control. In a much calmer voice, he said, "I'm going to town to buy my wife a wedding band that I'm going to pick out. I'm willing to take a Scout with me, but I'm doing this myself."

"Okay, ten minutes and I'll have a car and a guard waiting," Brenda said. "We're doing this for your own good here, Chief."

Yeah, I know. Sorry I'm such a grouch, and thanks, Brenda, I know this hasn't been easy on you either.

"*De nada*," Brenda said and hung up.

Joy and Stasia went to town with Charlie.

"Are you guys okay?" Charlie gave Stasia a quick hug and an apologetic grimace. "Sorry we're so distracted. It's not that we don't care about you, we just need some alone time to work things out."

"We're fine, the Scouts are good company." Stasia grinned at Charlie. "Don't worry about us, we don't expect to see you much. Take all the time you need together. I wouldn't want you on my honeymoon either."

Charlie sighed. "I wish this was our honeymoon with just the two of us and none of this crap hanging over our heads. No guards or nightmares or spikes of terror."

"She's still not eating?" Joy peered at him in the rear-view mirror.

"Not a lot no, but she was completely depleted. Twice now in a week she used all her magic staying alive. I gave her some of mine, she's been giving it back to me and taking it again. The little she's regenerated wants my magic, so I have most of what she's regenerated. The magic only began to regenerate yesterday, and she used it all again. I think she hit the forty-eight-hour cool-down for a priest death twice now in a week. She'll need time to recover."

"She didn't die though, neither time," Joy said reassuringly to his worried tone.

"No, it was close though, and she did run out of magic trying to stay alive." Charlie shrugged. "It's just a theory. I'll make sure she gets a lot of sun and as much of my magic as she wants. Now that we're married it stays with her,"

"It's not depleting you?" Joy asked.

"Not at all, I have plenty. I'm regenerating it normally, faster than normal actually. My magic is rage based, and I have lots of rage whenever I think about what they did to her." Charlie took a deep breath. "I can't dwell on it, she'll know I'm angry, but not the cause, and she'll worry." With a half-smile at Joy, he leaned forward and took Stasia's hand and kissed it, setting it down before his touch could become painful. "That will give her nice thoughts instead. My love for you is much better for her."

Stasia turned in the seat and smiled at him. "It's complicated, huh? I was sort of jealous of your connection, but now... Well, it must be hard to sense someone's feelings, but not their cause."

Charlie shrugged. "Most of hers are easy, a lot of fear and guilt. The ones for me are very clear, I don't confuse them. I'm sure it will get harder though as she gets better, and we spend time apart." His smile changed to a grin, and he winked at Stasia. "You should be jealous. It's amazing being that connected to someone. I wouldn't trade it for anything." He leaned over and whispered. "I know exactly what she likes and doesn't like, I never have to guess."

Stasia blushed and laughed. "That must be awesome for ordering food."

Charlie rolled his eyes and laughed. "That too," he agreed.

"What's awesome for ordering food?" Joy asked.

Charlie and Stasia laughed.

Stasia helped him pick out a wedding ring and made him get one for himself. "Trust me, she'll want you to have the matching one."

Charlie spent a few minutes talking with Oz and Hawk when they returned to the resort before returning to Sara. Asleep in the sun, he woke her when he came in. "Brenda is setting up our picnic. When she calls, we can go. I've talked to the entire team, and everyone is fine."

Sara tugged him down to her and kissed him. "We'll break the chair," he laughed as she pulled him on top of her. "We need an air mattress or something out here," he murmured as he kissed the bare skin of her collarbone. The blanket wrapped around her fell to the ground unheeded when he placed her on his lap as he continued trailing kisses across her bare skin.

When Brenda called, they were dozing in the morning sun. They dressed and met her on the beach and then hiked for almost two miles along the shore.

"How's this?" Brenda asked with a wide-armed gesture, displaying the small sandy cove as if she'd invented it. Steep cliffs ringed the small beach on two sides. A dense thicket of trees blocked access on one side, and the ocean casted gentle waves on the shore. A tumble of rough boulders ringed the closest side. The boulders continued out to sea, disappearing under the turquoise water. Most people would be deterred from crossing the sharp, uneven, slippery rocks so the beach should remain private.

"Perfect," Charlie said. A beach umbrella

already stood on the white sand with a blanket beneath it beside a large cooler and a stack of towels. "We'll be here all day, and I'll keep my phone on. If you need us, call. But please don't need us."

Brenda laughed. "Relax, have a nice day at the beach. We won't need you. Call me when you leave here though."

"Thanks, Brenda, we will," Charlie assured her.

Sara thanked her, and they went to the blanket and sat, both watching Brenda worm her way between the thick trees behind them. Unseen from where they sat, a member of the recon team guarded the cliff approach. Someone would guard both entrances while they were in the cove.

Charlie opened the cooler and took out a fruit cup, which he shared with Sara. He helped himself to a muffin, which she declined, and investigated the supplies Brenda had supplied. Under the stack of towels lay a bottle of suntan lotion.

"This is perfect," Sara said as he rubbed the lotion on her back.

Charlie grinned at her. "Sure is," he agreed. "I'm going for a quick swim" he added with an inviting lift to his eyebrow.

"I'll watch," she sat cross-legged in the sand.

Charlie removed his shirt, slipped the ring box into the shirt pocket, dropped the shirt on the damp sand by the water's edge, and jumped in. After a few minutes, he left the water. Not bothering with a towel, he ran a hand through his short hair, flinging off the excess water and grabbed up his shirt.

Sara sat with her head on her drawn-up knees, admiring him.

"Keep feeling like that and I'll get a swelled head," he said as he sat beside her.

She giggled, and he laughed. *This was better than he hoped it would be, her happiness sparkled. Calm with no fear or guilt just love for him. The perfect time to give her the ring,* he thought.

"What?" She asked seeing his smile and sensing his excitement, she smiled in return.

Charlie knelt before her, reached into his shirt pocket, and took out the small black ring case. The two rings nestled together in white velvet. "Becoming Sara Hayes is just a legality for me. In every way that counts, you're my wife. Someday, we can have the big ceremony my mother wants and exchange these again. Meanwhile, I want everyone to know we're together forever." He slipped the smaller ring onto her finger.

Eyes bright with happy tears, she placed the bigger one on his finger.

The embrace she gave him contained so much love and happiness his own eyes filled. Stasia had been right to make him get a ring too. Sara appreciated the symbol more than he'd thought she would. The warm sun relaxed her and nestled in his arms she was perfectly content. His magic was sated, making no demands to touch her. The sunlight had sped her magic regeneration. Another day of sun and rest and she would be fine magically.

Later that afternoon, when they made love in

the hot sun, was the most intense experience of his life. Whether from the sunlight or her returned magic or just that she felt better, he neither knew nor cared.

When she curled into his side afterward and fell asleep, he thanked God for the gift of her. This moment was one he wanted to remember forever, the smell of the soft sea air and bright, warm light. Relaxed against him, Sara's golden blonde hair glittered on the white sand, her sun-warmed skin damp from perspiration. The kisses he'd given her in the past now felt shallow and without depth. The way Sara felt when they made love, knowing her emotional response to his touch was amazing, and he pitied everyone without magic of their own. Relaxed and content he drifted to sleep beside her.

Neither of them wanted to return to their room that night. Charlie called Brenda.

"Nothing is wrong, but we're staying overnight."

"Do you need more food?"

"No thanks," Charlie said. After a brief conversation checking on the rest of the team, he hung up. "Nothing to worry about, she isn't upset. The team is fine. Tonight, we can watch the stars all night just the two of us."

Brenda sent for more guards and made a few adjustments to the schedule, putting the female Scouts on night duty. "Every hour visually confirm they're still there. "A quick glance, just enough to confirm and don't be seen. If they think it isn't private, they'll both be angry." Pink climbed her cheeks as she gave the order.

Joy remained as Brenda returned to the resort. After checking on the other three, she passed the log over to Glen and headed to the restaurant.

Two fancy drinks with umbrellas sat on the table before Mike. When she approached, he stood and smiled. Heat in his eyes, he handed her a glass and raised his. "Here's to no call outs for at least a day."

Brenda laughed. "I'll drink to that."

-27-

THEIR NEW HOME

Charlie left Sara sleeping in their bed and went to Liz's apartment to pick up the kitten. The previous day they'd returned to Pendleton where Charlie's parents had greeted them with enthusiastic relief. After he gave Sara her present, they would go to his parent's new house and spend the day with them for a belated Christmas celebration.

Liz answered the door dressed in her uniform, carrying the box he'd dropped on the floor of her apartment.

"Thanks for taking care of the kitten, Liz. I forgot all about her. How did you even know what was in the box?"

"The officer at the scene saw her, and I figured it out pretty fast," Liz handed over the box.

"Man, I need to send him a thank you card. I

felt horrible when I remembered."

"Well, I suppose you could be forgiven for having it slip your mind," Liz said with a smile. "And, no harm done, she's a sweet little thing. Prince will miss her."

"Hawk and I talked about training her; he could probably train Prince too. The plan is to teach her where it's safe to go outside. You're only two blocks away; they could hang out together doing cat stuff."

"He could do that permanently?" Liz asked in surprise.

"He thinks so. First, we'll try it inside for a year, and if it works, he'll add an outdoor area for her."

"Inside?"

"Yeah, just keep off the counters, things like that," Charlie said.

"I would be very interested. I was under the impression Hawk could only control them actively, not that he could set commands."

"He can do both. Usually, the commands wear off, but he thinks with enough reinforcement he can make them stick. You know he got a dog on this last mission, right?"

"Yeah, I've met Tank. Yesterday, we took him to my vet here for shots. Do you think he'll get another?"

"I'm not sure. He's been debating the merits of a big dog or a small one."

Liz laughed. "I hope he gets the teacup Yorkie, they're so darn cute."

Charlie laughed too. "We ran some scenarios, and believe it or not, a small dog would be helpful in a lot of them, but it's more likely to be Jack Russell than a Yorkie."

"Well, give Sara my love. I'm sure she'll love her Christmas present." Liz held her door for him. "What did she get you? Or haven't you exchanged gifts yet?"

Charlie blushed and laughed when Liz tried not to giggle. "A car she spent way too much money on before we were married."

"I don't think it's about the money for her. She really tries to find things people will like." Liz held out her wrist and showed him a watch. This was my grandmothers, and I meant to get it fixed forever and never got around to it. Sara fixed it herself for my Christmas present. She got your mom recipes, and your mother loved them, and they didn't cost a thing either."

Charlie snickered. "Yeah, those were from Stasia too. You know how they got them right?"

"No, I thought they were like family recipes or something."

"They were, other people's secret family recipes. My mom had a list of recipes she was trying to reproduce. Things her friends made, but wouldn't tell their secret ingredients. Well, Sara and Stasia hunted them all down. They had Oz casting disguise and pretending to be the spouse or whatever and asking for the dish and Stasia would spy and watch them make it."

Liz laughed. "Oh, my god. No wonder she loved them so much!"

"Yeah, the girls put a lot of thought into gifts. Sara keeps a gift idea notebook. Never, ever, mention you love something unless you really do because she writes it all down."

Liz laughed again and kissed his cheek as he left.

Sara was still sleeping when he returned home. Except for their bed and stacks of unpacked cartons, the apartment remained unfurnished.

Charlie took his clothes off, slid under the covers beside her, and placed the kitten on his chest. Paws so soft and light they barely dented the sheet padded about him as it began exploring the bed.

Sara snuggled closer to him. "Mmm," she murmured.

"Mmm yourself," he said and pulled her into an embrace. He kissed her and smoothed her hair back. Desire for him rose, and he smiled, tempted to postpone the introduction, but not wanting to crush the kitten. The kitten strutted up his chest, tail waving in the air, and he chuckled.

"Merry Christmas, sweetheart."

Last night, when she'd given him the keys to the jeep, he told her Liz had her gift, and he would get it in the morning.

Sara smiled, opening her eyes as she pushed herself into a better position to kiss him again and spied the kitten on his chest. "Oh, Charlie," she exclaimed as she rubbed between its ears. "Is it a boy or girl?"

"A girl. She has papers we can fill out to register her name."

"She's the cutest thing ever. Thank you so much!" Sara gave him a quick hug and sat cross-legged on the bed.

He laughed, Sara's desire had fled completely.

With a soft croon, she coaxed the kitten into her lap and cuddled it as it purred. Perfectly happy, Sara leaned against him, petting the kitten. He stifled a chuckle at his thoughts, tempted to give her a kitten every day it made her so happy.

"She'll need a name, and I thought we could stop at the store and get her some things."

Charlie grinned as the kitten batted at Sara's fingers and continued, "The breeder sent a bag of food with her, but she'll need more. I had planned to take you for Christmas and let you pick out toys and a tree house for her."

"She's perfect, Charlie. I love her already. What kind of cat is she? Will her eyes stay blue?"

"Yeah, she's a blue-eyed ragdoll. They're supposed to be real friendly cats. What will you call her?"

"I don't know. What do you think?" Sara held the cat up and inspected it, a thoughtful frown on her face.

"Lucky," Charlie said. "Her name should be Lucky." *That cat was lucky in so many ways. She was lucky that Sara loved her and that she hadn't died in the box. And, she was lucky to own. If I hadn't bought her, Sara might not be here right now.*

"Lucky it is." Sara kissed the kitten's nose.

The next day, Team Valor gathered in the pool area awkwardly, unsure how to communicate with each other for the first time in years.

Charlie eyed Stasia thoughtfully as she kicked the beach ball and watched it roll into the pool. It was clear something was troubling her. The peacefulness of the day felt surreal to Charlie, and he wondered how long it would be until he felt normal again or if he ever would.

"I'm calling an officers meeting!" Oz said abruptly. "We need to straighten out our ideas on where this team is headed."

Sara sat up from where she had been lying in the grass and took Charlie's hand.

Anxiety spiked then smoothed. Charlie didn't know if she had really calmed or was blocking her feelings, which she managed easier than he did. He kissed her hand, hoping his calmness would calm her. Her emotions changed rapidly, much more so than she let on and he wondered if that were always true or her magic influencing her or a side effect from the last week. The surge of anger that accompanied that thought made her stiffen, and he was annoyed with himself for upsetting her.

"It's nothing," he murmured and mentally yelled at his magic to knock it off. He gave her a half-smile, his emotions changed quickly too. The smile seemed to ease her, or maybe it was his amusement over his mood swings, but she turned back to Oz with a smile on her face and a calm demeanor.

Hawk turned to them and removed his sunglasses.

"First," Oz held up a finger. "Is everyone committed to remaining on Team Valor? Be honest. It's okay if you don't want to do this anymore. We can still be friends even if you don't want to do any more missions."

Stasia regarded Hawk and Sara with a frown on her face. "I still want to do missions, but it feels as if we're out of control here like we're all on different pages. As if everything I want is out of my reach or I'm waiting for it."

"We're a team now more than ever," Sara said, "but I do think we need to discuss where we see this team heading. Everyone needs to be completely honest here, we'll stick together. Any differences we might have can be worked out."

"I agree," Oz said. "The last few weeks have shown me we've been drifting with no clear goal. We sort of just slipped into this, but we need a plan. Honestly, I think the scientists have learned as much as they're going to from us and while we did the right thing turning ourselves in, I don't think we need to dedicate our lives to the military either."

Stasia looked troubled, and Oz put his arm around her. "No, I'm not saying I don't want to do missions. But, I don't want to join the military."

"I think I do," Hawk said.

Stasia kissed Oz's cheek and then sat by her brother. "I do too, but not as an enlisted soldier. I want to be an officer and run the missions."

"Charlie?" Sara asked. "What do you want? Don't worry about what I want."

"I have to worry about that. If it were just me, you know I would enlist. That was my plan before this. Now, well, I wouldn't enlist either. If

I join, I want to be an officer too. The problem is, if we join, they can separate us, send us anywhere, and I won't be separated from you, Sara, from any of you."

"I don't want to join," Sara said. " If that's the only way we can be together, I will, but I would rather not."

"What do you want to do, Sara?" Oz asked.

"I want to go to college and study medicine, history, and science, and anything else I think of to understand our magic better. I want to make it impossible for terrorists to harm us— to harm any American."

"Me too." Oz nodded his head. "I want to study math, computers, science, and engineering. I would still train with you, but I want to work on programs of my own. Ideas are bouncing around my head to make a better computer language."

"Well, if we want to be officers, we need college degrees," Stasia said.

"Then what?" Charlie said.

"Then I follow you," Sara said. "Wherever you're assigned, I'll go. There's schools and teachers everywhere, and I can always study online too." Sara hugged him, shining blue eyes peering at him hopefully.

"We would have to be separated during boot camp." Charlie tugged a lock of her hair.

Sara grinned. "They could try, but I bet we could sneak out and meet. Maybe not every night, but we would see each other."

"Do you have a school in mind, Sara?" Oz asked.

"It has to be a good one, but no."

"Well, how about Johns Hopkins?" Oz asked. "They have good programs for both of us." Excitement growing, Oz turned to Stasia and Charlie. "It's close to the Naval Academy. Sara, Hawk, and I could get a place close by. Charlie, you would have to be apart more than a few weeks though."

Sara nodded, pursing her lips and turning to Charlie. "Are you thinking of making the service your lifelong career, or just for a few years?"

"Forever, I guess," Charlie said slowly, knowing she felt his excitement over the idea. "But, Sara, I don't have to do that."

"I know. We're just talking here," Sara said and turned to Stasia. "What about you, Stasia, and Hawk?"

"I don't necessarily want to be an officer. And I sure as hell don't want to go through the academy when you guys are done," Hawk said as he rubbed Tank's ears.

"So, you'll what, enlist at eighteen?" Stasia asked. "What will you do between now and then?"

"School, I guess," he said and frowned.

"Don't be silly, Hawk," Sara said. "You'll go to college with us. You don't have to study medicine. They have general programs. I'm sure you can pass any entrance exams they have."

Hawk brightened, then frowned. "I could afford one year, Sara."

"Well, that isn't a problem. I could afford tuition for all of us," Sara said. "And, before you go turning me down, we could all probably get scholarships."

"Yes, they did say that when they talked to Mom," Stasia said. "Hawk, if I attend the Naval Academy I won't need tuition. You can use my money."

"Seriously, guys, don't worry about the money," Sara insisted. "I have a lot of it. What's mine is yours. My mother left me very well provided for. I need you guys near me. If it takes her money to do that, so be it."

"Yeah, security— we need to discuss that as well," Oz said, giving Charlie an apologetic grimace.

"Well, the Naval Academy must be pretty secure. I can't see Guthrie complaining on that score," Stasia said. "But, you guys living in an apartment somewhere? I don't know."

"Not somewhere, as close as we can get to you guys," Sara said. "I'm willing to be separated from Charlie only if he's nearby."

"Let me see your phone, Stasia, I want to look up the rules," Charlie said. He frowned as he scrolled through the website.

"We can't do it anyways, no married midshipman," Charlie said.

"We aren't legally married."

"Midshipmen only get one afternoon off a week, Sara."

"Well, that will suck, I agree, but again, we're highly trained. I'm sure we could sneak either in or out once in a while," Sara said and smiled when he did, taking his hand and squeezing it. "Someday, you'll be General Hayes."

Charlie laughed and continued reading the website. "Seventeen is the youngest they'll accept."

"So, Stasia stays with us one year, but I'm betting they'll make an exception for her," Oz said.

"We're agreed then?" Sara asked, glancing from face-to-face.

"I suppose," Hawk said doubtfully. "We should study up on these exams just like we studied for boss fights. If one of us doesn't get accepted, most likely me, we'll have a problem."

"Nothing we couldn't overcome," Oz insisted. "I'm one hundred percent sure they'll be thrilled that Stasia and Charlie want to attend the academy. If you don't get into the same school as us, other schools are available. I don't think they'll love us going to a regular school, but they can't stop it."

"Okay, we study hard on our own," Stasia said. "This spring, we take the tests and put in our applications. If one of us doesn't make it, we rethink our strategy just like every other fight."

"Team Valor." Oz held out his hand.

"Dork," Charlie said and punched him in the arm, laughing when Oz winced.

THE END

Upcoming book!

BEYOND VALOR

Charlie learns actions and inactions have consequences

And when you possess magic those consequences can change the world.

Charlie just wants to be one of the guys, and thinks he's learned to balance his magical nature. He's making friends and enemies at the Naval Academy, and while he has problems, they all seem mundane. But his magic has needs of its own. Needs it makes known with a vengeance when he leaves the zone to do his first tour on an aircraft carrier.